The Singular

Jacy Mautz

Text copyright © 2018 by Jacy Mautz

ISBN 978-1-7326810-1-9

For Wayne.
Who never stopped believing in me.

ONE

It was a bright Tuesday morning when the first silvery glow appeared on the horizon. There was nothing special about the day at all, although later on, many would compare the day to the Biblical warning, *"While people are saying, "Peace and safety," destruction will come on them suddenly, as labor pains on a pregnant woman, and they will not escape."* In less time than it took for a JPL employee to lean forward and squint at the small dot on the radar screen, the sky was suddenly filled with hundreds of thousands of gleaming gray aircraft. They flew in a tight, straight line, in a thousand mile-wide formation from east to west and every craft left behind it a wide trail of red smoke. In the hours that followed, the crimson smoke filled the atmosphere and blanketed the earth with the clouds that stung the eyes and the lungs and left thousands choking and weak.

As the days went by and the thick smoke didn't clear, the focus was no longer on finding the silvery crafts and finding the reason behind what was being called "the cloud attack." People stopped caring about the *why* behind the attack. They began to simply try to survive. It wasn't as bad as a nuclear winter. The sky still lightened in the morning and darkened in the evening with a surreal red-orange-pink glow. But the sun struggled to force its way through the layers of clouds so the light that did filter through appeared somehow damaged or tainted.

The plants that thrived on sunshine fought for whatever weak light made it through, but it was a losing battle. By day four the fields of green had become pale and stunted and they had become stunted and pale. It wasn't until the second week of suffocating clouds, that the people who should have noticed things sooner, finally noticed that the rains had completely stopped. Everywhere. By the time the farmers were unable to harvest enough to make their daily deliveries to the granaries, the damage to the crops was already too far gone to recover. Grocery stores tried a weak form of rationing before the government sent their troops to stem the tides of panicked citizens. Restaurants served what they could and tried to do business as usual before the frenzied crowds broke in and overran the kitchens and freezer until they all too, shut their doors and ran.

After a time, people stopped showing up for work as it was becoming clear that no one was intending to pay their salaries. Those with means were negotiating with people they weren't sure they could trust to get them into fresh air shelters to ride out whatever it was that was taking over the planet. Those without means were rushing from place to place, trying to find a place, any place, with breathable air and to get help for the lung diseases that were slowly taking them down. And it was a sure bet that with no governments left to back them, the coins and paper money that had once held so much value and wielded so much power were already worthless remnants of a former time.

Ben Richardson stared up into the sky and tried to find some break in the thick billows of red that spanned from horizon to horizon. His tall frame and wide shoulders cast a long shadow on the parched ground.

"We don't even know what we're fighting." He complained bitterly, even though complaining normally wasn't his way. Staying silent and trying to contain his anger was his usual response. But normal times were long gone. "If they would at least show their faces then we would have something tangible to fight."

"Then let's make them show their faces." Ella's brows had drawn together tightly and she watched him closely.

"Us? We make them? Just like that?" His laugh was short and without humor.

"Just like that." She repeated with a confidence he should have known to expect from her.

"And then what?" Ben brought his two fingers up to his lips.

The gesture was automatic but the cigarette was imaginary. He had been trying to quit for years. He guessed with all the tobacco crops gone and cigarettes no longer available in any store, he was finally going to be forced to do it.

"I don't know." Ella said this with no concession. She might not know the answer but she was convinced that Ben did.

Dark curls played beside her temples and she lifted a hand to brush the hairs aside, her gaze far away. If he broke, they were doomed. If he stopped being angry, she knew it was all over for them. They had already lost so much and in truth, Ella didn't want to fight. She wanted everything to end and she wanted to close her eyes and not see a lingering image of the red, smoky sky or a spreading pool of blood. But sitting back and closing her eyes to the new world around them was no longer an option. A promise made to a dying man had scraped her soul raw enough to bleed and pushed her firmly ahead.

Ella knew if she pushed Ben hard enough, he would fight. That was something about him she had seen right away. She had initially flinched back from the smoldering light that settled behind his eyes when he was angry. Glowing like a lantern, his gaze would pierce her and then he would turn away, wrestling with his anger and finally taking back control. His anger was one of the reasons she went with him that day that seemed so long ago. She learned quickly that she could push him with her words. She learned if she could get him angry enough to fight that he wouldn't give up until he won or until his heart stopped beating. She had learned a lot of things about Ben but that was the one and only thing she deliberately took advantage of.

"I don't know what else to do for us, El." He had finally said gruffly and stalked away from her in that hot, suffocating air, shutting her out and closing himself away from her.

Ella slowly followed him at a short distance, her head down and her long hair draping over her eyes. She needed to let Ben grind away at the problem and find his way back to where his strength lay, brooding and waiting. But they didn't have much time. She felt that urgency within herself the same way she felt his soft touch on her hair when he thought she was asleep. The red clouds were getting thicker and the air was filling with more and more poison. They wouldn't last much longer without fresh air and without a support structure to sustain them. Ella picked her way slowly over the hard gravel behind him. Her small feet in the too-big boots made short scrapes in the dead grass. She allowed Ben to gain a small lead on her, but she never lost sight of him as he plodded forward.

Ben couldn't see any options left to them. Both hands came up to shield his tired eyes. The morning sky had dawned a deep red that mirrored the red hot rage in his soul. The heavens had been crimson every morning for the past two months and he breathed in a harsh sigh. With the breath came a lungful of bitter air that caught sharply in his throat. Time was running out. There was nowhere to run and no place on earth where the air was clean.

They had heard rumors that even the supposedly safe underground bunkers with manufactured fresh air - paid for with cash when government money still had some value - had been compromised. No one knew for sure if the sabotage was by angry citizens trapped above, or if it was the work of the non-human enemy who was determined to destroy them. Either way, all hopes to withstand the aftermath of the cloud attack were already dashing away like wet paint flung from the bristles of a brush. The heads of governments and those chosen few in the bunkers now had even less chance of survival than those trapped on the stifling surface. The irony of it was galling. With the world's elect out of the picture, who would wind up ruling what was left of the world? Ben had to wonder if an alien race ruling the world could be any worse than an ill-prepared horde of desperate humans whose only true goal was personal survival.

"We're not going to make it, are we?" Ella's tone was despairing as she laid a hand gently on his waist. Her words burrowed into his mind. She wasn't as discouraged as she wanted him to believe. But she needed to make him even angrier than he was. His anger made him restless. It pushed him forward. There was no turning back so forward was all they had.

"I don't know." He was always direct with her and there was no reason to change that now.

It was time to leave again and they both knew the end was coming sooner than either of them hoped. The horizon was an indistinct blur, inflamed with an ever darkening haze of soot and smoke.

"Let's go back home, then." She leaned her head against his back and her hand slid down and away, finally settling loose at her side.

He hadn't made any promises to her. When she had followed him to this remote area, her trust had been unsettling to him. "I'm coming with you." She had continued packing even as he had stood shaking his head, willing her to stay where she was. "You'll find a way for us."

Putting the ruined horizon to his back, Ben spun on his heel and looked into her hopeful face. His mind roiled as he held her gaze. Who did she think he was? He was a fourteen-dollar an hour "picker and packer" warehouse worker for a company that hadn't even bothered to call or text him to say he no longer had a job. The thick alien clouds had created a perfect barrier between satellites and cell towers so that people could rarely get enough of a signal to get online. And when they were online, no one was taking a chance on buying products that may or may not ever appear on their doorstep.

Forcing his smoke-filled lungs to take in another choking breath, Ben had shown up one day for work and found the employee entrance boarded shut. A hand lettered sign tacked at a crazy angle on the edge of the wide door frame simply read;

"IT'S OVER."

He wanted to tell Ella to go away and let him stay and suck down the burning, soot-filled air so she wouldn't see him give up. He had no idea what to do and didn't know who the enemy really was or what he could do to fight against it. But she lifted her dark eyes up to his. After a long moment in which he frowned at her intently in hopes she might relent and leave him alone, he saw clearly in her dark eyes that she was never giving up on him. Her trust in him frightened him and at the same time made his flesh tingle with pride. Surprising himself, Ben found himself smiling down at her and letting a tiny pinprick of hope enter his chest.

"There's one more place we can try." He reached for her hand and as the germ of an idea churned and took root in his mind, he sighed out a breath full of smoke and dread.

TWO

The cabin in Alberton was set back at the end of a long gravel-packed road in a sparsely populated, heavily forested community. Ben drove while Ella slept, her breathing light and easy in the quietness of the car. As he piloted the car around the last turn that would take them down the driveway to the cabin, Ben spoke aloud.

"We're here." He said this without raising his voice.

Ella sighed deeply for a moment, her eyes closed, but she soon blinked awake and lazily stretched her shoulders.

"I could sleep for days." Her tired eyes scanned the trees lining the driveway and then turned to gaze at Ben.

"I don't know if I can let you sleep for days, but I promise to be quiet so you can at least sleep through the night."

Even when they were alone together, Ben and Ella talked quietly. He had learned early on in life that it paid to be soft-spoken and so thirty-five years later, he still rarely raised his voice. Ella was tired. She hadn't had the strength to shout about anything for a long time. Gathering her small pack of belongings, she pushed open the car door and stepped outside.

****

Once inside the cabin, they both felt the relentless quiet filling the place and it made them both want to keep their voices low and their hands busy. Flinging the dusty sheets off the worn furniture, they worked in silence to make the small house ready. They had no idea how long they would have to stay in the cabin, so they busied themselves with the small jobs that brought the old house back to life.

The wood frame building had been in Ben's family for as long as he could remember. At their "city house", as his father would always call their main residence in town, the dark haired boy would listen, fascinated. His father would lean back in his faded cloth recliner chair and prop an ankle on his knee as he bragged in a way that he hoped didn't sound too much like bragging.

"It's not like we're rich." His head would tip forward at this point in a faux-humble way. "It's just that we know the value of investing in real estate. Most people in this neighborhood can barely afford one house, let alone a primary residence and a vacation cabin."

Ben had heard the story so many times, with always the same proud inflection in his dad's voice. By the time he was twelve, Ben understood the difference between a real vacation cabin and his family's one thousand square foot, two-bedroom ranch house with a dank, unfinished basement. Only the fact that the small house had been built in an area surrounded by tall pine trees, set far from the dirt road, made it qualify, albeit peripherally, as a cabin.

Ben missed his dad. His mom had been gone for so many years that he barely remembered her. *Gone* was really just his pretty word for saying she was dead. The cancer that took her also took a big chunk of his dad's soul. Even though the memories of a five-year-old boy might be fuzzy and faint, those of a grown man, a husband still deeply in love, were powerful and strong. So strong that on some days, the boy wasn't sure his dad would ever stop staring at the TV to talk to him. The boy knew his dad wasn't really watching whatever silly show happened to be on. Because his eyes never moved to follow the scenes and when it was over, his dad could never remember enough details to answer any questions the boy had.

When the coughing had first begun, it hadn't seemed like much at all. His dad had been smoking for as long as Ben could recall and his harsh coughs often woke him up in the middle of the night, hacking out of his abused lungs. But the new cough was different. The new cough got uglier. And after the doctors had run all their tests and delivered their diagnosis with lowered voices, Ben hadn't batted an eye. He was a man by then and used to hurt and pain and fear. This was nothing new. Only more of the same. He would deal with it the way he dealt with everything else. Logically and practically. And he wouldn't get angry. He would hold his emotions in check like his dad had taught him.

Ben only made only concession to his internalized fear. Walking out of the clinic with his dad, Ben had tugged the blue and white box of Newports out of his shirt pocket and tossed them into the round metal trash can by the walkway. The box landed with a dull ringing thud into the empty waste can and the gong carried with it a finality that reverberated through his chest.

Months later, when the strange ships had appeared in the sky, blasting out their fiery clouds that never thinned or dissipated, Ben had started to get angry. He had felt the stinging in his lungs as the choking smoke settled into all the small pockets. His dad had lay on the bed and struggled to breathe air into his diseased lungs and he stared at the ceiling as his efforts failed. Ben had rushed from place to place searching for any remaining oxygen tanks or respirators to help his dad, but there were none left. He hadn't moved fast enough. Then the anger flared to life inside him at the senselessness of it all. The government and the military had done nothing while the thousands of alien craft had spewed their pink poison over the earth. By the time they realized the clouds weren't going away, there was no weapon they owned that could punch through the dense choking layers.

Listening to the ugly rasping cough pushing out from deep inside his father's lungs, Ben had seethed with anger at whoever or whatever had thrown that poisonous cloud over the earth.

"I don't need to stay here any longer anyway." His dad had barked out the despairing words and coughed so deeply that Ben wanted to turn his head away. But he didn't. He kept his eyes on his dad and pressed a hand to his shoulder, and watched him struggle as the relentless red clouds choked away the last of his breath.

Shaking his head against the memory, Ben became aware that Ella had been staring at him. The cabin was small and standing in the middle of the dusty living room, he hadn't expected the old thoughts to completely immobilize him.

"If you don't need me," His stiffened fingers pressed hard against the side of his leg, willing him to focus. "I'll go get the furnace going in the basement so we can have hot water." He looked steadily at Ella and waited for her response.

Her eyes flicked up at him. He knew she was still wary of being alone but he also knew he couldn't babysit her every minute of the day and night. If they were going to make it together, she would have to move past her fears. She would have to move past the memories of the night he had found her, sitting stiffly on the cold pavement, staring unblinking into the late afternoon sky. Her hands were still clutched tight to a man who was a sad casualty of a war they hadn't even realized they were fighting. He knew she had only gone with him that night because she lacked the strength to pull herself away from the rapidly cooling body of her husband. She had relied on Ben to pry her cold fingers away from her husband's shoulders and she had watched blankly as he laid her husband's crushed head gently on the pavement. It took only a minute to convince her to stand and follow him to his car.

Ella hadn't followed Ben because she trusted him. Not at first. In the beginning, she followed him because she didn't care if she lived or died. Everything had gotten too hard and she was so tired and her heart hurt so much. Ben had been fine with that at first. It gave him a reason to keep putting one foot in front of the other and a reason not to simply sink down on the road beside her and call it a life.

"Go ahead. I'll be fine." Her words were clear and strong and she swung the dust rag around in her hand, venturing a half-smile. She wasn't sure if she would be fine alone in the dusty living room of the cabin, but she told him what he wanted to hear. And at that point, whether it was the truth or not didn't matter so much to Ben. He was just glad she was trying.

Ben's heart softened at her gesture, and he reached out and tapped a finger to her cheek. Her weak smile grew at his touch. She was stronger than she knew and he relaxed as she turned to begin brushing the dust from the small coffee table.

When the small mouse darted across the dark wooden floor, Ella screamed and instinctively threw her dust rag at the scampering rodent.

"Uuuuugggh!" She recoiled and shook her shoulders in a mock shudder. "Nasty!"

If Ben hadn't been so irritated by the idea of a mouse invading his cabin, he would have laughed at Ella's response. Her nose wrinkled and he had to resist the urge to tell her that in that moment, she looked a bit 'mouse-like' herself. He pushed an armchair to one side, hoping to find the mouse hiding behind it. Unfortunately, what he found was a hole - slightly smaller than mouse sized - in the baseboard of the wall behind the chair.

"I'll go find it and get rid of it." Ben's tone of voice was firmer than it needed to be.

Ella hesitated. "It's not that big a deal. It's just one mouse." She had seen so much violence and death in the past few weeks and she was tired of it. Even if the death was of a mouse and not a man, it was more than she wanted to be responsible for.

"No. It'll think it can stay as long as it wants and where there's one rat, there's usually more. If we don't do something now, soon there will be more of them than we can handle." He spoke the words in a tone that allowed no argument.

She understood immediately what was going on. He was choosing to fight a battle he was sure he could win to take his mind off of the battle he was afraid he might lose. The color of the sky had been shifting from red to black then back to red and they hadn't been able to leave the house in the city for days. Once the food had run out in all the stores, sealing the two of them in the old cabin in the woods was their temporary solution. There was a small amount of food and some basic supplies and they might be able to last a little while longer there.

The house had been a retreat set deep in the woods until the first of the flames had chewed mercilessly at the surrounding tall fir trees. The drier wood had literally exploded into the hot air when the roaring blaze bellowed through the trees alongside the dirt road. When the inferno was only a few feet away from leaping the last few feet and consuming the old building, the winds had abruptly shifted and fell back the way they came. With nothing left to feed on, the flames had crackled in frustration, and then quickly died away.

"I'll take care of the mouse." He said with a sigh. He was exhausted. He hadn't slept well for longer than he wanted to think about and his mind was getting foggier every day. But he rebelled against the exhaustion. They couldn't let their guard down. The fire in the sky wasn't his only concern. Something more was coming and there was a restless, nagging feeling in his gut that wouldn't let his mind settle. Every night since his father died, when Ben's body would finally collapse into a fitful sleep, shadowy, fleeting images assaulted his mind. As the images grew stronger and more menacing, he struggled against himself, clawing at consciousness to break free from their fearsome grip.

Snatching up the heavy metal toolkit, he turned his back on Ella and descended the steps to the basement.

THREE

"Where did it go?" Ben's voice was loud in the stillness of the cool, dark basement.

A stale gust of fetid air wafted past his nose causing him to lift a hand against the assault. The basement was full of shadows but there was enough light filtering from the open door behind him to allow him to see…something. His eyes squinted trying to focus on the darkish, quickly moving shapes skimming across the hard, cement floor. His first thought was that it was water trickling across the floor. Maybe one of the rusty old pipes had finally burst open and was laboriously spewing its contents like an unhappy drunk. But there was no sound. Surely he would have heard the sound of rushing water or the hissing from the jagged seam of a burst pipe.

He had a brief thought that he should go back and get his flashlight, but quickly tossed the thought aside. This was his basement in his cabin and he shouldn't have to be afraid in his own house. Chasing the dirty brown field mouse through the crack under the kitchen door into the basement was what brought him down the old wooden stairs. But those shapes were what held his attention and caused him to hesitate with his foot still lingering on the last step. Enveloped in a wonderment that wasn't exactly fear but wasn't exactly ease, he leaned his head closer to the wispy moving shapes.

* * * *

Lying tiredly on her back on the lumpy tan couch, Ella wondered why Ben hadn't returned yet. She was so tired she could barely move. There was no sound coming from the basement and Ella wondered if he had dispatched the mouse and was sitting quietly in the dark. That wouldn't surprise her. During the time they had been together, he would often settle away from her. His eyes would cloud in thought and his face would tilt up as if there was something pressing calling his attention to a spot high on the ceiling.

Oddly, she caught a faint whiff of sulfur wafting through from the kitchen. But unable to keep her eyes open much longer, Ella turned her head toward the back of the couch, preferring its musty smell over the sulfur. And she slept.

* * * *

In the darkness of the basement, Ben flinched at the intensity of the sudden brilliance. Throwing up his hand too late, a vivid white-black-red light flashed around him and his horrified eyes watched the skin of his hand glow translucent to the point of seeing sinew and bone. He opened his mouth to scream but his breath was gone.

* * * *

Ella woke from a restless sleep. She didn't open her eyes, but from the stale smell of old fabric too close to her nose, she knew she had fallen asleep on the couch. Hearing the stamp of heavy boots on the basement stairs, her mind worked to figure out how long she had been lying there. Was Ben just now coming back up from chasing that mouse?

She knew before she saw him that something was wrong. Ben's breathing was tortured and came in short puffs as he stomped across the floor toward her. Opening her eyes fully, Ella sat up and blinked drowsily at the man she had unquestioningly followed as the sky burned above them. His face seemed oddly blurred and she reached for her glasses on the small table beside the couch.

"What happened?" She said and coughed lightly to clear her throat.

He shook his head and gave her the tiny smile that told her he was amused at something. His eyes slanted to one side and Ella stretched groggily to her feet, her arms lifted overhead.

"What?" She asked again and flicked her eyes down as he quickly moved to hide his hands behind his back.

"Come with me and see." He said and a cool hollowness followed each syllable like a murky echo between his lips.

He was the one she chosen to spend the rest of her days with. Although she had qualified that with, "No matter how long that might be".

Waking next to him one morning, she had insisted that he find someone to marry them before she would go any further with him. He had lifted a skeptical eyebrow at the firm set of her lips. However, he wasted no time driving to the closest church they could find and pressing the startled pastor into marrying them. The wedding was quick and efficient but all she cared about was that it was legal.

"As legal as it can be these days." The sad preacher had intoned as he had them sign a register and a license application and then pronounced them husband and wife.

Ella had decided that Ben would be the last man she would ever share her life with. She had run with him as the fire in the sky chased them from place to place and seared their lungs and sucked their breath away whenever they dared to venture outside. She had made her choice.

But assessing the man who now stood before her, his eyes blank and cold and the smell of smoke circling around him, she hesitated.

"Nothing has changed." The man intoned and Ella knew then that everything had changed.

"Why would you say that?" She shook her head slightly and a movement behind him made her flick her eyes to the left.

"Everything has changed." A second dark haired man staggered through the door leading up from the basement; his eyes wild, his skin ashen and so, so pale.

Ella forced herself to look and she forced herself to choose. It was only a split second but the man who wasn't Ben glanced away behind him and in that instant Ella jerked to one side and the real Ben lifted the shotgun and fired.

Hot pellets of wet flesh blew through the air and the awful moistness splashed on Ella. She shrieked and slapped at the hot places as the propelled lumps splattered on her skin and begin to sizzle. Too weak, Ben fell backwards from the recoil of the rifle and he slammed his left foot down to steady himself but he was too close to the top stair. Yelling a curse, he stepped back into empty air.

Ella's feet slipped in the hot stickiness that was all that was left of the creature that looked like Ben as she rushed toward the basement door. She felt as if she was moving too slow and Ben was falling too fast. Then she was at the basement door and grabbing him, her fingers clutching tight at his shirt. But his momentum had already propelled him too far and they both fell back and down and the black shapes moving and writhing along the basement floor began to stir.

FOUR

Darkness had never bothered Ben. He drank it in and swallowed it whole and dared it to come at him again. But Ella hated the darkness. Her nightmares always found her in the darkness. The darkness was where she slid down, choking for breath and flailing out a desperate hand. The darkness was where the lies became truth and the horrors became real. She avoided the darkness at all costs. But it was into the darkness they were falling. Swiftly. Silently. Painfully.

The fall from the top to the bottom step hadn't been a long one. But they fell awkwardly and hard and it was a full minute before Ella could catch her breath. When she finally did take in a deep, gasping breath, the stench of sulfur filled her lungs and she gagged and spit and tried not to vomit. Before her rebelling stomach could completely recoil, her mind suddenly cleared and she remembered where she was. Ella twisted her body around to grasp frantically at Ben who was lying too still beside her on the cold cement floor. His face and head were shrouded in the murky darkness and she squeezed her eyes tightly shut for a second. He couldn't be dead. She refused to let the thought take root in her mind. He was always the brave one and she counted on him for his strength.

Out of the corner of her eye, she spied a stealthy shifting of the shadows in the blackness beyond then. The dark shapes had fled to the far corners of the room when the two bodies had come crashing down the rickety stairs and slammed onto the hard floor. The smell of ozone and sulfur prickled its way into her nostrils again. They had recovered from their surprise and were regrouping, sliding across the floor toward where he and woman lay. She had to get them moving. Ella had no idea what had happened to Ben in the basement. And in truth, she didn't want to know. Whatever those shapes were, they had sucked him almost dry and tried to trick her with whatever that was that spoke to her upstairs.

Scrambling to her knees on the hard, damp floor, Ella wrapped her hands around Ben's legs and yanked on his dead weight, inching him toward the stairs until her strained back began to ache. She didn't want to look at his face. His head had been blanketed by the rank darkness and she was afraid of what she would see as it came into view. So she continued to pull and stare at a point on his stomach. She pulled even harder, her head twisting around to gauge the distance left to reach the bottom stair. The narrow wooden stairway was close and she should have been happy about that. Her gaze shifted to the top of the flight of stairs and she groaned, wondering how she would ever get him up the stairs. Settling her shoulders, she leaned further backward, her back screaming in protest.

"Let go of me!" He rasped out the command. His voice was weak, but she was absolutely sure it was his voice. She forced the sound into her memory and vowed she would never forget again.

"No." Ella continued to tug on his legs, pulling him toward the stairs, inching on her knees across the damp floor.

"Stop it. I can walk." He muttered testily and slapped ineffectually at her hands.

"Then walk."

She released her hold on him and scrambled to her feet, biting the inside of her jaw to stop the tears of relief. Ben's head slowly came into view in the dim light filtering down from the top of the stairs. Ella held her breath and fear stabbed at her heart as she waited to see his face. She wasn't sure what she would see but as more of his face inched into view, the more the noose of fear tightened around her throat. Ella was stunned at much she loved him. She was completely floored by the idea that she could love him as much as she did in such a short time. Staring at his pale, but unmarked face, Ella breathed out deeply and blinked back her tears. She watched him lying on the floor for another second, willing him to get up and follow her out of the basement before it was too late.

"Ughhh." His groan was low and long and he was moving, but not fast enough.

"Get up!" Ella finally yelled at him and even in the darkness she saw the irritation flash in his eyes.

"Woman..." He started to grumble, but at the same time, he stretched out his hand for her to help him up.

His other hand was still splayed out on the floor behind him. Ella twitched as a furtive dark movement caught her eye.

"It's there!" Ella yelled and pointed.

She felt herself rising to the brink of hysteria and she was trying to hold it together but the dark shapes were so close and they began to wriggle closer to each other, four shapes became two, then two became one as they bonded together in the shadows.

Just as the leading edge of the slithering darkness licked out to snag the tip of Ben's finger, he jerked himself forward and up and seemed to spring to his feet. His arms flew around Ella's waist and he shoved her in front of him and toward the basement stairs. She staggered on the first step, her shins cracking angrily against the wood but still he pushed her up. Her bruised flesh screamed at the injustice as she forced her feet to move and her hands to grapple with the railing as the two of them gasped and clawed their way to the top of the stairs.

Fiery red light blasted through the windows, bathing the kitchen in a deep red glow. It looked to Ben as if someone had upended a bucket of hot fresh blood and splashed it from wall to ceiling to floor. As Ben slammed the basement door shut behind them and threw the latch, he shook his head, knowing that wouldn't stop anything or anyone from getting through. And he had no idea if the dark shapes were a "who" or a "what", but he knew they had to get as far away from them as they could. His skin was still pale and the dark stubble of his beard made him look even paler. But he was alive and he was walking and most importantly he was angry. His anger made him stronger and Ella knew he would fight harder when he was mad.

"Let's go." He called out sharply to Ella.

"Go where?" She threw out a hand toward the blazing sky and tried not to lose hope or lose her mind. "We're running out of options."

"I don't know where we're going." He grabbed her hand and pulled her behind him toward the front room. "But I know we can't stay here."

"Grab a few things and let's get to the car." He staggered just slightly, his strength momentarily lagging, but he shook off Ella's outstretched hand. "I'm fine. Get your stuff and let's go."

He spoke quickly and firmly and averted his gaze from the shadowy shapes already wedging and pressing their way under the closed basement door.

The instant Ben and Ella left the safety of the cabin, their eyes began to sting and their lungs began to ache from breathing in the thick smoke. Ella was carrying too many things in her arms and she lagged a little behind him.

"I told you to leave all that stuff behind." Ben grumbled curtly.

But even as he said the sharp words, he turned to Ella and grabbed the largest of her burdens; a fully stuffed tan backpack.

"We'll need something to eat." Her voice was barely a whisper as her lungs hitched and fought against the burning air.

Ben pressed his lips together and breathing only through his nose, he sprinted the last few feet to the car. Jamming his thumb down on the remote, the click-clack of the doors unlocking was a dim sound compared to the rushing of the blood in his ears. He yanked open the back door and tossed in his bag and then the tan backpack full of food. By then, Ella was right behind him and when he turned, she shoved the rest of her bags at him and he flung them in the backseat, not caring how they landed.

"Hurry." He huffed and they raced, leaping awkwardly into the front seats. They had to get moving.

"What direction?" She glanced over at him.

Ella pulled out a paper fold-out map and a decades-old compass he had found in the cabin. Their cell phones had been useless for days. When the fire in the sky had begun to shoot out sparks like fiery red lightening, all their power had burned out within seconds.

He frowned slightly into the fiery distance and Ella waited with her eyes averted.

"I know you're not happy about having to leave the cabin." She stated the obvious and received a sarcastic snort from he in reply."

"No. But I don't think we had much choice, did we?"

"No." Ella looked out the window of the car and tilted her head up to look at the dense clouds covering the sky from horizon to horizon. "Do you think it was…them? Those shapes in the basement and that…thing that looked like you? Do you think they did that?"

"Yes. I'm sure it was them but I don't know how or why or what that copy of me was supposed to do."

"Do you think it was planning to kill me? Or take me to the basement and make a copy of me, too?"

"I don't know." He answered honestly and shook his head. "I wonder too, why didn't it kill me? It had to know I was still alive and would try to stop it. I don't understand that at all."

How they heard the slight rustling sound from the backseat would always be a mystery to them both. Ben heard it first and before he could swing his head fully around, Ella was already doing the same.

"Did you hear that?" He asked Ella.

"Yes." She answered quickly and her fingers tightened around the old round compass.

He quickly considered their options. Leaving the car again meant sucking in a lungful of the poisonous air, and he could try to crawl into the backseat to grab for it, but there wasn't much room for him to maneuver, if…

"Get out." He spoke abruptly.

Ella hurriedly tossed the map and the compass to the floor. Taking a deep breath, she pushed open her door and took two long steps away from the car. Flinging the back door wide open, Ben snatched up the food bag with both hands and prepared to sling it into the yard. Just as he lifted the bag off the car seat, he saw it. The small brown field mouse popped through a small opening near the top flap of the bag and scurried between the other two bags on the seat. Not hesitating, he grabbed for the creature and managed to pinch its long tail between his fingers.

"Here's our stowaway." He stalked around the back of the car and presented the mouse to Ella who shook her head and recoiled.

"Was it in the food bag?" She asked and wrinkled her nose.

"Yes."

24

"Did it poop in there?"

"Yes. I told you to leave the food behind. We'll find something along the way."

"Bite me." She muttered and ignored the slight smile on Ben's face.

He threw the pack of food onto the burnt remains of the lawn and gently slung the small mouse toward the pack. Not liking the slightly greasy feel of the mouse's tail, Ben rubbed his fingers absently along his pant leg. He watched for a moment as the mouse dashed toward the pack, its nose and tail twitching. Settling into the front seat of the car again, he glanced one last time at the mouse who had sat up on its hind legs on top of the pack, guarding it like a treasure. Training his eyes toward the horizon, he prepared to let Ella know what direction they would take. There wasn't anywhere he knew to go except north. The ocean was to the south, but the thought of the fire and the water and the heat all rolled together was too much for him to bear. It would be cooler in the mountains. He started the engine and put the car into gear. A movement outside his window made him flick his eyes back toward the small mouse. It was still sitting on top of the pack, watching him with tiny black eyes.

Ben blinked and sucked in a harsh breath as the image of the grey-brown mouse wavered and then dissolved into jet black, inky tendrils that spread like a black scar on top of the tan colored pack. Slamming his foot so hard on the gas that Ella's head snapped back against the headrest, the crumpled map shot forward off her lap and onto the floorboard.

"What's wrong?" She hissed her question and rubbed at the back of her head.

"Everything." He replied and pressed the gas pedal to the floor.

FIVE

Ben's eyes began to droop from weariness and his head bobbed forward. There weren't any other cars on the road so there was no danger of a head-on collision. However, careening off the road and rolling into the steep ditch on either side would cause them a world of problems. Ella knew he didn't want to make a stop until they had reached the point on the map he had selected; his finger stabbing determinedly onto a small dot on the paper. Driving into the deep angry red of the setting sun had creased a deep furrow into Ben's brow. He was tense and too tired and finally Ella grew weary of watching him and waiting for something to happen.

"Let's stop for a bit." She laid a hand on his knee and pressed lightly.

"I'm fine." He shook his head to clear the fogginess.

"Are you sure?" She asked.

When he turned to stare directly at her, Ella stifled an eye roll and looked away. He was so stubborn. She wanted to argue with him, to tell him it wouldn't help either of him to tire himself out so completely. But she knew he wouldn't listen. He would rest when he was ready. Ella watched him a moment longer out of the corner of her eye and then her full gaze returned to scan his profile. Everything about him was attractive to her; the lightly tanned skin of his face, his tall, athletic body and especially his mind. It was clear she would never have survived this far without him. His strength made her braver and she prayed every night not to disappoint him.

"Stop staring at me." He said gruffly but with a tiny bit of a smile. "You're supposed to be watching for our turn off."

"I can do both." She returned his smile but finally looked away.

The past few days had given them little to smile about, so they took their smiles when they could. Ben still hadn't told Ella exactly what happened to him in the basement or what he had seen when he glanced back at the field mouse. And he was beginning to see that not telling her scared her more than hearing the truth. He had always told her the truth. He wanted her to know what was happening every step of the way so she would be prepared for whatever came next. The events that transpired in the darkness of the basement and the fate of the field mouse were cavernous wells in Ben's mind where truth and reality grappled and tussled like Jacob and Esau in the womb. But he couldn't hold back telling her the truth for very long. In the long run, keeping that secret wouldn't help either one of them, and as it turned out, the secret itself forced the truth out of him.

The dot on the map Ben had selected wasn't random. Morgan Valley was a town well known to Ben. As he and his dad had traveled from the city to their vacation cabin in Alberton, Morgan Valley was the last stop for gas and food. It was nestled in a valley between two high peaks. The name Morgan was given to the valley when the town was founded by Willard Morgan.

Willard had hoped to use his considerable railroad wealth to drive a spur of the main railroad through the valley, making the small valley town a money-generating stopping point half-way between the two larger towns. The fact that Willard Morgan owned all the land in town and would make a hundred percent profit on the deal wasn't lost on anyone. When the deal eventually fell through and the railroad skipped over the valley, a bitter Willard Morgan refused to leave his town. He and his family stayed in the valley and as his children and their children married and had children, they all paid homage to him by naming several of their male children after their ancestor. Wandering through the streets of Morgan Valley as a boy, Ben maybe should have been amused, but he was usually simply annoyed at men and boys calling out to each other, "Hey, Willard!"

Lost in his thoughts and memories, Ben could almost forget what had happened at the cabin in Alberton. But forgetting wasn't going to be that easy. When Ben first saw the thick tree lying across the road, he narrowed his eyes and glanced left and right. He suspected a trap of some kind and as he slowed down he came fully awake and aware. Swinging her head to look from him back to the tree, Ella folded the old compass into the map and bent over to slide the packet onto the floorboards. As she lifted her head, he shifted in his seat, tense and prepared. Ella pulled the gun from the glove box, thumbed off the safety and held the weapon tightly on her lap. There were trees growing on both side of the road. Not many, but enough that a fallen tree might not be such an unusual thing. So much had happened to the sky and the ground over the past few weeks that the earth might easily be unable to support large trees any longer. But the couple was still wary and their eyes scanned the roadsides, searching for any sign of a trap.

"What do you think?" Ella's throat was tight and her words came out high-pitched and airy.

"I think it's a tree." Ben slowed down even more.

"I know it's a tree. What do we do?"

A chuckle bubbled from his lips as he looked over at Ella. "We're going through it."

"Seriously, Ben? What are we going to do? I don't think we should stop."

Ignoring her question, Ben gave the sedan a little gas and gritted his teeth. "Shoot for the middle of the tree. Three shots. On my word."

Ben waited for Ella to say something more. He waited for her to tilt her head to the side like he had seen her do so many times and demand some answers from him. As if on cue, Ella tilted her head to the side, hesitated a half-second, but this time was different. This time, she said nothing. Ella pressed the button to lower her window. Ben focused his eye on the road as she extended her arm out of the window and aimed the pistol toward the thick midsection of the tree. Hot wind blew into her lungs and she blinked and held her breath, as she steadied her aim.

"Now." He said calmly and Ella fired.

He pressed harder on the gas as the three bullets collided with the tree. Ropy black filaments flew up and out of the tree and he was aware of Ella screaming an obscenity as she yanked herself back into the car and jammed on the window button. Ben stared straight ahead as the gap in the middle of the tree grew wider. The entire length of the tree began to shimmer and waver. Then the tree disappeared.

Five miles down the road, well past the thing that was a tree but wasn't a tree, Ben lifted his foot off the gas and slowly coasted to a stop on the side of the road. His adrenalin was still flowing thickly through his veins and pried his damp hands off the steering wheel and wiped them off on the knees of his pants. Turning to Ella, he stroked one hand along her trembling cheek and tried to give her a smile but no smile came.

"I need to tell you some things that shouldn't be true, but are."

SIX

The inside of the car was blazing hot but neither one of them reached to open a window, not wanting to let more of the choking air drift inside. The clouds blocked out most of the light from the sun, but a weak pinkish glow filtered through to give the air a surreal, rose-colored radiance. The soft shimmering light would have been exquisitely beautiful if that same air hadn't also been exquisitely deadly.

Ben turned off the car engine and checked the road in front and behind them. They had driven far enough away from the tree that really wasn't a tree, so there was no need to search the road, but still, he looked closely. Tall trees with grayish green leaves still lined the road even on this stretch of the highway. All the trees in Ben's view looked real enough, and none were materializing in the road. But still…

The sky wasn't as red as it had been earlier and there were actually streaks of pale pink in the otherwise deep crimson color. He didn't know if that meant anything or if it was simply his mind wishing so hard for something good, that he saw things that weren't really there. But the fake tree? That had looked as real as any fake tree could be. Ben began to eye all the scenery around him, searching for some way to know if anything else had been manufactured.

"I can't believe that just happened." Ella whispered nervously, interrupting his contemplation.

Blasting their way through the false tree hadn't been as unnerving for Ben as it had been for Ella. When the black smoky tendrils had exploded from the middle of tree, Ben's mind had flown back to the black shapes in the basement and the sight of the gray mouse dissolving into inky ropes on top of the back pack.

"Yeah." Ben replied. It was all he could think of to say.

He knew he needed to say more but he dreaded telling her everything. He knew she could handle the truth, but after a few

30

weeks with him, she had become so full of optimism. He hated to take that from her.

"I know you were hoping that the clouds would simply blow over one day and things would slowly go back to the way they had been." Ben spoke her thoughts and she nodded her head.

"Yes. But things will never ever be the same. Will they?"

They had both lost so much, but she was right. That part of both their lives had moved on and would never return.

"I can tell you what I saw, but I can't tell you yet what it means." Ben said.

"Fine. Tell me what you saw."

"Because I don't want you to think I'm not telling you everything. I just don't know what it means." Ben didn't know why he was hedging. Maybe he didn't want to think about what he saw and what it meant so he had tried to avoid the discussion altogether. Maybe he just didn't want to admit that what was happening was real and they couldn't hide from it.

"Stop stalling and just tell me." Ella's small fist punched into his side and a low grunt flew out of him.

"Woman…" He rubbed at his side and frowned over at her.

Her eyes flashed with impatience and she leveled a finger at him. "Then talk!"

Ben let a tiny smile ghost his lips before he replied. When they had first met and were still in that 'getting to know each other" phase of their relationship, Ella told him she didn't have a bad temper. It soon became apparent that she hadn't been telling the truth. Her temper was quick and fierce and he loved her calm as much as he loved her fire. She had gotten hotly angry when he told her it was too soon for them to be more than friends. He explained quietly and sensibly that she needed more time before she should look to him as anything more than that. He never saw the punch coming that ricocheted off his jaw and rocked him back on his heels.

"I'll never be good 'friend' material." She had said with a fierceness that made her green eyes blaze. "I'd always be jealous and you'd never be able to trust my words. So we won't be 'just friends' but we don't have to be lovers. We'll simply be 'together'."

She had made the pronouncement with her narrow chin tipped up at him and Ben hadn't argued. He hadn't wanted to argue. Over the weeks, they had grown so close that he hardly remembered what his life was like before her and before the fire in the sky. Well...that wasn't exactly true. The darker years from before they met were always a murky, gray memory that often pushed into his dreams and stole his sleep. Ben spent a great deal of the nighttime hours forcing those memories to the back of his mind. He was getting better at keeping them trapped back there and some nights he was able to sleep four to five hours at a time.

Sitting beside Ella in the small car, hot, stale air seeped through the vents like an angry mist. Ben sighed and turned to Ella and prayed she would stand with him after what he had to say. She was stronger than she was a few weeks ago. But strength was fickle and eager to flee when truth battled with fear.

"Do you want to know what happened in the basement?" He asked again and was rewarded with her narrowed eyes and raised fist.

"Yes. Please. Tell me now before I beat it out of you." Ella growled her threat at him.

Ella knew Ben didn't want to tell her. But he needed to understand that she could deal with whatever it was that had left him pale and shaking and staggering up the basement stairs. Since they had been together, Ella had woken up beside him when the nightmares would pummel his mind and shake his body like a flopping rag doll. He was always angry when he woke from the dreams and sometimes he would let her hold him but he would never talk. When holding him wasn't enough and she began to kiss his lips gently, he would sometimes grasp her tightly and mount her quickly until the shaking turned to a hot, shuddering orgasm. Other times he would roll away from her, not wanting her touch or her words. Those were the times she would lie on her back, staring up at the round circle of the ceiling light and try to ignore his heavy, torment-filled breathing beside her.

"I saw them move toward me and then the light flashed." He began in a monotone voice. "Black shapes like the ones that blew out of the tree when you shot it."

"Okay. And then what happened?" She prompted.

"There was light, then dark, and then red. Then I saw…" He hesitated before continuing, but not for long. There was no need to stop when he was almost to the part she truly needed to know. "I saw you sleeping on the couch."

Ella rolled her head to one side and frowned out the passenger side window. She had already known this part, hadn't she? Her mind was prepared for this, but she also had prepared for another possibility. She had prayed that he would say he was sick or delusional or just plain crazy. It was funny, but she could handle that much better than what she knew would come next. Closing her eyes for one second, she pushed down her fear and the horde of butterflies fluttering in her stomach.

"And then what did you see?" The words slipped with surprising effort from her lips.

"I saw myself lifting a hammer over my head and bashing in your skull."

Ella gritted her teeth as she remembered the way the false Ben had held his hand behind his back. She remembered how he had shuffled resolutely toward her, and his cold, hollow request to 'come with me and see'. The butterflies in her stomach turned to bats and her gut churned with the realization that she had been only minutes away from being no more than a splotchy red stain on the old musty couch.

"Thanks for not letting it kill me." She said and looked out the window again.

"I love you." Ben professed and let his thumb slide against her cheek.

"I know. I love you, too." She turned her face back to him.

His dark eyes held such sadness and a grief that went beyond the loss of his father and his mother and the loss of a job he hated. What Ella saw in his eyes was a look of resignation so strong that it both frightened her and comforted her at the same time.

"But At least now we know what they want." He said quietly with an understanding that numbed his soul.

She nodded. "They want us all dead."

"Yes. Except... Ben squeezed his fingers around the steering wheel and let his head fall back onto the headrest. "They didn't kill me. They left me in the basement and made that copy of me and sent him up to kill you. Why didn't they kill me?" His head rocked from side to side on the headrest and he wrestled with trying to put all the pieces together. "They had to know I would get up and come after them if they hurt you. They had to know I wouldn't just lay there and let them…"

Ben's voice trailed off, unable to say the unbearable words again. What he also left unsaid was how his resentment had been building, day after day, like brick upon brick, as what little time he had left with his dad had been stolen away by the poisonous clouds.

His dad's voice telling him to keep his anger in check had been a constant in his life. An old memory from his childhood elbowed its way to the surface and Ben was powerless to shove it back away. The memory was one he hated. It was the one time he had let his anger fully rage - fully control him - and hurl him explosively to the edge of reason. His fists were tight knots of fury and Ben was advancing on the unsuspecting teen who had unknowingly pushed him beyond his ability to back down. Out of the corner of his eye, Ben had seen his dad trotting toward him, with a fierce urgency on his face that the young boy had refused to acknowledge. Ben had taken another step forward, his fury propelling his legs and lifting his curled fists, ready to pound them into his tormentor over and over until the red rage subsided or the other boy was dead. But his dad had reached him in time and yanked him aside and slammed him hard against the side of the car. His dad's thick chest pressed his body tight against the hot metal of the car. All Ben could hear was the rushing of the blood surging past his ears, but then slowly, like on old record stuck in a groove, he finally heard the deep timbre of his dad's voice, harsh and panting in his ear; "Push it down, Ben. Push it down…Push it down."

Now, Ben's dad wasn't there to help him. He was no longer there to get in his face and remind him to rein in his anger before that awful but vague 'something' happened. Ben glanced back over at Ella and watched as she fiddled with the paper map, folding and refolding it to try to give her hands something to do. He stared up at the red clouds covering the sky and snorted out a grunt. Something awful had happened and he couldn't see that it had anything to do with his anger. The entire world had stood looking up in passive amazement as the crafts sped across the skies, blanketing the planet with the red choking clouds and then diving down toward the earth. News reporters had focused intently on the massive clouds overhead. When they finally turned their eyes, stinging from the acrid air, down to the places where the aircrafts had descended, no evidence of their landing could be found. Even though no one had reported seeing the aircraft rise back into the air, no unusual craft or spaceship had yet to be found anywhere on earth.

Ella's heart pounded a beat inside her chest as she watched him struggle. She had heard him moaning in his sleep and she had witnessed the fierce anger in his face as each day with the choking clouds had passed to the next.

"I was hoping we could continue to run for a while." She laughed and the sound clutched at Ben's heart. "I honestly hoped we could find us a place in the mountains and we could lie down together and close our eyes and wait for the world to come to an end."

Ella really had embraced that dream, but as she spoke, she acknowledged there was a formless notion inside her that gave her reason to hope for more. Ben might not know why they let him live, and maybe he lived in spite of what they did to him. But Ella had an inkling of an idea of why they had left him alive.

There was something about him that made him special. Standing over six feet tall in a town where most adults were well under that height would have made him unique anyway. But it wasn't only that. And it wasn't the way his dark eyes would bore into you as he spoke with you. Although, if pressed, Ella would admit that his intense gaze could sometimes make her uneasy and cause her to drop her eyes down and away. There was something more. What happened to him as a child had definitely shaped him and there was a quiet restlessness about him, if that contradiction was possible in a person. There was a fire in his eyes when he spoke of the red clouds in the sky that was more than just righteous indignation.

When the red clouds had swept over the planet and blotted out most of the sunlight, no one was really surprised when the climate changed and the crops began to fail and solar power no longer meant anything. The weather didn't change drastically – it wasn't like a nuclear winter. It wasn't dark during the day and there weren't chunks of ash falling from the sky. It was a subtle change for humans but the change was devastating on the crops that provided for all the food in the stores and restaurants. The attack had come in the fall with the devastating effect of destroying all the crops that were only days away from harvest. The clouds acted as a kind of reverse filter, where they amplified the sun's effect on small crops and the green leaves. Overnight, the world awoke to fields that were withered and appeared to be sunburned. Biologists tried to figure out how the phenomenon worked. Millions of acres of trees and plant life still survived; however nearly all the edible plants seemed to be targeted for destruction. The survivalists said it was the alien's plan. Starve out the entire world and only the fittest would survive. For once, no one argued. It was the only explanation that made sense. So the survivalists had grabbed their rifles and their survival gear and headed for the hills to wait for the inevitable.

Even before the president made the announcement that the entire country was in a state of emergency, most stores had already been stripped during the panic of the first two weeks after the ships had left their red poison in the sky. Only the smaller towns still had some food left in the stores and much of that had already spoiled, leaving only dry good and canned item on the shelves.

"It all seems so unbelievable." Ella tipped her head back against the headrest. "Spaceships? Aliens? Come to take over the world?" She shook her head grimly.

"Maybe it's not so unbelievable." Ben pronounced with a surety that sent a chill up Ella's spine.

"Ok." She turned in her seat to face him. "Tell me the rest."

Ben took in a deep breath and pushed it out. "I've always had dreams. Angry dreams. In some of the dreams, I'm running and fighting and my mind is black with rage at something I can never quite catch hold of. My hands are almost always useless. They seem to be trapped at my side as if they're being held by a tight metal band, but when I look down, I can see that they are not bound at all. It's a frustration so maddening that I want to scream and pound my fists against the first thing I see but I'm helpless to move. And that too makes me even more enraged." His breathing quickened as he recalled the dream and Ella wanted to press a hand to his chest to comfort him, but she didn't touch him. She let him continue. "My thoughts are so consumed with this rage and I'm screaming at whatever this is in my mind to get out but it keeps coming at me and I can feel myself rising up on my toes, straining to get free and destroy…whatever or whoever was holding me down."

Ella sighed long and deep. A miserable, disconcerted feeling spread through her. His dream may have meant nothing, but her heart told her that wasn't the case. She had felt the heat from his anger as he talked about the fires in the sky and how it took his father's breath and left him helpless and weak too soon. His rage was building. She could see that clearly. Every time they talked about the fires in the sky and what to do next, it took him more time to push down the bitter rage.

Outside the too-warm car, a black bird hopped across the vacant pavement. Ella wondered if the bird was real. Or was it as fake as the tree they had just blasted through?

"Ka-pow." She whispered and shot at the bird with her forefinger. As if hearing her, the bird stopped and swiveled its dark head to look at the two of them in the car. One beady black eye regarded them solemnly and a twist of fear rose in her chest. But the bird was only a bird and finding the couple in the shiny white car of no real interest, the bird flapped its inky wings once and took to the air.

"Tell me about the mouse and the tree." Ella prompted.

"Okay."

Ben dropped his hands from the steering wheel and took in a deep breath.

"They can make things."

"Okay." She said again.

"They made the mouse and they made the tree. When I told you I saw light and then dark, these filmy black shapes were in the dark." He frowned deeply with concentration. "No," He corrected. "They weren't in the dark. They were the dark."

Ella forced herself not to say 'okay' again and waited with chilly goosebumps rising on her forearms in the warm car.

"The black things were wet." Ben's left hand worked against his left, remembering the sticky feel as the inky tendrils sprayed the liquid on his upraised hand. "It hurt, but not like crushing pain. More like a million needles. Like a tattoo."

"Yes." Ella nodded.

"And then when I looked at my hand, I could see through it. Like they were taking my skin and flesh and then I felt this pulling. I don't know how to describe it but it was like these black things were pulling at my mind and my body, but here's the funny thing. I opened my mouth to scream and I couldn't scream. I felt that same helplessness that I felt in my dream."

Ben looked over at Ella and the crease in her forehead told him this was hard for her, but he didn't stop. He had to finish and tell her the rest.

"When I couldn't scream and I felt so defenseless, I started to get angry." His own brow began to crease with the telling of the tale. "The rage rose in me so fast that I couldn't have stopped it even if I wanted to. But, El?" His eyes closed tightly. "I didn't want to stop it. I knew it was the aliens, or whatever you want to call them, trying to take me and it made me so angry that I wanted to bash them into the floor." Ben's breathing came faster. While goosebumps rose on Ella's flesh, beads of salty sweat rose on his.

"The angrier I got and the more I pushed back at that pulling feeling, the more they pulled. It was like a tug of war but I couldn't see any rope, I could only feel it. The more I pulled back from them, the weaker I got and I could feel myself strong one second and then weak the next. I don't know how long that would have gone on until finally the black shapes sprayed – that's the only way I can describe it – they sprayed this red mist at me. I brought my hands up to grab at my eyes but in less than a second, everything went black."

SEVEN

"How did you know we could shoot our way through the tree?" Ella asked with one finger absently stroking the side of her mouth.

"I didn't." Ben's mouth twitched with a smile at her raised eyebrows.

"That was quite a gamble you took with our lives."

"Not really." Ben put his hand out and captured a lock of her long hair and wound it between his fingers. "I can't tell you how I knew it would work, but I just knew."

After telling her a tale that should have left her scared and angry and maybe even a little suspicious, Ben's heart constricted tightly when Ella reached for him. He knew she loved him and would fight to stay with him. But he was asking so much of her to believe what had happened in the basement. His eyes softening, Ben wrapped his arms around her as best he could in the small car while Ella tried to understand why she couldn't cry. She was hurt and sad over what he had to endure in the basement, and what they still might have to endure, yet no tears would come to her tingling eyes.

She was also more afraid than she would ever tell him.

When Ben slid his hand down tentatively to the warm place between her legs, she didn't hesitate. Ella shifted slightly and opened herself fully to him. The car was small, so she yanked on his shoulders to guide him over to the passenger seat and she settled herself on his lap. Their lovemaking was slow and gentle with a sadness to it that they both felt deeply but neither would ever admit. His orgasm was deliberate and intense and Ella's eyes flew open when she realized they had forgotten to use a condom this time. It was too late anyway as her own passion overtook her and his climax exploded inside her and filled her completely.

* * * *

The rain was heavy and full of black grit as fine as sand. Each drop that smacked against the windshield made Ben blink but he made no other reaction.

"Is it real rain?" Ella asked wearily.

"No."

Ben stared up at the sky and at the water droplets falling from the red clouds. It was water, but the black flecks inside each drop made it clear that it wasn't just water. Whatever it was that came after him in the basement and what made up the false mouse and the tree, were made of the same stuff. After a moment of intense fear that the alien rain would eat its way through the metal of the car, Ben noticed something.

The strange rain wasn't so much falling out of the sky, as it was *dropping*. Random gashes in the dark clouds overhead had opened and the rain seemed to be tumbling to earth from the slitted openings. Ben struggled to hold in the anger that made him want to leap out of the car and yell curses into the ruined sky. It wasn't fair that these things could simply appear one day and destroy his world and the people he loved. His teeth ground together as his hands gripped the steering wheel so tight that his knuckles ached.

Ella watched Ben's face with growing alarm. She couldn't bear the thought of losing him and she could see he was only minutes away from jumping out and racing through the feral rain to…what? What exactly would he do besides put them both at risk? No. It wasn't time for his anger to take him over. Not yet. Ella clamped a hand on Ben's trembling thigh. His head snapped around to face her and she tried not to flinch at the hot fire in his eyes.

"Push it away, Ben." She soothed with her words but clamped down harder on his leg with her fingers. "Come on. Push it away."

The sound of his father's words springing from Ella's mouth startled Ben to the point of speechlessness, but still, he fought against the calming words. He didn't want to push the anger down. He had spent his whole life being forced to deny the rage whenever it poked its furious head up from the depths where he had been repeatedly required to thrust it.

"It's not time, yet." Ella's voice was soft but it was like a knife piercing his ear. "You know that, don't you? You feel that, right?"

"Really, El?" He tried not to shout. "They stole all the air from my dad's lungs and killed your husband and you can sit there and tell me it's not time to get mad about this?"

Ben's teeth ground down so hard on his jaw that his head began to pound. Ella's fingers were like a vise on his leg.

"Yeah. That's what I'm saying, Ben."

Hot blood rushed past Ben's ears and his eyes blazed. For a moment he was sure he would finally tip over the edge. A wetness dripped from his nose and for a horrifying instant, he imagined the alien rain had somehow found its way inside the car. He swiped quickly at his nose with the back of his hand. With a sort of relieved shudder, Ben's eyes focused on the slick red blood on the back on his hand.

"I told you to push it down, Ben." Ella reached into her purse for a Kleenex and flipped the white tissue over to Ben. "It's not time."

* * * *

Driving toward the pale gray peak that was the start of the mountain range to the west, Ella counted the distance and the times in her head four times before she spoke.

"One more hour before we get to the foothills."

"Probably more than that." Ben replied with a confidence that made Ella narrow her eyes and bite her lip.

"No. I think it's right at an hour." She swiveled her head to look at him as he turned his head to look at her.

He was looking at her and smiling. Ben was always up for a challenge but this time Ella knew she was right. The challenge would also help to take his mind off the unsettling black specks in the softly falling rain. They plopped onto the windshield in greasy wet globules that seemed to leap back off the glass and back into the air, only to crescendo down again once more.

Ella turned her gaze back out the passenger side window and kept an eye on the fiery red clouds far above their heads. As the droplets of grainy water hit the leaves of the trees along the roadside, the droplets exploded and splattered and left oily looking splotches on the faded green foliage. Although the thought had been in Ben's mind since the rain started, Ella finally began to consider what those black flecks might actually do to them when they had no choice but to venture from the car. She remembered the way the false man had burst apart when Ben shot him. She remembered the hot sizzling feel as the wet particles that made up the body had landed on her skin. Her hand instinctively went to the place on her arm and her cool fingers rubbed at the slightly puckered flesh.

Shaking her head to dispel the disturbing thoughts, Ella's eye fell on the speedometer. Brushing a stray strand of hair from her eyes, she idly wondered why Ben was driving the posted speed limit of 65 miles per hour. There were no other cars on the road and they hadn't seen any police cruisers in days. Just as she tipped her head up to ask him to please drive a little faster, Ben pressed his foot down on the accelerator and the small car shot forward. Ella's heart dropped into her stomach for fear of what he might have seen on the road.

"What?" She asked Ben sharply.

"What?" He echoed and looked back at her with a frown perched above his dark eyebrows.

"Why did you speed up just now?"

Ben shrugged and turned his head back to the road. "I don't know. Just realized there was no point in driving the speed limit." He said calmly as he pressed down even further on the gas pedal. "And we haven't seen any other cars on this road for miles and haven't seen any police cruisers for days."

"Riiiiiiggt." Ella drew out the word as she glanced warily at the side of his face.

Leaning over to peer at the speedometer, she watched the needle lean more and more to the right until the car was speeding down the highway at just over eighty-five miles an hour. Ben was holding the steering calmly and loosely in his hands. Ella turned her face away again and stared out the window at the graying trees flying by, and she traced a finger along the cool glass. She didn't want Ben to see the look of speculation on her face.

There was zero possibility that it was a coincidence she and Ben had the same thought about the speed limit at the same time. And there was a less-than-zero possibility that he would say the exact same words she had been thinking. Never mind that it wasn't possible. Never mind that telepathy wasn't supposed to happen without a deck of marked cards and an accomplice assistant. Never mind that she was sure it had just happened anyway.

It was less than an hour of driving through the valley before the land began to rise and the tall trees gave way to shorter ones. The range of high, gray mountains rose up before them and the curve of the road yawned around to take them west toward the narrow pass.

"We'll need to stop for gas here before we head into the mountains." Ben sighed. He was tired. He frowned up at the red sky, made a dark pinkish color through the light haze of the rain.

It was surreal, watching the rain fall from a sky that was at the same time burning with fire. Ben lifted his foot from the gas pedal and steered the car to the right. Ella blinked. Why hadn't she seen that gas station before now? It seemed to have appeared out of nowhere. She shook her head and told herself she needed to pay more attention. Too much was happening too fast and she needed to focus better. As they cruised to a stop beside the first of the silvery metal pumps, Ella was grateful to see the metal overhang that would shelter them from the peculiar rain.

She slipped the heavy handgun out of the glovebox and rolled down her window, wincing slightly as a gust of warm air threatened to blow a few beads of rain inside. The hot wind made her almost dizzy and she angled her body slightly away from the door. Ben had already reached under the dashboard to release the door covering the gas cap. In four strides of his long legs, he was standing beside the 97 octane gas pump. His hand hesitated.

He didn't want to touch the wetness on the side of the car. He didn't know what it could or would do to him, but he didn't want even the slightest bit of him on him. Ben dug into his pocket and yanked out a dingy white handkerchief. His dad had instilled in him the value of always carrying one with him, although he could count on one hand then number of times he had ever needed to use it. Until then.

"Is there anyone inside to pay?" Ella called out of the window at the same time she tried to stare through the glass doors of the station.

"No." Ben answered flatly and continued to hold the nozzle, the sweet smell of the gasoline wafting past his nose.

Ella watched as Ben finished filling the tank and replaced the gas nozzle. He had left the driver's side door open to be ready for him in case they had to drive away quickly, but the cross-breeze of hot, bitter air was starting to make Ella's eyes water.

"I can't believe the rain isn't washing away some of this bad air." She grumbled and coughed lightly into her hand.

"That's because I don't think it's really rain." Ben replied.

No sooner than he had slung one long leg into car, than the tortured screeching blasted from inside the station and made Ben freeze in that awkward positon. Even from where she sat inside the car, Ella could see the commotion from inside. Two figures were being whipped back and forth viciously like giant rag dolls. As the two figures, men it appeared, continued their horrible dance with some unknown assailant, a bright flash of blinding white light streaked across their faces. In an instant, they both seemed to glow from within like some horrible human jack-o-lanterns. The anger shot into his brain and Ben's hands clenched into fists. Did these aliens think they could just come and take everything and everyone and that no one would do or say anything to stop them?

Ben yanked the gun from Ella's hand and strode toward the glass doors.

"No!" She yelled. "You can't go in there. You know what's going on inside there. You'll get yourself killed!"

"What do you want me to do? Just walk away and let it happen to them?" Ben shouted back and continued walking steadily toward the glass door.

The heavy gun looked so small in his large hands. He held it at chest level, yanked open the ad-covered glass door and pushed his way into the station. Ella didn't dare leave the car. If he did make it out of the station alive, he would be moving fast and she didn't want to be the one to slow him down.

The boom of the four gunshots roared inside Ella's head.

She didn't scream. She kept her eyes on the glass door and tried to keep her breathing even and to keep her heart from racing. When the first of the gunshots thundered, the rain stopped. With the second shot, the gash in the fiery red clouds healed itself leaving not even a seam. With the last two shots, Ella felt a supercharged gust of blazing hot wind tear through her open window and shoot straight out the open car door on the other side.

Ben pushed through the glass doors and Ella closed her eyes for a half a second. She didn't doubt it was him. She had kept sight of him the entire time he was inside. Climbing into the car, Ben thrust the still-warm gun to Ella who reloaded it before tucking it away in the glove box.

"Was it too late? Were they already...transformed?" Ella asked even though she already knew the answer.

"Yes." He said and began to drive.

In the cold fluorescent light of the station, the black wisps moved swiftly across the graying tile floor.

EIGHT

For forty-five minutes, the white sedan ferried its two passengers steadily upward, climbing the east face of the mountain. At the top, the view was breathtaking but neither occupant was in a mood to enjoy the scenery. Ben drove with his right hand clutched tight on the wheel and his left elbow propped on the narrow window ledge, two fingers restlessly kneading his scalp. Ella's hand stroked Ben's leg from time to time, eager to maintain a connection with him. They didn't talk, but the silence was comfortable and they felt no need to fill it with idle words.

Ella's head swiveled her view from window to windshield to Ben's profile then back again in a slowly moving, repetitive arc. She was tired but she was still alert, and her gaze swept the landscape from right to left and back again. Then as her eyes shifted left again, they settled on Ben and stayed.

"I'm hungry." She said and tried her best to keep her voice from rising to a whine on the end.

"I know." Ben kept his eyes on the road and on the steep ravine on the right. "The last sign we passed said there's a town over this rise. We'll stop there to eat and find a place to sleep for the night."

Ben knew that it had been hours since they had last eaten. He was hungry, too. His stomach had been battling for his attention but his mind was occupied with thoughts of more than just food. He didn't want to stop in the mountains. He wanted to reach the other side and make it into the valley beyond well before nightfall. There were no streetlights along the stretch of the highway they traveled and he couldn't imagine what the aliens might create to snare them in the darkness.

Glancing over at Ella's weary profile, Ben smiled and the worry left him a little. He watched as she reached under the seat for an almost empty bag of candy. For a small woman, she ate a lot and often. It had threatened to become somewhat of a sore point between them since they had begun traveling together. It

46

seemed she was always about five minutes away from starving even after a full meal. Ben often found half-eaten bits of pungent beef jerky or crumpled silver-lined bags that once held chips or crackers in her new backpack.

Once, and only once, he had reminded her that her food stash might attract real rodents. Ella had stared at him for a long two minutes without saying a word; her green eyes cool and emotionless. Ben had finally dropped his gaze, shrugged his shoulders and walked away.

"Yeah...that's what I thought..." She had muttered too low for him to hear as she stuffed a small package of Twinkies in her bag. Ben no longer commented and he no longer complained, but he did check her bag every morning and every night for stowaways. So far, his hand had encountered nothing but snacks and empty wrappers. Her favorite snacks, since the small cakes found in the stores were now stale and dry, had become the colorful Skittles candies which she scooped up by the armfuls. It kept her satisfied and the extra bonus? Her kisses always tasted of candy and sweetness.

"Look." Ben jutted his chin toward the road ahead.

The crest of the hill was behind them and the valley spread out before them like a multicolored blanket. Night was fast approaching and the tiny amount of sun that pushed its way through the flaming red clouds gave the entire town an eerie pink glow. It was a bigger town than Ben had expected and that was both good and bad. It was good because that meant they could easily get food and supplies and the gas they needed for the next leg of their journey. And it was bad because that meant there were more places for the things that may or may not be real to hide and wait and create their malevolent traps.

A vibrant memory of flashing bright lights slammed into Ben's mind. He blinked and shook his head against the battering and the painful emotion that came with the memory. Whatever had assaulted him in the basement and replicated him, had fully intended to kill Ella. And it had intended for the last thing she saw on this earth was the man she loved and trusted slamming an iron hammer onto her skull over and over. A sudden white-hot anger shot through his whole being and Ben jerked the steering wheel sharply to the right. The edge of the mountain road was bordered by only a short metal railing that offered little protection between them and the drop off to the valley below.

Ella sucked in a breath at the erratic movement toward the edge of the road and clutched at the seatbelt that was already tight across her shoulders.

"What are you doing?" Her voice was high and shrill with fear as she stared hard at Ben.

But Ben didn't hear her. The car was no longer moving and Ben had both feet jammed down hard on the brake. His breath was ragged and his eyes were open wide and staring but he wasn't seeing anything in front of him. Ella kept her eyes on his strained face, willing her own panic not to rise. Unsure of what else to do, she reached over, pushed the gear shift into Park and turned the key in the ignition. The abrupt silence in the car was dizzying, like a vacuum, broken only by the harsh gasps from Ben.

Ella had heard him breathing in that same rough way when the nightmares would overtake him. The sight of his eyes rolling restlessly under his closed lid was always chilling. Even more chilling to her was that this time, his nightmare wasn't happening while he was asleep. He was fully awake.

Ella wanted to run. She wanted to leap out of the car and hop over the small metal railing and scramble down the hillside, not caring about the dangers lurking in the waist-high brush or the towering trees. For a split-second Ella wanted to run from Ben and his nightmares and from the responsibilities of loving another person she was scared to death of losing. She wanted to race through the woods as fast as her feet could carry her and pretend she had never met him and that she didn't love him.

But she had made her choice long ago. She slipped the handgun out of the glove box, twisted a little in her seat to better see him, and waited for it to be over.

****

The road was on fire.

Ben watched with dread filling his unblinking eyes as the fire in the sky flickered and deepened and the flaming clouds dipped down and ghostly red fingers crawled their way toward them. Ben yearned to scream at Ella to get down, to crawl into the backseat and hide from the fire that was almost on them. But he couldn't move and he couldn't utter a sound. He could only stare as the flaming cloud danced through the air and seemed to bounce on the pavement in front of him on the way to where he and Ella sat trapped in the car.

Setting his jaw, Ben tried once again to move his arms or legs as he waited for what he knew was to come. He hadn't expected it to end that way; without a fight or a battle. He hated for Ella to have to suffer and his eyes ached to blink as he tried not to think about what was about to fall on them. As he waited, Ben began to feel that stinging knife of anger deep in his gut. His life had never been easy and his future had always seemed murky and unclear. But as bleak as it was, it was his future and he had always refused to let anyone or anything choose it for him. Being with Ella had never been part of his plan, but once she had leaped into his heart and refused to let go, Ben realized he wanted her there. He wanted to see what a future with her would be like. He wanted a future without fires in the sky and without graying dead trees and without beings who roamed the planet, taking what they wanted.

As Ben grew angrier, the red-tipped clouds that advanced on the small white sedan seemed to hesitate. His rage caused him to grind his teeth and his brow furrowed with fury. The feeling of being pushed and manipulated fueled his rage until he felt a sensation like a dark thick bubble begin to rise from inside him. The bubble rose up in him and as he aimed his anger at the advancing red cloud, he felt something. As hard as the red mist was pushing toward the car, the pressure inside him was pushing the cloud back. Ben strained his muscles and focused his anger and the cloud receded and as the pushing rage grew stronger and stronger, finally his frozen throat snapped open and one word burst from his lips.

"NO!" He screamed and in that instant, the red cloud vanished.

Ben blinked.

Ella shifted in her seat but didn't take her eyes off of his profile. His scream was loud in the stillness of the car but she didn't flinch. She had no idea what he had seen. She could only watch with alarm as his eyes had fixed on the empty road in front of them and listened as his breathing become more labored by the second. When the one word propelled from his mouth like a sharp verbal missile, it was as if something had broken inside him.

His eyes snapped shut for an instant and then back open. Swinging his head over to look wildly at Ella, he blinked over and over, moistening his dry eyes.

"Did you see it?" His voice was low but strong.

"No." She replied.

There was no reason for her to ask what 'it' was. She knew he had seen something and she didn't need to know what he saw as long as he had faced it and shouted it down and that he had won. Ella longed to believe that what had just happened was random and not related to the fire in the sky and the black shapes. She wanted to chalk it up to another one of his nightmares that somehow had crawled its shifty way into his head during the day. But she knew better. She knew nothing with him was random and nothing with him was simple. And she knew from the moment she met him that he was going to be both the life of her and the death of her.

And the knowing brought her more fear than she ever thought possible.

NINE

It was Ella's turn to drive. She sat easily behind the wheel of the car as she maneuvered it down the steep hill toward the valley. Her long hair was loose and fell across the seatbelt where it was stretched across her shoulders. Every so often, she would drop her head a little, reaching into the dwindling supply of candy cradled in her lap. Ben smiled as he glanced at the side of her face, shrouded by the veil of hair. He liked it better when she pulled her hair back. He liked to see more of her face. But she had long ago gotten tired of trying to keep up with hair ties and barrettes and now left it loose most of the time.

Ben reached out and snagged a strand of her thick hair and twisted it around his finger.

"Stop touching me." She said with a smile that belied her demand.

"Never." He replied and wound the hair tighter around his finger.

When she didn't complain or resist any further, Ben kissed the dark strands wrapped around his index finger then released them. They were comfortable with each other now. Their first few days together had been difficult. Ben was indifferent and Ella was distant and the silences between them were long. Their eyes never met or searched for the other and too many troubling thoughts kept them apart. But things had changed. Finally.

There was a slight thump from beneath the wheels of the car as the texture of the pavement changed from the mountain road to the valley street. Ella was a good driver, but as Ben had seen, she was also easily distracted.

"Oh look!" she suddenly exclaimed as if to prove his point. "A moose!"

"Just drive, woman." He pointed a finger to the road ahead, drawing her gaze away from the large animal standing stiffly on the side of the highway.

"Probably wasn't real anyway." She muttered and stuck her lip out a bit.

"Probably not."

Knowing what the dark shapes could do; how they could transform into whatever they wanted, was no longer a surprise to Ben and Ella. It was simply a truth that they would learn to deal with in order to survive. They talked quietly as the car wound its way into the valley where the trees ended and the small industrial buildings began.

"How can you just accept that your vision meant what you think it means?"

Ben shrugged at Ella's question and offered her as much explanation as he could.

"They've come after me twice. For whatever reason, they couldn't take me over like those two poor guys in the gas station. You didn't see them, El. You didn't see how their bodies were still there but their eyes were...*empty*." Ben struggled to find the right words to describe what he had seen and to explain why he hadn't hesitated to shoot two complete strangers to death.

"So was it like a body snatcher, pod-people kind of thing? Is that what you mean?"

"Yes. And no."

"Tell me about the yes."

Ben shifted in his seat and rotated his shoulders, releasing the stress from his tired muscles. "Yes, their bodies had been taken over and their eyes were dead. Like cold." Ben concentrated his gaze down at the dashboard. "But they weren't zombies. They didn't shuffle and drool and stare through me. Their eyes were cold, but they were *crafty*."

Ella winced at the word 'crafty'. That word told her that whoever took them over, whoever was controlling them, wasn't just a simple organism making random actions. It confirmed to her that the takeover of the bodies was deliberate and done with a specific plan in mind. She was being forced to move further away from her hope that the beings would simply fly away one day without any confrontation.

To Ben, it was all very simple. He understood that the vision meant they would keep coming for him until they killed him. There was no other explanation that made sense. He knew he would die sometime. Everyone died. It was only a matter of when and how. His greatest fear now, the one that caused his heart to clench and ache, was that in trying to kill him they would also kill Ella or perhaps even worse, they would torture her or make her watch what they would do to him before they killed him. For one brief instant, Ben was sorry she had followed him to this place. He was sorry he hadn't left her where he found her and let someone else gather up the pieces and stand guard over her while she healed. But the feeling only lasted for an instant. In reality, it lasted much less time than it took to explain it. His love for her quickly reasserted itself and he leaned over and planted a soft kiss on her temple.

In the valley, evening softened the flaring red of the sky as the car rolled into town.

****

Parking the car in the large, mostly-empty lot in front of the grocery store, the couple sat for a moment watching the entrance. The town was small enough that there hadn't been a desperate run on the store like in the larger towns, so there might still be quite a bit of food left to choose from.

"Don't get a ton of stuff." Ben spoke to the side of Ella's head.

"Sure." She bounced a little in the driver's seat, too eager and hungry to really pay attention.

"I mean it. We can't keep it all and it's still an active store, so we have to pay for it. I don't want to waste money."

"No problem."

She moistened her lips with her tongue as they watched an older couple make their way out of the store with their arms full of grocery bags.

Once inside the brightly lit store, Ella veered off to the left where the deli counter and cheese selections beckoned.

"No cheese, El!" He called out and saw her hesitate, her shoulders drooping for a second.

"Ok." She tossed the words over her shoulder.

Ben knew she would buy cheese anyway. That was one of the first things he had learned she loved. In the beginning, when he hadn't been able to get her to eat anything else, she would always accept a small piece of cheese. Later, it had become their private joke. Whenever she was in a bad mood or her fierce temper threatened to spill over and burn them both, Ben would stand up, retrieve a small chunk of cheese from her pack and hand it to her with a smile. He would always get a smile in return.

When Ella picked up the first wedge of whitish, yellow cheese from the open case, she felt a tiny twinge of guilt. She had promised Ben. But when she picked up the second wedge of cheese, bringing it to her nose for a light sniff, the guilt was washed completely away in the delicious yeasty scent of Gouda. She leaned to one side to pry a third wedge of cheese from a tight circle of cheddar in the waist-high case.

"What are you doing?" The voice from behind her made jump and almost drop the orange wedge.

"I'm buying cheese." She snapped, more frightened then mad. "What does it look like I'm doing?"

Turning around to face her accuser, Ella sucked in a breath. There was a thump as the wedge of cheddar tumbled from her fingers back into the cooled cheese case.

"What do you want?" She worked her throat, trying to keep her voice steady.

Ella's eyes shifted from left to right as she took in the crowd of six people who stood much closer to her than she had allowed anyone other than Ben to get. The six faces and six pair of eyes all held the same cool anger. Ella took in a breath and narrowed her eyes, trying to decide what to do. She flicked her eyes toward the front of the store and wondered where Ben could have gotten to. He usually wasn't too far away from her. Where had he gone?

****

Taking a quick look around the store and committing its layout to memory, Ben took the opportunity to slip into the small musty smelling toilet. Ella would never use a public toilet. Smells bothered her so much that she would rather pee in the tall grass on the side of the road than squat in a narrow stall in a funky public restroom. Ben smiled as he recalled the "protector" stance

54

she required him to assume while she yanked down her jeans and rocked back on her heels.

****

Ella took a step backward and tried to keep her eye on all six of her accusers at once. The two remaining wedges of cheese in her hands felt so small and there was no way they could be used as a weapon of any kind. How long had Ben been gone? Scanning the crowd surrounding her, Ella couldn't tell if the people surrounding her were real or not. She needed to hear their voices. She would be able to tell by the tone of their voices.

"What do you want?" She said loudly, her hands tightening around the cheeses now clutched tightly in her grip.

"We don't know you." The same person spoke again. "We don't need strangers coming in here buying up all our food." His voice cracked a little at the end and Ella stared into his frightened eyes. She relaxed and breathed out a short sigh of relief at his fear. He was real.

"Come with me." A new voice croaked from the small group. "I'll show you the way out."

Ella's hands clenched involuntarily. The new voice was all wrong. It was cold and gravelly and the hollowness of it matched the sudden hollowness in her chest. She looked wildly around. In the group of six who were beginning to press closer to where she stood, how many were real and how many were the other ones?

****

Washing his hands in the grimy porcelain sink, Ben stared at his reflection and tried to remember as many details of his vision as he could. The advancing cloud, the way the fiery cloud hesitated as his anger grew and the way the cloud burst apart when he yelled were all emblazoned in his memory. But there were other things he struggled to recall and he knew he had to remember everything. Everything was important. But he was so tired.

****

As Ella faced the group and shifted her weight from one leg to the other, ready to run, she realized she had backed herself up against the waist high case of cheeses and the group had begun to spread out to trap her. Her right side was already blocked, and a man with a shock of dirty white hair was moving slowly to her left to close that escape route also. She leaned back and brought her hands up slightly. Her mind was racing and she was fighting against her own brain that was trying to shut down from fear. It was clear now that not all of them were the 'other ones', but she couldn't tell which was which without hearing all their voices. Ella knew she could fight her way past the real people because they were afraid. And their fear would make them easy to defeat. But if one of the "Others" grabbed her; she was convinced she was dead where she stood.

****

In the bathroom, Ben stared into his reflected eyes. His short dark hair had begun to grow out and he saw the beginnings of soft curls appearing near the nape of his neck. His mother had always kept his hair slightly longer when he was a child. She would often run her long fingers through his soft curls as she settled him into his bed at night. The lips of his reflection began to lift in a slight smile at the memory, but then Ben jerked hard. A sudden bright image of Ella flashed across his vision. His teeth ground as a cold, hard anger suddenly burned from his middle up to his throat and the word, "NO!" was already screaming from his throat before he knew what was happening.

****

Glancing to her left, Ella saw the man with the dirty white hair hesitate, one knee bent as his foot halted in mid-step.

"Get away from her!" Ben yelled in a voice that made Ella drop her hands. Her eyes widened and a whoosh of air pushed from her mouth.

Her breath came fast and hard and her heart pounded in her chest. Ben's voice was too loud and too shrill. In those seconds as Ben advanced on the crowd, pushing his way toward her, she had only a moment to realize she didn't know where he had gone or how long they had been apart. Since the fires in the sky and the time in the basement, they were never apart for more than a few minutes. Anything could have happened while he was away from her. Anything.

Ben shouldered his way through the huddled group, pushing them aside with a fearlessness that unnerved Ella. She cut her eyes to the left. The man with the dirty white hair had disappeared. By the time Ben had pushed past the last person and turned his back on Ella to face the crowd, the remaining five people stopped their threatening advance. Seeing Ben's face, tight and angry, they too backed away, and then all were gone.

With her back still pressed tightly against the cool metal case, Ella eyed Ben and waited. She wanted to believe it was really him but his voice when he yelled was so cold, so different.

He turned to face her and Ella couldn't breathe.

"It's me." He stepped closer and flinched as Ella pressed even further back.

"I...don't know." She stammered and shook her head, praying the tears wouldn't come and blur her vision. She needed to be able to see him clearly.

Ben's throat worked and he nodded. He was hurt and angry at the reason for her doubt, but he understood. They had been through so much and he thought she should know him better than anyone else. But he also knew things were happening that neither of them had ever faced. He nodded his head again and infused his smile with all the love and trust that he could possibly display.

"Ask me anything." He said.

Ella thrust out her narrow chin and tilted her head to one side, thinking carefully as her eyes took in his eyes and his face and slid down to appraise his body. She didn't know how much the "Others" might know about them and their relationship. But there was one thing she and Ben had smiled about but never spoken about out loud. Yes. That would be her question. Ella blinked up at Ben and allowed herself a tiny speck of hope.

"What do my kisses taste like?" She bit her lip and waited.

Ben blinked at the unbidden tears that sprang to his eyes. "Skittles." He whispered confidently and held out a hand to her.

Ella tossed aside the remaining handful of cheese and threw herself into Ben's arms.

TEN

Standing at the reception counter of the brightly lit "Stay-Put" motel, Ben kept his eyes trained on the clerk.

Ella had told him about how the 'Other' in the grocery store with the dirty white hair had looked much more real than the first 'Other' she had seen; the one they had copied from Ben's body and tried to kill her with. She would never forget that one. They had decided on their name for them - 'Others' - because it seemed the easiest word to describe the beings that the black shapes had created. But also, the word 'copy' held too much pain for Ella. Her eyes had dipped away from Ben's as she remembered how the copy had shuffled toward her in the cabin, looking so much like the man she loved. But she was careful to explain that the copy of Ben she had encountered in their cabin hadn't looked as perfectly human as the man in the grocery store with the dirty white hair. Ella hadn't speculated on the reason, but Ben knew it came down to two options: The aliens were either getting better at taking on the human form, or another option was that some humans – like him - were harder to replicate. Neither option gave him much comfort. And in the back of his mind, he wondered if it was possible that both options might be true.

Ella stood with her front pressed tightly to Ben's back and he resisted the urge to tell her to back up a bit. He felt a small well of irritation from her crowding him, but he also felt the fear emanating hotly from her. So he said nothing and moved his shoulder slightly to free his arm to sign the hotel registration card. Ella was tired. On the way to the motel, she had explained to him what happened in the grocery store, and then said nothing more. She had kept one hand wrapped tightly around the handle of the gun and the other hand on his leg as he drove. He hadn't minded her touch then. He was glad for it and it made him feel safer somehow, as if her touch kept the darkness and anger at bay that was continually threatening to rise up within him.

Knowing that his anger was one of the things that caused the Others to hesitate was still a surprise to Ben. He had spent most of his childhood learning to keep his fears and anger pushed down inside. His father had told him that his constant nightmares were caused by a host of negative feelings battling inside him and were his mind's way of trying to let them slip loose. And having them slip loose was something he was told could never happen.

"You can't let your bad thoughts and feelings control you." Ben's father had whispered to him as he lay in his small child's bed, trying to calm his racing heart and his muddled mind. "If you don't stay in control; if you let all those bad feelings out, someone will get hurt. Maybe you will get hurt. And I don't want that for you."

So the nightmares had become his enemy and it was an enemy that he fought on a nightly basis. Ben had never understood why his father had pushed him so hard to deny his feelings and to ignore the dreams. When he tried to talk to his father about a nightmare that was particularly disturbing, his father would shake his head and lay a finger over his son's lips.

"Leave it alone." He would say in a hushed tone and walk away.

But Ben couldn't leave it alone. Every evening the nightmares were waiting for him, and cold, gray lights and shadowy figures lurked in all the corners of his dreams. Now, with Ella standing so close to him as he waited and watched the hotel clerk for any sign of 'otherness', Ben began to consider his father's actions in a new light. It was in those times when his father dismissed his fears and urged Ben to leave it alone, that the exact opposite happened. The dismissal of something that was clearly troubling him to the point of distress made the young boy seethe with anger. On those nights, when his furious mind roiled and churned, the dreadful night visions fled from him and brought him brief fragments of peace. Snapping his gaze away from the motel clerk, Ben rolled that thought around in his mind and the tip of a realization danced like a busy firefly in the corner of his brain. But the illumination was still too dim to fully reveal the answer.

Leaving the thought alone for the moment, Ben turned his attention back to the clerk. The corners of the man's mouth were turned down so deeply that he gave the impression of a perpetually sad comic character. Ben wondered idly if the man was still getting paid a salary. The thought brought a twinge of worry at the dwindling supply of cash in his pocket. How long would his money still be good? It was no longer worth anything in the bigger towns and Ben was sure it would soon be worthless in the small towns too.

As the clerk trudged tiredly from one end of the long counter, Ben was satisfied he was a real human and took the key card from his hand and then turned to leave.

"Check out is at eleven." The clerk's voice was apathetic but real.

The clerk's sudden words made Ella twitch against Ben's back. She uttered a little sigh and sagged against him. Turning, he slipped an arm around her shoulder and his heart clenched in his chest at the relief on her face. That expression and her expelled breath told him she had been expecting the worst. She smiled a weary smile when he looked down at her, but even then, she tried to be brave for him, straightening her back and lifting her head.

"Hungry?" Ben asked as they walked down the long, narrow hallway to their room.

"No." She replied and grinned at Ben's stunned expression.

"No? You're not hungry? Who are you?" He pressed a smiling kiss to her forehead.

"I'm real. Don't worry." She snagged the plastic key card from his hand and pushed ahead of him into the dimly lit room where she promptly fell facedown onto the double bed.

Later, stirring slightly on the lumpy bed, Ella groaned in her sleep. She had been too tired to make love and Ben hadn't pushed her. Her sweet tasting kiss had been soft and drowsy as her head flopped back on the too-soft, hotel pillow. He had watched her for a few minutes, gently combing through her long hair with his fingers. Then, he moved away to fold his long frame onto the desk chair, pulling it close to the drapery covered window. Loving her as much as he did frightened him. It made Ben vulnerable and a bit uneasy. He knew in his heart that he would fight to the death for her and he wouldn't give her up for the world. Even as he hoped with all his heart that it would never come to that, he felt a tight stirring in his gut that told him in the end, the truth might be otherwise.

Sitting upright in the hard chair, Ben's eyelids pressed heavily down and he longed for sleep. But a growing tension inside him kept the sought after sleep at bay and kept Ben open and watchful. He wasn't exactly sure what he was watching for, but he had no doubt that something was going to happen and he wanted to be ready. Rising up slowly from the chair, Ben stepped to the window and drew back the heavy curtain, blinking owlishly at the darkness outside. But it wasn't that dark anymore. The red fires in the sky that were normally deep, almost black at night, had bloomed and blossomed into a bright red and yellow fire that lit up the night and threw hot dancing shadows onto the cracked pavement.

When the first few people began trickling into the street, their eyes focused upward on the ever brightening sky, Ben's eyes widened and his stomach heaved. He wanted to scream at them to go back inside – to stay away from whatever what happening in that poison-laden sky. But to his horror, more and more people began to flood out of their rooms and houses onto the narrow sidewalk, seemingly drawn like moths to the flaming sky. And as he watched with a dismay that held little surprise to him, the seam in the red clouds began to open and within seconds, the strange rain began to fall. The silvery droplets of water were as before, heavy and full of black grit as fine as sand. Ben only had a second to be glad that both he and Ella were safely inside.

As the first drop of rain splattered onto the people gawking upwardly on the sidewalk, Ben saw the flash of bright light and heard the first of the screams.

ELEVEN

The loud screams blasting through from outside the hotel window startled Ella from her fitful sleep. Her nightmarish dreams of the 'Other' with the dirty white hair and the re-living of the dreadful pressing of the crowd in the grocery store, all flew from her mind in an instant.

"What's happening?!" She leaped up and ran toward Ben.

"Get back!" He shouted and threw up a hand, shielding her from the pulled back curtain and the miserable scene outside.

The bright explosions of light flashed through the window and lit up the inside of the darkened hotel room. Ella flinched at the brilliance and stared with wide eyes at Ben. Panic fluttered in her throat like a trapped bird and she sucked in a deep breath and held it.

"What's happening?" She said more quietly as her hands found his waist and she slid around, holding him tight.

"It's taking them all." Ben kept his eyes on the street outside.

She knew exactly what he meant but her mind couldn't help but focus on the one word that she hoped wasn't true.

"What do you mean, taking them *all*?"

There was a part of Ben that still wanted to protect Ella from everything. He wanted to pull her to himself and tell her gentle lies so that she would feel safe and happy and not have to worry about a thing. But of course, he couldn't do that. He had never lied to her and he was determined not to let them force him to start. She had to know everything he knew in order for them to be able to fight back. She needed to know the whole truth so that she would be prepared for whatever was coming next. With a sigh, he reached for her.

"Here. Look." He drew her around in front of him to peer through the small crack in the pulled back curtain. Ben wrapped an arm around her waist to hold her as she went rigid and unbelieving at the sight.

The dimly lit sidewalk was slickly wet with water from the strange rain and the street was filled with people. That is, if you could still call them people. Some had already been transformed and others were in the process of being transformed. Ben and Ella stared speechless as the drops of strange rain splattered onto a short resident with large wire-rimmed glasses who had made the unfortunate decision to step outside to see what all the commotion was about. The couple heard a sharp, searing sizzle just before the man began to scream and snatch at the glasses on his face. The man screamed and screamed until the blazing white light enveloped him and his shrieks suddenly stopped.

A group of five newly transformed 'Others' stood in a tight group near the front entrance of the motel about a hundred yards away from their window. Ben wasn't sure how he knew they had already been transformed, because they looked very ordinary, very real. But he knew. His eyes couldn't see the difference between them and real humans, but his mind knew the difference. It was as if his mind could see beyond their flesh, glistening and wet from the strange rain, and see the tiny black sand-like grains writhing just below the surface.

"Are they all changed?" Ella sagged back against him, her voice low and weary.

"Not yet." He said just as a bright flash of light lit up the night as another one was transformed.

"You can recognize them now, can't you?" She asked without turning around. Her body pressed against his as she realized she already knew what his answer would be.

"Yes."

"For how long?"

"Since the gas station."

Ben waited for her to pull away. He waited for her to look at him in a way that would crack his heart in two. He was still the same man she had loved for so long. But he was also changed in a way that made him feel almost as alien as the Others. A feeling of aloneness and sadness washed over him as he waited for her to respond. He knew he had always been different. Even as a child he hadn't been able to push away his nightmares and dreams to be able to view the world the way others did.

He had known he was taking a risk by letting Ella get close to him. There were places within him that he never wanted her to see. Places where the darkness was so black that even he couldn't tell exactly what was lurking there. But she kept pushing at his mind and his body and his heart. When he first realized he had lost and she had won such a large place in his heart, he had been angry. How dare she force her way in when he needed to keep her away? He needed to keep her at a safe distance from the anger that sometimes overtook him until his personality was nearly unrecognizable. But there she was, nestled deep inside him and so much a part of him that he didn't know what his life would be like without her.

He kept his arm around her waist and let her stare out of the window as the horrifying transformations continued. The flashes of light came less frequently as the grisly task was almost completed. The pain in Ben's heart was huge. He hurt for what the people had become and he hurt for what he might have to do to them if they tried to attack him or Ella. As his anger at the injustice of it all, Ben began to get angry again. He hesitated, wondering if his anger would somehow reveal his location to them. Would they be able to find them in the hotel room and come for them? Or would his anger make the Others sense him but cause them to turn and run? He heard Ella take in a deep breath.

"If you die, I'll kill you." She turned to look at him as she spoke. Her eyes glistened with unshed tears and her bottom lip quivered.

"I'd never leave you." He said without hesitation.

Ella turned around in his arms and butted his chest lightly with her forehead, each thump accentuating her words.

"I. Can't. Live. Without. You."

"You won't have to." Ben lifted her chin and looked into her eyes. "I promise."

Kissing her should have been the last thing on his mind, but in that moment, it was the only thing he wanted to do. Maybe he wanted one more moment of normalcy before they had to leave everything normal behind. He lifted her chin further and tipped his head down to hers.

"Where are their bodies?" She asked suddenly when his lips were almost on hers.

Ben frowned. He glanced off to one side as he recalled his own transformation in the basement of the cabin. Except with him, it wasn't a transformation. He slid his eyes down, frowning in concentration as he remembered the black, shifting shapes on the basement floor. He remembered the blinding white light and how he threw up his hand to shield his face. But what he remembered most vividly was hauling the heavy shotgun up the basement stairs and blowing away the Other who would have killed Ella.

His mind scrambled to put all the pieces together. Ben looked down at Ella's questioning face, then his gaze when back to the window. When the last flash of light and the final shriek of agony shot through the night, Ben felt a glimmer of understanding and he opened his mouth to ask a question whose answer might set him free or drive him insane.

That was when the frantic pounding on the motel room door made Ella scream out loud.

TWELVE

When the hammering on the door began, Ella clutched Ben so tightly around the waist that it hurt. Her scream pierced though the stillness of the hotel room and Ben flinched as both the banging on the door and her scream assaulted his ears.

"Hush." He silenced her with two fingers pressed over her lips.

A few weeks ago, if he had silenced her that way, he was sure he would have lost a couple of fingers and maybe more from the fury that gesture would have unleashed. But they had been through so much together and Ben was grateful she gave him this leeway. Her eyes were still wide with fear but she was quiet and still against him.

"Where's the gun?" Ben asked with an edge to his voice that might have been anger or might have been fear. He didn't stop to try and figure out which one.

Silently, Ella moved to lift the corner of a shirt that was lying on the small side table. Handing him the gun butt first, she opened her mouth to speak. Ben silenced her again, but this time with a slight shake of his head. As Ben took the gun and began to turn toward the door, Ella grabbed at his arm and silently pleaded with him. Her eyes filled with tears as she mouthed the words 'please' and 'don't go'.

"It's ok." Ben whispered with his lips right on Ella's ear. "Get in the bathroom."

"No." She shook her head and stood staring at him, her temper already rising.

"Woman…" He began. But her mouth was set in that tight line that told him she wasn't going to do anything more than what she wanted to do. "Fine." He pried her hand from his arm. "Just get down."

Ella turned and dropped down behind a square wooden table a few feet away. It wasn't much cover if bullets began to fly, but it was enough. Ben watched as Ella tried to still her trembling hands. Even though he understood her fear, he realized he could no longer share it. He was suddenly certain there wouldn't be an Other behind that door because he was positive of one thing. An Other wouldn't knock. If they really wanted him, the Others would simply burst through the door and take him and whatever else they wanted. The danger from the Others was real, but whoever was at the door wasn't a threat.

Ben strode to the door and took a quick look through the peephole. He experienced a moment of confusion that was almost dizzying. There was no one there. But then the loud pounding came again from a place much lower on the door than he would have expected. His furrowed brow cleared with understanding. Ben yanked open the door and dropped his gaze and lowered the angle of the gun by two feet.

When the little boy saw the firearm pointed directly at his head, his mouth dropped open and then he burst into tears. He took in a sharp breath to let out a scream but Ben grabbed him by the shirt and yanked him roughly into the room. The little boy appeared to be about nine years old and his small brown face was splotchy with tears and he was hiccupping with fear. His hands were tugging at Ben's fist, trying to pry the strong fingers away from his shirt.

"Don't bring him in here!" Ella shouted and leaped up from her insubstantial hiding place, nearly falling backwards trying to scurry away.

"Hush. It's fine. He's real." Ben replied calmly and Ella clamped her lips together, clearly angry, but still willing to obey.

Ben slammed the door shut and shot the deadbolt. As he stared down at the young boy, his mind churned with questions. He certainly wasn't an Other. Ben was sure of it. Then what was he doing there?

The boy's jet black hair was still dripping from the strange rain and the curly locks were shiny and full. Why hadn't the rain transformed him? Backing up slowly, his fist still clutching the boy's shirt, Ben stepped further into the hotel room. As he passed by the open closet, he slipped the loaded handgun into a small gap at the top of the clothes rack and then pulled the little boy over to the bed.

"Sit." He commanded and lifted the boy, releasing him as he thrust him gently onto the bed. The boy's feet, clad in bright blue tennis shoes with green laces, bounced against the edge of the mattress.

Ella continued to stand at a distance. With suspicious eyes she watched the little boy as he squirmed and folded his thin legs beneath him. His hair and clothes were still damp from the rain and she shot a quick, wondering glance at Ben.

"He's wet." She whispered and Ben nodded, keeping his eye on the boy.

The frightened little boy sat huddled on the flowery bedspread and tears continued to stream down his cheeks. He was obviously still scared, but the look in his golden brown eyes showed that he was resigned to whatever might happen next. Ben pulled up the desk chair close to the bed and sat facing him.

"Why are you here?" Ben asked in a firm, quiet voice.

For a second, it seemed like the boy might not answer. His eyebrows twitched together as he stared at Ben and then he shot a glance over his shoulder at Ella.

"You knocked on my door." Ben stated the fact sharply and lifted a dark brow. "So tell me what you want."

When fresh tears burst out of the little boy at Ben's tone of voice, Ella pushed down her fears and rushed to stand between him and Ben.

"Wait." She whispered to Ben, her head bobbing up and down. "Okay?" Then she turned to face the boy. "What's your name?" She asked him quietly.

The boy's sobs hitched in his small chest as he looked up at Ella. She blinked approvingly at the way he was dressed in faded blue jeans and a blue t-shirt peeking from under a green and blue plaid button down shirt. He was clean and although his curls were long on top, his fade and clipper-cut were still fresh. He had been well cared for and for some reason that hurt Ella the most. If he was so well cared for, why was he there alone? Her smile was slight as she waited for her answer. The boy was clearly scared but he was also desperate, so he latched onto her smile and gave her a tentative one in return.

"Amos." His voice was barely above a whisper.

"Amos?" Ben frowned. The name was so old fashioned.

"Amos Alexander Anderson." The little boy gulped out the words, then dropped his head onto his knees and his sobs began afresh.

It was clear Ella was conflicted. The boy apparently had been through something that had terrified him and if he had seen his father transformed, she completely understood his terror. She wanted to throw her arms around him to give him some comfort. But she was still afraid of the rain. What would happen if she touched him and the strange water touched her skin?

"Look." Ben said from behind her and Ella jumped a little.

Ella let her eye follow the pointing of Ben's finger. He was drawing her gaze to the water that was still dripping from Amos' wet hair.

"It's clear." She said just above a whisper and leaned forward to get a closer look. "No black grains."

Ella rubbed her hands together, trying to make her decision. The boy had drawn in on himself, pulling his legs in tight as if he wanted to become as small as possible. He wasn't a large boy and his wrists poking out of the sleeves of his shirt were thin and knobby. Ella hadn't been around children very much, but she had seen enough pain in fear in the past few weeks to recognize the signs. Although he wasn't running and screaming, the boy was still desperately afraid. But as Ben had announced, the boy had come to them and they needed to find out why. Her confidence buoyed by the lack of black grains in the rain, she moved to sit beside him on the bed.

"Will you tell us what happened?" Her voice was calm and full of genuine concern.

Amos didn't raise his head to look at either of them. He was still crying and the sound was low and miserable. Ben and Ella waited and sadness swept over them both. Where their losses were a few weeks old, Amos' grief was fresh. But he finally nodded his head and snuffled once before he spoke.

"My dad…" Amos' voice was high pitched and it quavered with each word.

"Did he tell you to come to us?" Ben prompted.

"Yes." He sniffed and slowly lifted his head.

"Tell me exactly what he said." Ben tried to keep his tone neutral, but a fear and dread began to press hard against his throat.

As he waited to hear Amos' reply, Ben's thoughts skipped in his head like a stone skimmed across a pond. A feeling here. An idea there. A notion that made his mouth dry with apprehension. But none of them prepared them for the words that came out of Amos' mouth.

Amos squeezed his eyes tight and he shivered once and said, "He told me; *Go to the One.*"

Ella wanted to gather the little boy in her arms and hold him tight and wipe his tears away, but his words left her cold and stunned. A sudden hiss and a pop from the ancient mini-fridge startled them and all heads turned toward the appliance.

Ella was the first to move and she rose up, pulling Ben behind her to stand closer to the bolted door. Turning her back on Amos, she placed her lips close to Ben's ear. "His dad sent him to you. To 'the One'."

"I suppose." Ben answered tiredly.

"So just like that, you're 'the One' and we have to pretend that's just fine? Like you're some kind of freaking Neo in a Matrix movie?"

"I guess so."

"You guess so?" Ella's voice rose with her temper.

Ben rubbed a hand over his face and his gaze traveled from Ella to Amos then back again.

"What do you want me to say? Do you want me to say he's wrong and this has nothing to do with me? Because I can say that. I can say those exact words even though you know that's a lie. It's been about me from the beginning and you've seen it, too. So I'll ask you again. What do you want me to say, El?"

Ella closed her eyes and drew in a shaky breath and held it. He wasn't wrong. She was angry at him for shoving the truth at her the way he did, but he was right. She had suspected he was different from the moment she met him. Call it intuition or call it premonition, but the 'oneness' had been there all along. What made things worse for her – at least for her weary heart – was that she had seen the uniqueness in him and yet she hadn't walked away before her life was too intertwined with his. Ella lifted her eyes back to Ben's and inspected his face before she threw herself into his embrace so quickly that he staggered back a bit.

"You can say 'I love you'." She whispered.

"I love you." Ben held her closer.

"Okay." Ella conceded as she pulled away slightly to look into his face and began talking softly again. "So are we to assume that this little guy's dad, with his last rational thought before they transformed him, sent his son to you? To 'the One'?"

Ben only shrugged.

"Okay. Maybe you can tell me this. Why didn't the rain transform Amos, too? Why weren't there any grains of black stuff in the water that was dripping off of him? And how did he know where we were? And how did he know we would let him in?" The questions tumbled from her lips.

"Is that all you want to know?" Ben asked sarcastically, but it was missed on Ella who was already forming her next set of questions.

"No. I want to know why his dad sent him to you. Was it because he knew you would protect him? Or is it because he's a plant? Like a spy?" Ella's eyes went wide with the idea and her brain worked trying to get her mouth to spill out all her thoughts. "And one more thing. We know all the people who were outside in the rain were changed into...whatever they are now. But what's going to happen to the rest of the people who never went outside? Do you think the aliens will simply wait until they eventually come out or will they use the black shapes on them?"

Ben closed his eyes and with mounting horror he recalled how his copy had moved resolutely up the basement steps, on his way to find Ella. His mind tried to forget how the copy had hidden the hammer behind his back. But his mind wouldn't let him forget his vision of the creature lifting the hammer and smashing it down onto her skull. That scene in his head was a nightmarish dream he struggled vainly to forget. But with his flesh prickling and his heart pounding in his chest, Ben knew it wasn't a dream at all. It was a premonition.

With his eyes still closed, Ben fought to control the rage building inside him. He should have known what would happen when the rain started and the transformations began. He should have been prepared to fight. But it was already too late for this town.

It should have been impossible for him to hear it. But Ben heard everything as if it was happening right inside the hotel room - no - right inside his head.

In dozens of houses in the small valley town, the transformed Others were returning. Returning to their families. They were going home.

And the homecoming would be unspeakable.

THIRTEEN

"Let's go. Now!" Ben yelled and grabbed up his bag at the same time he reached for the gun.

Ben couldn't possibly be hearing the screams from inside the houses. If he was hearing them with his ears, then Ella and Amos should be hearing them too. He glanced at their faces and saw tension and lines of worry that could be from fear. But what he wasn't seeing was the absolute terror he should have seen if they were hearing the same sounds he was hearing. In that instant Ben understood that he wasn't actually hearing the screams as the transformed Others brutally slaughtered those who hadn't been transformed. He was *feeling* the screams and his mind clenched in on itself trying to shut out the piercing din as it assaulted him and tore at his heart. Ella caught Ben's eye and a long look passed between them. She could see he was overcome by some emotion or sensation but she had no way of knowing the agony he was enduring. Ben immediately saw the change in Ella's expression and the intense alarm that began to take over her features.

"I'm fine. Let's go." He affirmed before she could ask the question.

Whether she believed him or not, Ella didn't argue. She left her questions to herself and quickly ran to the small hotel bathroom. She scooped up bottles of body wash and lotion and jammed them hurriedly into her brightly colored cosmetics bag. Ben trailed behind her, not meeting her eyes in the tall mirror over the sink. His hands moved to grab his only two items, deodorant and a toothbrush and flung them into a clear zip-lock baggie. It was only after they had gathered up everything and were moving toward the door that they looked behind them. Amos was still sitting quietly on the bed, unmoving.

"Come on." Ben ordered sternly and worked hard to keep a frown of irritation from creasing his forehead. They didn't have time for this.

Shaking his head resolutely, Amos drew his feet back under him and clasped his arms around his legs. He buried his shaking head in his knees and the sleeves of his long sleeved shirt tugged back as one russet colored hand grasped the other. Ben stared at his wrists and flicked a glance over to Ella and then nodded his head, drawing her gaze to Amos. A sharp intake of her breath confirmed she had seen what Ben needed her to see. The purplish-red bruises on Amos' wrists were fresh. Whatever had happened between Amos and his dad that had brought the boy crying to their door, hadn't been gentle.

"I'm not going back out there." Amos sobbed, and the cry in his voice sliced through Ella's heart like a hot knife through butter.

"It's ok." Ella pleaded with Amos as she moved closer to the bed. "We'll be fine. He's… different." She nodded her head toward Ben. "If we stay with him we'll be fine."

Ben bristled a little as he listened to Ella try to convince Amos to come with them. He wasn't sure at all if they would be fine if they stayed with him. His heart slammed thickly in his chest with the new responsibility. After the red clouds had sucked away his dad's life, Ben hadn't wanted to take care of anyone else except himself. His plan had been to sit in the darkened room and wait for the poisoned air to choke the life out of him, too. He had been too angry at life and too angry at the alien force that came to destroy his world that all he wanted to do was let death end it all for him. What he hadn't counted on, in that dim room with the smell of smoke and death all around him, was that he would be too angry to die. Then Ella had come and his life was no longer just his own and her trust in him scared him but also made him strong. He still had his doubts that he could do anything to fight this new enemy. And now it seemed that Amos' doubts about Ben's ability were even greater.

"I don't believe you." The boy said simply and looked up to meet Ben's eyes even though it was Ella who had spoken to him.

After being transformed, Amos' dad had known exactly where Ben and Ella were and had sent Amos to them. And if he knew, did that mean all the other transformed ones knew, too? Or was Amos' dad given special instructions by the aliens to send

Amos to them? The rest of the transformed Others had left Ben and Ella alone and hadn't tried to force them to come out, and they hadn't tried to force their way in to attack them. As Ben turned the new thoughts over in his mind, trying to understand what it all meant, he became aware of how quiet it was outside. The silence was a heavy weight on his heart. All the transformations were done and the rain had stopped.

Ben dipped his head and stared down at his heavy black work boots as if he could find his answers there. His mind began to run through all the past events once more trying to fit all the pieces together. There were so many shadowing memories from his past coalescing with the present and now he had to worry about dreams and visions that were premonitions of the future. He couldn't put it all together fast enough and he was afraid that failure might come back to haunt him. All he knew right then was that they had to get moving.

"Fine. If you don't want to come with us, then you're welcome to stay here." Ben tossed the cold words over his shoulder to Amos and then continued walking toward the door.

"No!" Ella shouted and her head swung around to Ben so fast that her long hair whipped at her face.

She stepped so close to Ben that for an instant he thought she was going to kiss him on the mouth. Kissing him was the last thing on her mind. Ella's frown was deep and Ben had to fight the urge to rub a finger over the skin of her forehead, smoothing down the puckered flesh.

"We can't leave him." She hissed quietly and her confused eyes traveled back and forth between his.

"Sure we can leave him." Ben said loudly enough for Amos to hear. "If he wants to stay here all alone, with only a flimsy wooden door between him and the outside, then that's his choice."

Behind them, Amos's eyes immediately widened at Ben's words.

The disturbing images of his father and the blinding lights and the ghastly change that had come over him tussled with the hurt and fear in Amos' mind.

"Wait." The boy leaped from the bed, scurrying close to Ella. "Maybe...maybe I could go with you for a little while."

This time when Amos slid close to her, Ella didn't hesitate. She turned and dropped to one knee and pulled him close. She tossed a glaring look back at Ben.

"How can you be so mean?" She hissed as she stood and took Amos by the hand.

"It worked didn't it?" He shrugged and pulled open the door.

Working their way silently across the now empty parking lot, the trio held their hands over their mouths to keep out the acrid smoke from the red clouds. The streets of the small village were desolate and still. All the strange rain had already dried up and not even black-flecked puddles remained on the streets. Popping the locks to the car, Ben made a quick scan of the front and back seats and then the trunk to make sure there weren't any unwanted stowaways.

As he approached the car, Amos stopped a little ways away, his hand slipping from Ella's grasp. Ben watched as the boy's sad gray eyes shifted over to a point further down the lamp lit street.

"I want to go home. I want to see my mom and dad." The plaintive sound of his voice nearly broke Ella. But Ben stood firm.

"They're gone." He stated coldly and Ella flinched.

"Please…" She turned her judging eyes on Ben and he blinked at the gleam of tears in them.

It only took her a moment to kneel down and scoop the trembling boy into her arms. Hugging him tight, she pressed her lips softly to his cheek.

"Where did they go?" he asked, not fully understanding Ben's words.

"I don't know for sure." Ella said truthfully. "But I'm so sorry, Amos. If Ben says it's true, then it's true." Her words were soft and gentle but they were still a blow.

When the rain fell from the sky and landed on his dad's flesh, the bright flash of light had nearly blinded Amos. When his father had begun to scream and tear at the skin of his face and hands, Amos hadn't been able to move. His eyes grew so round with fear that they seemed to take over his whole face. Finally he was able to force his feet to move – to take one step back. It was in that instant that the transformation was complete and the light in his father's golden brown eyes, that had always looked so much like his, poofed out like a snuffed candle. By the time Amos had gathered his wits to turn and run, the creature was on him, grasping him by the wrists so tight that the boy thought his bones might break. Amos had screamed then, a loud, thin keening sound that welled up from the deepest part of him.

"Go." The creature who was no longer his dad had uttered in a voice so hollow, so empty. "Go to the *One*."

The creature had then shoved Amos hard toward the motel room door with the silvery numbers "195" tacked above a grimy peephole. Amos managed to stay on his feet, but barely. He had watched with horrified eyes as the creature that used to be his dad turned his back on him and began to run.

Amos shook his head from side to side, tormented, but finally accepting that Ben and Ella were telling him the truth. His dad was gone and now they were telling him that his mom was gone. His narrow shoulders began to hitch with his anguished tears. Ella let Amos cry against her shoulder for a few seconds, his thin fingers digging lightly into her skin. When his sobs finally slowed and he took in a long sighing breath, Ella led him by the hand and pressed him down gently in the back seat of the car. The seatbelt was too long for his thin frame and she had to adjust it twice to be able to fit him. But for the time being, he seemed to be secure.

Ben stood watching as the scene between Amos and Ella unfolded. All he could think of was how much he wanted to be alone. He wanted to hand her the car keys, kiss her hard on the lips and then walk far away into the night. It wasn't that he didn't love her, but he had always been alone. He had always taken care of himself and only himself until his father had gotten so sick. Now it wasn't just Ella he had to worry about, but here was this child. And this boy might very well have seen too much and felt too much and be damaged beyond repair. How would they be able to fight with him weighing them down? And there was no question that they would have to fight. Ella had accepted that she might have to give up everything in order to win this battle. But she was an adult and she was wiling. What would they do with the boy? How would they live?

Steering the car down the quiet street toward the edge of town, Ben spoke softly. "We haven't had a lot of time to talk about this or to plan."

"What options do we have?" Ella's reply was just as soft.

"I don't know. I'm still not sure what weapons or power we have. And I need to be blunt." He said and looked quickly at Ella who nodded. "What if they get to you again when I'm not close by? Will they take you or will they kill you?"

"Yeah. That's really blunt." Ella bit at her lip and tried not to think too hard about the answer.

They continued their slow drive through the quiet, dark town. The reddish glow from the ruined sky filtered through the car windows and settled on their skin like an angry rash. Lights were on in most of the houses and with the curtains open, the couple could have looked in if they wanted to. But they kept their eyes focused straight ahead and closed their thoughts to what horrendous scenes might be playing out inside.

"That's my house!" Amos suddenly yelled from the back seat.

His voice was high and shrill from excitement. When he began yanking on the handle of the back door, Ben realized his mistake. He hadn't disabled the child-proof locks so the heavy door immediately swung open into the night.

"Stop!" Ella's body twisted around and one arm flung out and behind her to grab at Amos's shirt.

Ben slammed hard on the brakes and Ella flung an arm back, holding Amos down as his small hands scrambled to press the button to unlatch his seatbelt. When the car jerked to a stop, the car door swung wildly back toward the car but didn't close.

"That's my house!" Amos shrieked again as the front door to his house slowly opened.

With a movement so quick, Amos jerked his shirt from Ella's grasp and leaped from the car, his small legs pumping. Ella gasped and sucked in a breath and began fumbling for her seatbelt, determined to go after him.

"No!" Ben yelled, his fingers digging into her arm. He waited for her to stop yelling and struggling and she finally looked him in the eye. "No." He said again softly.

They both turned and watched as Amos dashed down the sidewalk toward the front door of the white two-story house. Amos' excitement was palpable as he ran toward the door, yelling for his dad and yelling for his mom. And it was only when the Other who used to be his father pulled open the door the rest of the way and gazed blankly at him that Amos stopped.

And Amos began to scream.

FOURTEEN

Amos took two staggering steps backward, his bright blue tennis shoes barely connecting with the pavement. His terror filled screams had turned to a harsh rasping intake of breath, making Ben think the boy might hyperventilate right on the spot. In the darkness lit only by the overhead street light and a dust-covered bulb on the porch, a dreadful scene played out as Ben and Ella looked on.

The Other who had been Amos' father stood in the open doorway facing the street. He was covered in bright red splashes of blood from his neck all the way to his knees which made his dark skin shine in the dim light. The chaotic pattern of the blood spatters looked oddly to Ben like a big red question mark on the Other's chest. It was as if he was taunting Ben by throwing more questions at him when what he really needed was answers.

Taking another step through the doorway onto the small slab porch, the Other's head suddenly snapped downward and his teeth bared and he seemed to leap down the stairs toward Amos.

"Noooooooo!" The scream from the little boy was like a dagger slicing through the still air.

Unable to sit still any longer, Ella was out of the car and running by the time Amos had backpedaled his way to the end of the sidewalk toward the street. This time Ben didn't try to stop her. The Other was closer to the boy now and the fresh, wet blood on his shirt dripped crimson splatters onto the dark sidewalk.

For Ben, sitting in the driver's seat of the car watching the three people out of his window was like watching characters in a play. He was barely feeling any concern for Ella and the boy, and oddly, no fear. And why wasn't his gut twisting in fury for what the Other might do to them, exposed as they were on that pitted concrete sidewalk? Ben's eyes narrowed. Something wasn't right. His fatigued brain churned until he finally wrestled one small piece of the puzzle together. Giving a short grunt of understanding, Ben reached for the door handle. Deliberately controlling his now mounting anger, he slowly opened the driver's side door and then even more slowly, as if he had all the time in the world, he pulled open the back door, leaving it hanging wide ajar.

"We're taking him!" Ben shouted at the Other who stopped as abruptly as if he had been yanked taut by a string tied to his back.

Even as he shouted his threat, he knew the Other wouldn't fight him. The Other was only making a pretense of chasing after Amos. He never wanted the boy. That was completely clear to Ben. They didn't want children at all. As he thought about it, the only Others they had seen had been adult males. So whoever or whatever it was that was transforming these people into Others, they were picking who they thought were the strongest members of the human race.

Ben might have laughed as he thought about some of the women and kids he had known in his life who were stronger and tougher than any full-grown man. He was sure the Others would have a big fight on their hands if they tried to take on any one of them. But at the moment, Ben didn't let the thought bring even a hint of a smile to his lips. He stood calmly by the car and stared into the eyes of the Other.

"Come to me, Amos." Ella said loudly.

She had finally reached the place where Amos was still stumbling backward, almost about to step off the low curb into the street. Grabbing his narrow shoulders, she turned him around toward her. His face was so pale and his eyes were so huge that it frightened her for a second. He was closing in on himself again and she completely understood why. He had seen too much in too short of a time and his mind was trying to build up a barrier to protect him. Ella gently lifted Amos off of his feet and sat him in the backseat of the car. This time, though, she pushed his small body over to the other side of the backseat and slid in beside him.

The Other stood with emotionless eyes staring at Ben. Nothing about him seemed tensed or ready to attack. He simply stood there. His breathing was slow and even and his body was perfect and his flesh looked as natural as a real human. If Ben didn't know for a fact that he was an Other, he wouldn't be able to tell by looking at him. He looked that real.

Ben quickly feigned two forceful steps toward the Other. The Other took two quick steps back. From where he stood, Ben could smell the sulfuric odor of the transformed body. The smell reminded him of the smoke and the fire in the sky and brought back the vile memory of the basement way too vividly for his liking. It would be hard to say how long the stalemate might have continued, with the Other staring at Ben and Ben staring at the other. But quicker than Ben could blink, the Other turned and leaped and seemingly flew through the open doorway back into the house.

The slam of the front door was like a gunshot in the night and Ben blinked and noticed two things. The Other wasn't afraid of him, but still showed no intention of engaging Ben in any way. The second thing he noticed was that he was no longer smelling or tasting the foul smoke from the burning sky. He glanced upward and had to blink his eyes shut for a second. Opening them again, he had to acknowledge what he was really seeing. The sky was clear and he was seeing a host of bright stars littering the heavens from one end of the horizon to the other.

Without warning, Ben was overwhelmed with a weariness that threatened to drop him where he stood. He was too tired to even think any more. His mind was tired and his body was tired and he didn't understand what was happening and he was exhausted from trying to figure everything out. He didn't know why he was different and why they left him alone. And right then, he didn't care. All he wanted to do was get in the car and drive to a place where he could eat and sleep and give his mind a break.

****

Twenty-five miles down the road leading away from the village, Ella finally spoke up from the back seat.

"Can you stop for a minute? Amos is asleep and I need to come up front with you."

When she used the word 'need', it didn't surprise Ben. When Ella was drained from sensory overload or simply too dog-tired to function, she either ran away from Ben or she ran toward him. She had no in-between setting. She was either all his or all to herself when her mind was in turmoil. Ben immediately steered the car to the side of the road and pushed open the passenger side door. He left his hand outstretched and she eagerly grabbed onto it as she dropped into the seat and turned her wide, sad eyes on him. Ben drew her into his arms and she slid into his embrace, fitting neatly to him like the missing piece to a puzzle.

In the backseat, Amos twitched in his sleep and whimpered.

FIFTEEN

Finding a deserted cabin partway up the mountain pass seemed too good to be true. Pulling off to the side of the narrow dirt driveway, the weary trio sat in the car listening to the tick ticking of the cooling engine.

"Do you feel anything?" Ella clicked a fingernail on the passenger side window, trying to appear less nervous than she felt.

"I feel tired." Ben said mildly, not answering her question.

"I'm going to pinch you." Ella extended a hand and grabbed a small section of Ben's arm flesh between her thumb and forefinger. "And after I pinch you, you'll answer my question."

"And after I answer your question, can I pinch you back?" Ben tilted his head toward Ella and lifted an eyebrow.

"Try it." She quipped. "And see what it gets you."

Amos dropped his head to stifle a grin at their playfulness. He didn't want them to see him smile. It didn't feel right smiling. Not yet.

"I think the cabin is safe for now." Ben nodded as he spoke.

"You think?"

"Yeah. That's as good as I can give you, El."

Ben still didn't trust his intuition enough to give a definitive answer. He could feel a sort of calmness in his chest that settled between his ribs softly like a small fluttering moth. There was a tiny bit of trepidation, but the main emotion he felt was calm. It was strange to Ben to have these impressions and he was still learning how to interpret what the feelings meant. This time, however, he was almost positive. It was that *almost* that left his mouth a little dry and a frown of tension between his eyes.

"Let's go." He said and Ella glanced back at Amos.

The young boy was staring blankly out at the trees lining the long wooded driveway. Some color had come back into his cheeks and Ella breathed a tiny sigh of relief. She had been more worried about Amos than she wanted to admit and she wasn't sure what she would have done if he had continued to draw in on himself.

Standing at the front door, Ben wasted no time trying to pick the lock. Lifting one booted foot, he smashed the wooden door inward and stepped boldly inside. By that time, he was positive there were no Others inside. No more almost. He was sure.

Once the burning red clouds and the choking smoke had dissipated from the weary sky, Ben did seem to be able to think more clearly, even though thinking was the last thing he wanted to do right then. He was beyond exhausted and his only wish was throw himself on the nearest bed and sleep deeply and not have to think of anything for a while.

"Now that you've busted the lock so nicely," Ella said, moving through the door and pulling Amos behind her. "How are we going to lock the door?"

Leaning over to press a soft kiss to her temple as she passed by him, Ben shook his head. "They won't bother us. I'm special, remember?"

He gave her a wry smile and she rewarded him with a smile so genuine and so full of love that his heart slammed hard in his chest. He loved her so much it scared him. Never letting anyone get close to him was his way to avoid ever losing anyone. But it was too late. She held his heart and he couldn't imagine being without her. Ben tried to wrap his arms around Ella, but she was already moving past him. So he just slid his lips along her jaw until they found her mouth.

"I need more of that." She whispered.

"Let's get this guy to bed first and I'll see what I can do for you." His voice was husky with his need for her.

Later that night, after they both had satisfied their desire and need for each other, Ben lay wide awake in the double bed in the only bedroom in the cabin. They had bunked Amos down on the dusty couch in the main room. Lining the rough fabric with soft sheets and blankets they had found in the closet, Amos' eyes had fluttered closed within seconds.

Ben couldn't sleep. Frustrated, he worked to shut down his thoughts and give his embattled mind a chance to recharge. But as soon as the exhaustion overtook him and his eyelids almost closed, the dream image of his copy filtered through. He watched with a miserable fury as he saw the creature in the Alberton cabin with the heavy iron hammer lifted overhead. Too clearly, he saw Ella lying on her side on the musty old couch as her eyes moved restlessly beneath her lids.

For a few seconds, the images forced themselves on Ben and he observed the ghastly dream from behind a grayish fog like a spectator. This part wasn't new. He had long ago come to accept this role in his own dreams. He always felt he was on the outside looking in, even in his own head. But this time, just like all the times before with this grisly dream, right as the Other in the dream began to swing the heavy hammer down, ready to crush Ella's skull, Ben jerked awake. Shifting slightly toward Ella, he reached out with his left hand and felt for her hip. She stirred and immediately rolled toward him, her arm circling his waist and her leg slipping easily over his. He spread his legs a little to more comfortably position her thigh between his legs. The pressure against his balls was light and pleasant. Through all this, she never woke up. Embracing him in her sleep was automatic for her now.

Ben scrubbed a hand over his face as he rubbed his other hand down her back. Her warm body smelled faintly like flowers and sweat and the combination brought him to a distracting state of arousal. He shifted his hips a bit hoping she wouldn't feel his growing erection, but it was too late. Her hand slid down and stroked him and her eyes fluttered open.

"Again?" She asked and tilted her head back for a kiss.

"Too soon?" He could wait if he had to.

"No. I'm ready."

Her hand massaged his stiffening penis and after a few strokes, Ben rolled her over onto her back. He wanted to look into her eyes. He wanted to watch her face as they made love.

****

The next morning, Ben stood over Amos' sleeping form, watching the young boy's chest rise and fall. Small tufts of his curly black hair poked out on both sides of Amos' head, making him look like a tiny mad professor. Ella was in the kitchen, rummaging through her backpack for the makings for their breakfast. At the thought of food, Ben's stomach rumbled so loudly that the little boy flinched in his sleep and startled awake.

"Go away! Leave me alone!" Amos' eyes went wide and he dug his heels into the slippery blankets trying to push his body away from Ben.

"What's going on?" Ella flew into the room and ran straight to the couch where Amos had pressed himself into the farthest corner. The whites of his eyes had expanded and the fear emanating from him was palpable. Ella gathered both of his trembling hands in hers and rubbed them softly together.

"I was just watching him sleep and he woke up and saw me." Ben said tersely and took a step back.

He refused to feel guilty for simply standing there watching the boy. And he wouldn't apologize when he hadn't done anything wrong. Still, an unbidden wave of guilt washed over Ben and he felt angry at the same time. He was doing his best. He was trying to help them figure out what was going on and keep them all safe. And if Ella was going to start taking the boy's side of things without even asking him his side of things, then he wasn't sure how much longer they would last.

"Amos." Her voice interrupting his thoughts was soft and soothing. "We will never hurt you. Ben will never hurt you. You don't ever have to be afraid of him."

Ben blinked and mentally kicked himself for how quickly he had misjudged her. He should have known Ella would always take his side. The wave of guilt crested and then dissipated as she continued to calm Amos with her words.

"He's going to help us find a way out of this. A way to be safe. You don't have to be afraid. He's not always going to speak sweetly or nicely to you, but he will always tell you the truth and we need to be sure and listen to him and do what he says. OK?"

Amos sat with his back pressed tightly against the arm of the couch and surveyed Ben. He wanted to believe Ella. He really wanted to. But Ben could be so cold sometimes and it did scare him. Amos glanced down at his hands that were warmly pressed between Ella's two hands. He couldn't imagine Ben ever soothing him like that.

"OK, Amos?" Ella asked for his agreement and raised her eyebrows, waiting for a response.

Amos flicked his eyes from Ella to Ben and he tried not to sigh out loud. Ella was kind, and so easy to understand. But Ben made the back of Amos' neck itch. He longed to reach back and scratch his neck but he didn't want to let go of Ella's hands. Finally, the young boy nodded his agreement. Ben raised his eyes in surprise. He truly hadn't thought it would be that easy.

"OK." Ella said with a finality that settled the issue for them all and spoke to Amos once more. "How about you go get washed up and get ready for breakfast?"

The boy nodded his head once again and crawled quickly off the couch. As he stepped past Ben, Amos hesitated and glanced up at him. Ben stared down at him, not sure what to say or do. He was aware of Ella watching him and he began to get a little anxious wondering what he should do next. Before he could come up with anything to say, Amos impulsively pressed his small body against Ben's legs and wrapped his thin arms around Ben's hips.

"I'm sorry I was scared of you." He whispered. Then just as quickly, Amos pushed himself away and trotted across to the bathroom at the far end of the room.

"Ughhh." Ben intoned and then looked over at Ella. "Stop laughing." He pointed a finger at her and raised his eyebrows even higher at her huge grin.

"You'd make such a good Daddy." She slapped him lightly on the butt and returned to the small kitchen to finish fixing breakfast.

Rolling his eyes as he shook his head might have been juvenile, but Ben did it anyway. Opening the front door to the cabin, he decided that a little fresh air was just the thing he needed. Now that the skies had been cleared of the burning red smoke, Ben couldn't get enough of the clean air. Not having a cigarette in two weeks hadn't been as hard as he thought it would be. Thanks to the acrid smoke from the alien clouds, every breath he took was filled with enough poison to make him feel like he was still inhaling his beloved cigarettes.

But the clouds were gone and the air outside was fresh and cleansing as he took one deep breath after another. It hadn't taken long for the smell of smoke and the thick choking cloud to dissipate. Later, he might stop to wonder why it hadn't taken long for the skies to clear, but for that moment he didn't question it. He simply wanted to enjoy it.

"COME WITH ME!!!" The loud booming voice blasted through the quiet morning air.

Ben dropped down into a crouch as his head swung from left to right trying to figure out where the voice was coming from. He slapped at his hip and nearly cursed in frustration. He had left the gun inside. Hunkering down further, Ben slid behind a moldy old porch chair, knowing it would provide little cover but was better than nothing.

"COME WITH ME!!!" The voice boomed out again.

Finally locating the source of the sound, Ben snapped his head to the right and saw the man instantly. He stared hard, trying to determine if it was an Other or not. The man looked real. But then Ben remembered that it wasn't his eyes that let him see the Others. Struggling to still his pounding heart, he still kept his eye on the approaching man but let his mind show him. As Ben's eyes narrowed and his hands curled into fists, he was able to peer beneath the surface, beneath the skin and see the creature for what it was.

It was an Other.

With no warning, the Other suddenly leaped up from the flimsy cover of the trees and began running at full speed toward Ben.

SIXTEEN

Surprise is what Ben felt first.

The Other was running straight at him at full speed, his thick legs pumping and eating up the ground between them at a rapid pace. Ben was still crouched slightly on the porch behind the flimsy cover of the outdoor chair. He rose up a bit on the balls of his feet, ready to take the hit and hopefully fling the Other up and over his head and flat on his back behind him. The surprise Ben felt lingered. If the Other was afraid of him, he didn't show it. Then, there were only six feet between the creature and the bottom step of the porch. As Ben tensed all his muscles and set his jaw, ready to fight, the Other suddenly skidded to a stop just four feet from the bottom step.

"Come with me! Tell us!" The Other shouted and the veins pulsed thickly in its neck.

Ben was genuinely confused and he barked his words back at the Other. "What are you talking about? What do I have to tell you?" He frowned as he yelled.

"Tell us why you are Singular!"

When the Other shouted the word "Singular", a hot tingle shot through Ben from his scalp to his toes. *Singular*? How could that one word fill Ben with more dread than all of his nightmares combined? He needed to know more, but apparently patience wasn't high on the list of character traits for an Other.

"We have to go now!" The Other yelled his words at Ben and ventured one more step closer.

In the back of his mind, Ben felt the faint stirrings of a great fear. Not fear of the Other who had gotten closer to him than any had before, but at the staggering implications of that one word. Singular. Ben wasn't a stupid man. He knew being Singular meant there was something more than unique about him. As a child Ben had been quieter and more introspective than most children his age. After his mother had breathed her last breath and slipped away from him in that too-quiet hospital room, the sensation of otherness became so strong that Ben was convinced he wasn't anything like any of the other children who crossed his path.

The Other's face began to darken and beneath the surface of the pasty skin, Ben could see the black alien grains moving and coursing like blood through veins.

"What's your hurry?" Ben goaded.

He spoke loudly but didn't yell. He was hoping to agitate the Other into revealing more information. Whatever being Singular meant, the aliens, who had the knowledge and power to fly their crafts from their world to his and spread their poison all over the skies, still had sent this creature to fetch Ben like a common dog. Did they think he would simply smile and nod and follow the Other to wherever they wanted him to go?

"Come with me, now!" Agitation bloomed across the Other's face and the splotchy pink of its cheeks was becoming an alarming shade of red.

Ben almost laughed at the insanity of the situation. They had sent the Other on this quest, but the creature clearly had no other power over Ben other than a loud voice and a lot of shouting.

As Ben narrowed his eyes in thought, the Other began to twitch with annoyance. This time Ben did laugh. There was no doubt that the Other had been sent with one purpose. His mission was to find Ben and then deliver him to whoever had sent him. And once they had him, they would of course, kill him.

"Okay." Ben nodded and the Other's eyes widened with expectation. The excitement on the creature's face was unmistakable and Ben recoiled slightly at the dark glee in the Other's eyes. Ben had absolutely no intention of going anywhere with the Other. He just wanted to push the creature a little bit more...

"Nah." Ben shook his head and flapped a dismissive hand at the Other. "I changed my mind. I think I'll stay here."

A frightening transformation blew over the Other's face like a spark exploding into a raging fire.

"COME WITH ME!" The Other howled in fierce frustration and its lips peeled back ferociously from its teeth.

With a growl that sounded more animal than human, the Other lunged at Ben.

The bullet hit the Other square between the eyes, the impact pirouetting him up on his toes like he was preparing to dance a delicate ballet on pointe. But it was no dance. The Other landed down hard on its heels, then tottered backward and slammed to the ground with a solid thud.

Swinging around, Ben saw Ella standing in the doorway, her arm outstretched with the silver gun still pointed at the place where the unfortunate Other had been standing.

"I was hoping to get some answers out of this guy." Ben said with a slight tone of irritation.

"I was hoping to keep you alive." Ella said flippantly.

Ben could see that she was trembling slightly. Her glib words were a cover for her fear and his heart softened a little. She should have known he would be okay. By now she should have known that there was something about him that kept the Others from attacking him. But she was also scared to death of losing him. She came by that fear honestly. Ben nodded his head at the gun, which she finally lowered shakily to her side.

Reaching down with a grunt, Ben began dragging the Other across the gravel driveway toward the tall weeds off to one side. A dead body was the last thing Amos needed to see when he came outside. He had seen enough death and weird crap for a while. As Ben grasped the dusty jeans of the Other, a peculiar shifting beneath the thick fabric made Ben yank his hands away and take a step back. It was as if the skin and bones of the Other's legs had started softening…dissolving.

"Ben?" Ella shouted from the porch. "What's wrong?"

Ben didn't answer right away. He rolled his shoulders back, easing some of the tension and he gritted his teeth together. "Nothing. It's okay. Go on back inside."

Gripping the Other's legs once more, Ben began tugging on the dead weight that became lighter and lighter with every pull. By the time the creature's body was fully off the road and in the grass, Ben knew he was hauling only a pile of empty clothing. He didn't want to watch as the Other's head disappeared. He didn't want to see that scene and have it replaying in his dreams every night, but his eyes had a different plan.

At first, the ripples of fine black grit moved lethargically beneath the skin of the Other's face. Within the space of five seconds, the writhing became a fast moving shimmer that puckered the skin in places and bubbled it out in others. Ben watched the de-transformation in rapt horror. The skin of the forehead turned a grayish black, then began to soften and then in an instant, the entire head simply disappeared in a puff of black sand. No tendrils of oily black smoke rose from the body but the foul stench of sulfur and smoke blew past his nostrils in a sickening wave.

Ben flapped a hand in front of his face to dispel the stench and cocked his head to one side, thinking. He kicked lightly at the empty clothing with his boot. At the movement, a few black grains flew from the sleeve of the shirt and Ben stepped back quickly, thinking they might be reaching for him. But the grains weren't moving. They were dead.

****

"What does *Singular* mean?" Ella asked once they were both seated inside the cabin at the small kitchen table.

"I don't know. You shot him before I could find out."

"He got too close to you." She lifted her head and the fear in her green eyes pierced his soul.

"Yeah. He had a job to do and I guess he was willing to die to do that job."

"Did he really think you would go with him? Just like that?"

"I'm not sure what he thought or if he even was able to have an independent thought. And even if I had wanted to go with him – to find out more about them and about myself – I would never leave you, El."

Ella's head bobbed her appreciation at his words, but then she immediately bit at her lip and asked her next question. Ben was ready for it.

"When I shot this…guy, why wasn't there the same wet mess and black fibers like with the first…Other?" She picked at her short fingernails as she waited for a response.

"I don't know for certain, but I have a theory on that. Well, a partial theory for now." Ben rubbed his hands together as he talked as if he could rub away the disturbing feeling of the Other dissolving as he hauled him to the side of the road. "It may have something to do with how they were created. I mean, the copy of me died wet and messy. But the two guys in the gas station that I shot? Their bodies exploded in the same black tendrils just like the mouse and the tree in the road."

"Wait." Ella interrupted and leaned forward in concentration. "That doesn't make sense to me. If they made a copy of you, why was that copied body juicy? It was made up completely of black fibers. The transformed Others still had their human bodies so wouldn't you think it would be just the opposite? That the Others' bodies would be more gooey than the copy they made of you?"

Ben and Ella didn't have to worry about Amos hearing the conversation, yet they both instinctively kept their voices low. Once breakfast was over, Amos had wandered into the bedroom, climbed into the unmade double bed and fell asleep within seconds.

"I know what you mean," Ben continued. "But the fact is it was the copy they made of me that was messy. So here's what I think. What if the black shapes tried to convert me, but couldn't for whatever reason? Because, you know…I'm special. I'm Singular." Ben chuckled and Ella rolled her eyes. "But they had to try and copy a human body after touching only my hand and copying bodies isn't how they normally do things. So what if it was because they had to create skin and bones and blood and bile and all of that to be able to fool you. And that's why the copy exploded the way it did. But when the black shapes made the tree and the mouse, they were able to take over an existing form."

"Okay." Ella tried to keep up with his logic.

"I'm thinking that in a normal transformation, if you can call any of that normal, that all the wet stuff is absorbed by the black shapes and all the skin and blood and cells become like the black shapes.

"Okay." Ella conceded. The explanation actually did seem plausible. "What about the ones that were converted by the rain?"

"Right." Ben tapped a finger onto his palm. "Here's what I think about that and why this Other's body dissolved the way it did. Imagine the black shapes and how they seemed to have a kind of a form. Weird and wispy, but still a form?"

"Yes."

"In order to be disbursed through the rain droplets, I think they had to somehow dissolve themselves - tear themselves into tiny pieces. And the black grains we saw are what they transformed into and these grains are what did all the dirty work. I believe the rain was just the distribution system. So when you shot the Other, it was like the Bible verse talks about things going from "dust to dust.""

All of this, Ben spoke aloud with a detachment that made Ella a little uneasy. Seeing the Other dissolve into dust should have left him at least a little upset and unable to talk so easily about this. What she didn't know was that Ben's nightly battle for sleep had left him with a kind of mental strongbox. If it wasn't for this ability, Ben wouldn't have been able to deal with the horrors of his nightmares. In his eyes, it was his most cherished gift of all, to be able to file away the anger and the pain and the dread into the strongbox where it was safely contained and could no longer wound his bruised mind. It was one of the few benefits Ben enjoyed from his lifetime of suffering. It was his and he owned it and it had saved him time and again.

Ben reached across and snagged one of Ella's slightly trembling hands and held it between his own.

"You know they'll send another one." He stated the obvious truth.

"Yeah." She sighed.

Sitting at the kitchen table in a cabin that wasn't theirs, talking softly to keep from waking a child who wasn't theirs, Ben and Ella finally lapsed into silence. She picked absently at a thread on her tan pullover sweater, and Ben drew a finger under his bottom lip, both of them pondering. There was a host of unknowns and still more questions than real answers. They could make guesses all day long, but in order to know of what Ben's role in all this was, they needed to learn the truth. Ben's mind began to grow weary again as he rolled too many ideas around in his brain. One thing he should have been happy to accept without explanation still pricked at him like a spiky thorn. The fires in the sky that had burned their eyes and throats for so long were gone. That had been the alien's way of introducing themselves and taking out a good-sized chunk of the human and plant population. The finger under his lip rubbed continuously as if he could rub a solution into existence. Ben couldn't help wondering why the clouds would suddenly disappear. How would they be able to transform more people into Others without the clouds and the rain? Ben peered out into the cloudless afternoon sky and thought back to the night of transformations in the doomed town. Suddenly, his breath caught in his throat and his fingers tightened painfully on Ella's hand.

"Ow, ow, ow!" She squealed and snatched her throbbing fingers away. Frowning over at Ben, she blinked, trying to read his expression.

Ben had gone pale.

"What? What?" Ella searched his face for the answer.

"Back in the hotel when I said they were taking them all…?" Ben's voice was low and full of grief. "I thought it was just that village. That one town. But I was wrong. How could I have been so stupid?" He shook his head viciously as he looked up at Ella, his eyes clouded with anguish. "That's why the clouds are gone, El. They didn't just transform the people in that village. You saw the clouds. They covered the sky as far as our eye could see."

Ella dropped her head with understanding and Ben pulled her close.

"They're done, El. They've transformed the entire planet."

SEVENTEEN

Everything was gray.

The walls were gray, the ceiling was gray, and the floor was gray. No, that wasn't quite right. Everything was silver. There was a light sheen to everything, a reflectiveness that let Ben know he wasn't looking at gray paint, he was looking at silver metal.

Late in the night, in his restlessness, Ben reached for Ella. This time, she didn't stir. She was deeply asleep but so was he. His hand found her hip and rested gently on the softness. Ben breathed deeply but raggedly as the dream moved on.

In all of his nightmares, Ben played the role of a spectator. He would survey the unfolding scenes from the side or from above as if he were in the audience watching a high school play. Even when the hapless victims in his desperate nightmares would turn pleading, fearful eyes on him, dream-time Ben was powerless to lift a finger or an arm to rush to their aid. He would watch helplessly as whatever nightmare creature chased their prey from room to room, their sharp, snatching fingers grasping nearer with each turn. Ben's body shook with the exertion of trying to shake himself loose from whatever bonds held him captive, but his efforts were always futile. He was helpless and the helplessness made him angry.

However, this night and this dream were different. In the vision that played in his mind this night, Ben was standing alone in the large silver room. He glanced down at his hands and his feet then back up to the smooth walls. He looked around for something more but the room was large and square and completely empty. His eye swept along the four bare walls and up to the ceiling. He guessed the room was about ten feet square; a perfect cube. The reflectiveness of the room made it look so much like the inside of a 1940s sci-fi movie set spaceship that in his dream, Ben laughed out loud.

"Seriously? A silver spaceship?" The laugh echoed hollowly back to him in the bare room.

As he turned his head to the right a second time, a glowing red dot came into view. Had that been there all along? Ben shook his head in irritation. He hated games and puzzles and was already frustrated by the empty room. Peering closer, he could see that the red dot emanated from a small square box mounted on the far wall.

"Ok." He said out loud, sarcasm tinging his voice. "I assume that's a camera." He walked boldly toward the red light.

But it wasn't a camera. And as Ben approached the light, the red glow began to pulse and a feeling of dark malevolence washed over him in an instant. Even as he jerked his body quickly to the left, Ben knew it was too late. The red dot transformed into a blazing hot beam that shot directly toward him.

He felt the searing pain as the meat of his upper arm was sliced clean from him. There was the familiar instant of nothingness before an agonizing pain stabbed daggers of hot fire throughout his entire body. Ben groaned and gritted his teeth, forcing himself not to grab at the open raw wound.

"YOU ARE TOO WEAK TO WIN." The cold menacing words pushed into his mind and Ben staggered backward from the assault coming from deep inside his brain.

His damaged shoulder was still a searing fireball of pain, forcing his body to bend over nearly in half. The insistent sinister voice in his head was horrific. The personal assault deep into his mind was an onslaught like nothing he had never experienced before, and he fought with all of his strength to shove it away. It was taking all the force of his will to repel the insistent voice probing deep into his brain. But Ben thought of Ella and he thought of Amos and he knew he had to take control of his mind if he had any chance of keeping them safe. Finally, in desperation fueled by excruciating pain, he marshalled every ounce of his will and snapped his torso upright as he spread his feet and forced in a deep, full breath. Then he propelled out the held breath and shoved at the voice in his mind, "I WILL DESTROY YOU ALL!"

Jerking awake, Ben clutched at the tangled sheets of the bed. His left hand was still on Ella's hip and his fingers dug agonizingly into her flesh.

"Ow! Stop it!" She jolted awake and slapped at his tightened fingers. Ella flipped over to face him with eyes narrowed from pain and suspicion. But when her eyes focused on his pale face and she registered his heavy, labored breathing, her tone immediately changed and she pulled his hand to her face and kissed his fingers over and over.

"Sorry, so sorry. It's ok. It's ok." She chanted with her soft lips pressed to his knuckles. "Tell me about the dream." She prompted and her lips chased along from finger to finger.

His breath came in short gasps and he rolled his eyes upward. "It was just a dream. Like all my other nightmares." He lied.

That was how it started, he thought as he tried to still his rapid breathing. That was how the lies began and the trust dissolved. Ben's concern for Ella's safety pounded at his chest and was so strong it threatened to throw off the rhythm of his heart. He wanted to keep her safe but he knew he had to tell her the truth. He swallowed hard and rolled his eyes over to look at her face. She wasn't looking at him. She had her head dipped down and her mouth was on his hand and she was giving him time to think and time to form the words. Like she always did. She was giving him privacy to settle his breathing and chase away the last of the nightmare demons from his mind.

"Wait." He said softly.

"Of course." She replied.

It took only a minute for Ben to pull in a deep breath and begin to tell her about the dream. He didn't spare her any details and he kept his eyes closed as he spoke. When he came to the part about the laser and the excruciating pain, Ben felt a single drop of wetness on his hand, her tears warm on his skin. But he didn't stop talking until he had told it all.

"They were in my head." He ground his teeth at the memory of the invasion.

"It was only a dream and even in the dream, you beat them." She assured him.

"The pain was so real." Ben reached over and rubbed the skin of his shoulder, his mind almost registering a blistering pain, but then it was gone.

"It was a dream and it's over."

"They'll come back." He was sure.

"And you will fight them and win again."

"I'm not so sure." Ben sighed at a realization. "They waited until I was doubled over in pain before they dug into my head."

"They definitely fight dirty."

Ella rubbed her lips along the swell of his shoulder as if she could soothe away the memory of the pain. Ben threw an arm over his eyes as they talked, replaying the dream in his mind, trying to make sure he didn't forget any details. Everything was important. They both knew that. So he had to be sure to remember everything and tell her everything. In the quiet room, Ben talked softly and Ella nodded, committing his words to memory.

"Hey?" The low voice from the other side of the closed bedroom door was accompanied by three small raps on the wood.

"Come on in, Amos." Ben called out immediately.

He felt the smile on Ella's lips as they were still pressed against his shoulder. "Such a good dad."

"Oh, stop it." He chided lightly and shifted himself to sit up in the double bed.

Ben wasn't really sure what to do with Amos. He didn't dislike kids as much as he simply didn't know how to talk to them or understand what they wanted from him. In his experience, kids asked too many questions and stared at Ben as if he was from another planet. They didn't frighten him, but they weirded him out in a way he couldn't quite explain. But Ella was already crazy about Amos. And she was determined to keep him with them so Ben knew he had no choice but to make it work.

"I had a bad dream." Amos pursed his lips and stared over at Ben and Ella. He didn't have any other clothes with him except the ones he had been wearing when they found him. He had stripped down to his colorful Thor underpants to sleep and his thin brown arms hugged around his bare chest.

"Me too." Ben replied and held out a hand to the boy.

Amos' eyes tightened with initial distrust, but the residual fear from the nightmare made the offered hand more appealing. Gathering his courage, Amos scrambled up the side of the bed and nestled between them with his head resting against Ella's shoulder. Ella could barely hear the muttered the words as Amos immediately began to talk. But Ben heard him loud and clear.

"I dreamed I was in a big gray room." Amos whispered.

"Silver." Ben corrected and he saw Amos' head nod.

"Yeah. Silver. And I was all alone and I felt really scared 'cuz there was nobody and nothing in the room but me."

"Did you see a red light?" Ben asked and felt Ella stiffen at his question.

"No. I didn't see anything but the gray – I mean silver – room."

"Did you hear anything? Like voices?" Ben prompted.

"No. Well...Yes."

Amos hesitated a long time and Ben could feel his small body trembling against him. If the world had been a different place and he had been a different person, Ben would stop asking questions and let the boy forget all about the dream and the silver room. But he couldn't stop. He had to know why they both dreamed of the same room. He had to know everything.

"Tell us what you heard." Ben prompted and gave Amos' shoulder a little pat.

He felt Amos draw in a long breath and let it out.

"I kept thinking this bad thought." Amos' voice was low. "I kept wanting to scream at someone. Scream these words. I dunno why I wanted to do that 'cuz the words were mean. But it was all I could think about and finally I was so scared, I thought if I just scream the words then maybe they would leave me alone and I could get out of that silver room."

"Amos?" Ben asked as gently as he could. "What were the words you screamed?"

Amos tipped his head back and his golden brown eyes were round with fear and sadness. And neither Ben nor Ella were surprised when Amos finally said the words he had been forced to scream in the silver room...

"You are too weak to win!"

EIGHTEEN

The smell of smoke woke Ben from a sleep that was for the first time in a long time, restful and dream-free. Silver rooms with destructive red beams had been banished from his mind and all that remained was an angry sureness and his yelled words, "I will destroy you all!"

When Ben's eyes had slid blissfully shut, the sounds of soft inhales and exhales from Ella and Amos lulled him into that deep and dreamless sleep. But then his eyes snapped open and he breathed in the suffocating smoke and his first thought was that the choking red clouds had returned. A deep cough burst from him as his lungs sucked in the stifling air. One arm – slightly numb from being trapped so long under Ella's neck – tingled as though he was being stabbed by hundreds of tiny needles. Between them, Amos still lay with his knees bent and his hands folded and tucked under his cheek. Ben had only a split second to wonder at how much his life had changed in the past few weeks and how much these two now meant to him. But then the coughing overtook him and both Ella and Amos jerked awake.

"Get up! Now!" Ben sat up quickly and coughed once more, his eyes beginning to sting with tears from the thick smoke.

"What's happening?" Ella questioned him but at the same time, she was swinging her legs over the far side of the bed and yanking down on the hem of her nightshirt.

"Grab what you can!" Ben blinked hard against the acrid fumes. "Head out the front door to the car!"

Already lightheaded and dizzy from the lack of air and trying hard not to cough again, Ben wrapped an arm around Amos' back and hauled him up and stood him on his feet. Sleepy and groggy, Amos's eyes blinked rapidly. He also began to immediately cough as his lungs filled with smoke. Ben glanced up at the ceiling and although relief wasn't exactly what he felt, he was encouraged by one thing. The fire must have started on the roof because the hot flames were licking across the nubby texture of the ceiling. So far, the flames were confined to the ceiling so that literally gave them a bit more breathing room. Ducking low as the billowing gray clouds swirled above them, Ben swung Amos around to peer in his tense, tired face.

"Grab your bag and throw on your clothes and meet us on the porch!" Ben spoke loudly and firmly to the little boy and trusted he would understand and obey. He wasn't disappointed. Amos nodded his head up and down and quickly sprinted from the bedroom to the living area where his small bag lay. Ben hated to lose sight of Amos but he couldn't afford to baby him right now. He was going to have to learn to think fast and obey without question if they were to survive. A nugget of fear clutched at the man's gut for a minute and once more he wished he could fight this battle against the Others alone. But he loved Ella and would never leave her. And as he watched Amos' retreating form, he realized it was already too late when it came to him, too. Ben already loved Amos too.

Ben coughed into his hand and made eye contact with Ella who was yanking on a pair of jeans with one hand and grabbing up her bag with the other. When their eyes met, no words needed to be said. His eyes spoke his love for her and her eyes answered the same. Snatching up his own bag, Ben began shoving in a few shirts and underwear he had taken out to air, and then he strode over to retrieve the guns from the top shelf of the closet. They had found a small cache of handguns in the empty cabin and after checking them out, Ben selected two additional guns to keep with them. Things had changed, and not for the better, so they both needed to be armed and ready at all times.

Within less than two minutes Ben and Ella, eyes watering from the acrid smoke, ran from the bedroom to the living room. Their eyes scanned the small room and it was immediately apparent Amos wasn't in the living room and his bag and shoes were gone. Ella scrunched up her face, trying not to cough again.

"Where did he go?" She ducked her nose into the crook of her arm to avoid the smoke. The flames had begun to find their way to the walls of the old wood cabin and with so much fuel, it wouldn't be long before the entire building was ablaze.

"I told him to meet us on the porch. Let's go!" Ben coughed out a lungful of smoke and ran with Ella toward the front door.

When Ben tugged the wooden door inward and then stopped abruptly, Ella slammed hard into his back.

"Move, man!" She poked her bag hard at his butt and although Ben sagged forward on his toes, he didn't take a single step forward.

"Come with me!" The Other shouted at Ben and pressed the glittering knife blade tight to Amos' throat.

The thud as Ben dropped his bag on the wooden porch barely registered. Enraged, the hot blood rushing past his ears was louder than the roaring of the flames from the burning cabin. In his lifetime, Ben had been angry hundreds of times. He had been mad enough one time that he had ripped a cabinet door clean off the hinges and tossed it halfway across the room. Anger wasn't something he sought out and he truly fought hard to keep it pushed down and hidden away. He automatically recalled his father's words to not let his anger control him. If he let his anger rule him, someone could get hurt. Someone would get hurt. But right then, someone Ben cared about was getting hurt and the rage inside him was rising faster than he could push it down. He wanted to rip the knife away from the Other and make the creature pay for daring to attack his family. His intense anger should have been making the Other back away. The depth of his rage should have been enough to send the creature running. But this time, with this one, there was no effect. They were adapting too fast and that knowledge made Ben even angrier.

Amos' eyes met Ben's. The fear in the boy's eyes was bright and glittering. But when Ben gave him an almost imperceptible shake of his head, the boy blinked and swallowed. Amos didn't dare nod his head; the knife was already so tight against his neck that it wouldn't take much to slice into his delicate skin. But Ben saw the look in the boy's eyes change just slightly and the fear lessened a tiny bit. It was enough.

Ben shifted his gaze away from the Other and suddenly lashed out behind him with his left hand and gave Ella a hard shove. Her startled gasp as she overbalanced and tripped over the small porch chair struck like a painful stone in his heart. He didn't want to hurt her but he couldn't have her getting in his way again.

In the next set of seconds as Ella called Ben a name he didn't even realize she knew, Ben swung his body around, leaped off the porch and flew straight at the Other. Even though Ben's anger didn't make the Other hesitate, the surprise frontal attack did. The Other's eyes went wide and a gargling choking sound came from his throat and the knife pressed against Amos' throat dipped down a fraction of an inch. And that fraction of an inch was all Ben needed.

Ben's fist connected solidly with the bone of the Other's elbow. The sound of the punch was so loud Ben thought for a second he had broken the Other's arm. But broken or not, his blow had the desired effect. The Other's forearm and his fist that clutched the knife to Amos' throat swung out and away like a pendulum, the knife flinging wild from his grasp. At the same time, Ben shifted all this weight onto his left leg, rotated his hip and kicked forward with his right foot, throwing all his body weight into the blow. His booted foot caught the Other just above the knee and the muffled snap and the spongy way the leg gave way told him that the Other wouldn't be walking away from this fight.

When the knife flew away from his throat, Amos dropped like a stone and began scrambling away from the Other, his sobs thick and low.

The Other's mouth was a round "O" of pain and surprise and it occurred to Ben that there must have been enough humanness still left in the body it had taken over to still be able to register the mind-numbing pain. The Other stumbled a little, not fully aware of what the pain meant and in its ignorance, the creature stepped back and down on the ruined leg. The howl of its agony was enormous. Ben leaned forward and gave the Other a lightening quick jab in the chest, knocking it backward where it fell hard on its back on the packed dirt of the driveway. When the rippling of the fine black grit began to writhe beneath the Other's skin, Ben didn't wait around to watch. He didn't need to. He knew what would happen next and he didn't need to see it again.

Turning back toward the cabin the man's eyes scanned the porch for Ella and the grassy area for Amos. At first his eyes didn't want to accept what he was seeing. There was so much blood. It only took a second for Ben to understand. While he had been fighting the Other, Ella had been running toward them. Running to try and save Amos. When his punch had propelled the knife out of the grip of the Other, the wildly flying blade had soared through the air and driven itself deep into Ella's shoulder.

NINETEEN

Ben prayed it was a dream.

He had done everything he knew to keep her and Amos safe. It was the first thought on his mind when his eyes opened for the day, and it was the last thought when he closed his eyes at night. Yet, there Ella lay sprawled on her back on the gravel path with the handle of the large knife buried to the hilt in her shoulder. Her breathing was labored and her eyes were shut and Ben felt the most shameful feeling of all. He was grateful. He was grateful that with her eyes closed, Ben couldn't see the accusation her green eyes would have leveled at him for his failure.

Amos was kneeling beside her, his small hands clasped so tightly together Ben could see the paleness of the thin skin covering his knuckles. The tears streaming down his face almost crushed Ben's heart. It was tempting to just cut and run. How many times would that thought cross his mind? Ben looked at the boy and Ella and the enormity of his responsibility to them pounded at him and made it hard to breathe. There was an odd coldness in his mind as he stared down at the horrific scene and saw the blood running in sluggish rivulets from Ella's shoulder onto the dusty ground beneath her.

Ben was suddenly gripped by an anger that stiffened his entire body. He had tried to make Ella stay back while he dealt with the Other. She had known that was why he shoved at her as he stalked off the porch. Ben's anger mounted at this complication and his mind screamed at him to leave her there in the dust and let Amos take care of her and Ben would be free to go and do what he needed to do. And he would do it alone.

"LET HER DIE!" The cold voice slammed into his brain like a dagger of ice and Ben staggered forward and blinked hard against the new assault.

"Nooooooo!" He groaned out the word through gritted teeth.

Ben's fury at Ella fell away from him in an instant and it felt like heavy lead weights dropping from his shoulders. He shoved hard against the alien voice in his head. Ella was right. The aliens were playing dirty and shoving their vile thoughts into his head when he was the most vulnerable. Ben dropped to his knees beside Ella, his hands and his heart reaching out for her. He no longer wanted to be free of her searching eyes. He wanted to look deep into them and let her see his sorrow and let him share her pain.

Her chest rose and fell, and with each rise, the handle of the knife rose and fell like a dark, mimicking twin. Ben ached to reach out and yank the offending blade from her shoulder and ram it with all his strength into the ground. But the blade was serrated. He had seen that when it was pressed against Amos' throat. He knew it would rip through her soft flesh coming out just as much as it had going in. If she had been unconscious, he might have done it anyway. Just rip it out and be done with it. But she was conscious and she was aware. He could tell by the way her hands clutched at the rocks beneath her fingers and the way her forehead creased into deep furrows each time she drew in a gasping breath. A moment ticked by and Ben struggled with a new thought that came as a soft plea in his mind.

"No. I can't..." Ben finally answered as Ella's head turned slightly toward him. He was near tears and he hoped his voice wouldn't break as he shook his head.

Amos shifted a little on his knees and looked quizzically over at Ben. He hadn't heard Ella say anything. He had only seen her open her mouth to take in another harsh breath. But Ben was leaning away, his breathing faster now, his head shaking back and forth, "No. No."

Ella opened her eyes and looked directly at Ben. Her lips parted to take in a halting breath and as she exhaled, Amos heard her whisper, "Hurry."

This time the sob did break from Ben's throat and he jerked back at her word spoken out loud. He wasn't surprised that he had heard her anguished appeal directly from her mind to his. Nothing much surprised him anymore. But this was different. This would hurt. His fingers twitched with the knowledge that it would hurt him nearly as much as it hurt her. He was willing to share her pain but it was tearing at his heart to be the one to cause her pain.

"Hurry." She whispered again and her frown deepened and Ben clamped his jaw down on the next sob that threatened to escape.

"Amos?" He said loudly, then stopped and cleared his throat that was husky with pain. "Grab my bag off the porch."

"But…what about the fire?" The boy began to protest as he swung his arm to point toward the burning building.

They both looked up at the cabin and Amos' mouth dropped open in surprise. But again, Ben wasn't surprised at all. The blazing hot fire that had forced them out of the cabin and landed Amos in the grip of the Other, was gone. Not a hint of smoke or charred wood was left to indicate a fire had ever threatened to engulf the small structure. The cabin stood as it was before; a slightly ramshackle wooden building with the busted door hanging slightly askew.

"Grab my bag." Ben said again and drew his eyes away from the cabin. He knew if he looked at it any longer, his eyes would see what his mind had already revealed; the fine black grains dusting the roofline of the cabin and falling inert to the ground below. At Ben's command, Amos jumped up, still confused but obedient. As he trotted toward the porch where Ben had dropped his bag, Ben leaned his face down close to Ella. His lips met her cold cheek and he whispered in her ear, "Hold your breath."

Ben yanked off his shirt and folding it quickly, he held it in his left hand, ready. His eyes flicked up to locate Amos one last time. Sure that the boy was looking the other way, Ben grabbed the handle of the knife and yanked the serrated blade from Ella's shoulder in one swift movement. Trying hard not to think about the way the soft flesh ripped as he pulled the knife free, he forced his left hand to press the cloth down on the wound that was now spurting freely with blood. Ben also had to resist the nearly overwhelming urge to hurl the knife through the air into the woods behind him. Instead, he stretched his arm out as far as it would go and jammed the knife hard into the gravel covered ground.

Ben kept waiting for Ella to scream. He was waiting for her to open her eyes and open her mouth and let out a bloodcurdling yell or something. Anything but this quiet stillness. Her chest was still rising and falling and he was pressing so hard on the wound that he could feel her faint heartbeat against his fingers.

"I'm OK." Ella said and opened her eyes wide and looked over at Amos who had returned with the bag. She gave him a weak smile.

"I'm so sorry!" Amos' wail was loud and his tears left salty trails down his flushed cheeks.

Ben glanced up at the boy and tried but failed to keep a look of annoyance off of his features. "Amos, don't ever apologize for something that's not your fault. There will be enough things in life that truly are your fault. You'll make mistakes that you can't fix and can't change. Be sorry for those. But don't take on blame for something you had nothing to do with."

Amos sniffed back his tears as he shifted his gaze from Ben to Ella. Ben rummaged through his bag and found a clean white t-shirt. He tossed away his bloodied shirt and pressed the clean t-shirt to Ella's shoulder. He wanted so much for Ella to be okay that he thought he could already see the flow of blood lessening. He lifted a corner of the cloth and as if his eyes were willing to join his mind in this little trick, Ben was certain that the jagged edges of the raw wound were somehow softer. He closed his eyes briefly and then snapped them open. There followed a moment mixed with confusion and fear and wonderment as he peeled back the cloth once more. Ben wanted to believe what he was seeing, but his mind reeled with the realization of what this would mean for him and Ella and for Amos. With every new truth, came new responsibility.

Ella blinked.

It was then that Ben noticed the faint tingling in the fingers of his hand where it was pressed tight against her shoulder. The tingling was accompanied by a heat that he had thought was coming from Ella's body. But it wasn't coming from her. The heat was coming from him. And as he peered at the small part of the wound he had uncovered, he watched with stunned amazement as the bloody edges began to slowly knit back together.

Ben looked into Ella's eyes. She wasn't afraid. She reached up with one hand and pressed his fingers more tightly to her wound and waited for the healing to be complete.

TWENTY

One hour after having a serrated knife blade buried deep into her shoulder, Ella sat at the table in the completely intact cabin devouring a large bowl of hot chili. Ben stood at the stove, spoon in hand, absently stirring the reddish brown stew as he watched her eat. Ella showed no indication of ever having been in pain, and the wound in her shoulder was only a faint puckered line against her skin. Her body had revived with a hunger and Ben was cautious, but doing his best to keep up with her ravenous appetite.

"Any more bread?" Ella's voice was muffled with her mouth full of the last spoonful of chili.

"I'll get it!" Amos chirped and ran to the kitchen counter to grab the half-eaten loaf of bread.

"You really should slow down a bit." Ben said as he watched her carefully.

Ben had thought that nothing else would surprise him. He had been so sure of it. But as he held his tingling fingers to the deep gash in her shoulder, he couldn't deny that he was staggered by what he was witnessing. Every few seconds he had lifted the edge of the bloodied cloth pressed to her shoulder to peek at the wound underneath. At each viewing, the edges of the cut were smaller and smoother. Ella had been breathing heavily with the effort of lifting her chest against the excruciating pain. But with each passing minute, her chest rose and fell more gently. When Ben lifted the cloth for the last time, after only fifteen minutes, the wound was completely healed and he had dabbed gently at a pink smear of damp blood on her skin.

"There's no explanation." Ben snagged the bag of bread from Amos and pulled out a stale slice for himself. He nibbled on it absently as he talked.

"Yes. There is an explanation." Ella held out her hand for the bread and Amos happily handed her the remaining slices. She chewed and swallowed and looked Ben in the eye. "We just don't know what it is yet."

"It was so cool." Amos stared with wide eyes at Ben.

Watching them sitting comfortably at the table, Ben could almost believe they were a happy normal family. Any outsider looking in would surely think they were witnessing a quiet moment between a dad, a mom and their son. But normal was the last word Ben would use to describe this assemblage. Amos had been abandoned by his transformed father and was scarred from seeing too much and knowing too much about a group of creatures that didn't belong on this planet. His excitement at Ella's healing was understandable. He had already lost so much and seeing her brought back from what might have been her last moments with them on earth, Ben could easily see why he was in such a giddy mood. As for Ella, she was simply crazy. Ben knew that from the moment he met her, but he loved her anyway. She wasn't clinically crazy of course, just witty and weird and odd in all the ways that made him want to take her in his arms and love her even more.

"Skittles!!!!" Ella suddenly yelled and leaped up from the table, nearly knocking over the empty chili bowl.

Amos jumped in his seat, startled. His eyes darted from Ben to Ella's retreating form and back again. Ben rolled his eyes and waved a gentle hand at the boy, soothing his fears.

"She'll be back."

Ella returned within seconds with a huge bag of Skittles and she ripped open the bag with her teeth as she plopped back down at the table. Ben looked at her and at the piece of purple shiny paper dangling between her front teeth. He raised an eyebrow at her and she raised an eyebrow in return. When she turned her head slightly and spit the paper onto the floor, they both heard Amos suck in a startled breath.

"You're cleaning that up." Ben stated it as a fact as he kept eye contact with Ella and tried hard not to smile.

She stared at Ben and shook her head, 'no', as she popped one brightly colored lump of candy in her mouth.

"It's your turn." She insolently flicked some bread crumbs off the table onto the floor with the back of her hand. "Check the schedule."

Amos' eyes flicked from one to the other and finally a small smile turned up the corners of his lips as he realized they were joking with each other. He had been so afraid of Ben at first. Ben never smiled and his words were often harsh. Amos had loved Ella right away. She was sweet like his mom and she held him in her arms when he couldn't sleep. The first time Amos had seen Ben hold Ella in his arms, he had been a little jealous. The jealousy hadn't lasted long. Amos saw the look in Ben's eyes when he looked at Ella. It was the same way his dad had looked at his mom.

The loss of his family had been a fresh, open wound at that time. At the unbidden thought of his family, tears had flooded the little boy's eyes and he dropped his head. Ella had seen it right away and once again gathered him into her arms. Her soft hair had fallen around his shoulders and her words were just as soft and comforting. After that time, Amos didn't feel so jealous. He knew Ella loved him and she would often hold him and rub his hair and press her lips to his cheek whenever he felt afraid. He was willing to share her with Ben. Besides, she knew how to make Ben smile and Ben's eyes always danced a little when she teased him. Like now.

"I'm not cleaning up your mess." Ben was losing the struggle to keep the smile off of his face.

"Sure you are." She switched the bag of candy from one hand to the next and batted a wadded up napkin to the floor. "It's your turn to clean."

Ben strode the few steps to the table and leaned toward Ella. For a brief moment, Amos was afraid he might really fuss at her this time. But like every time before, when Ben leaned close to her, he softly pressed his lips to hers and came away with a smile.

"Sweet." He whispered as the taste of candy met his lips.

"I know." She replied and smiled and popped another piece of candy between her lips.

Ella poured a handful of the colorful candy in to Amos' waiting hands. Ben watched as the boy picked out one piece at a time, chewing slowly and smiling back at Ella. Ben's eye fell on the fading bruises on Amos' wrists and noticed something new. There was a shallow cut on the underside of his arm, near the bend of his wrist. Ben stared at the red edges of the cut and he was certain that with one touch, one moment of pressure from his fingers, the cut would heal itself and be gone within minutes. As that thought entered his mind and began to worm its way into his psyche, Ben cocked his head as a new question pushed its way to the surface.

He had been touching people and animals his whole life. His mother loved to hug him to her breast and pretend to squeeze him hard until he broke away, laughing and gasping. His father wasn't an affectionate man but he had often faced off his son, grasping his palm for a session of good-natured arm wrestling. Ben didn't remember any heat, any tingling or any signs that he was emitting any kind of healing force onto his family. So when did these powers come to him? He hated thinking of this new ability as a power. To him, power had always connoted something negative. Power was what the bullies in school used to demand things from him and to make him feel weak and helpless.

"It's not like that." Ella leaned toward him and peered into his startled eyes.

"Of all the weird stuff that's happening to us," Ben suppressed a shudder. "This mind-reading, mind-sharing thing is the weirdest."

Ella laughed and a wave of candy flavored sweetness wafted toward him. It had become her scent more than the soft floral perfume she sometimes wore.

"I can't hear your thoughts all the time." She didn't try to whisper. Amos had seen and heard so much already and it made more sense for him to understand everything. However, they would be careful. He was still only a child. But that part they would let him hear. "I can only hear your thoughts when you're focused clearly on one thing and nothing else."

She twisted the neck tight on the bag of candy and laid it on the table, her hand patting the bag gently like it was a sweet baby.

"But I think you're looking at this the wrong way. This is a power you have and it's a power you were given for a reason. I think there's a larger vision that we can't see just yet and you and your abilities are going to play a huge role in whether or not we win against what's happened to our world."

116

Ben knew perfectly well Ella was right. He had been consumed by those thoughts himself over the past few days and nights. He ticked them off in his mind, one by one: His ability to see the Others for who they were; the ability to keep them somewhat at bay by the force of his anger or will; the ability to hear Ella's thoughts and have her hear his; And now this new ability to bring healing by a touch of his hand. None of that was random and it was clear that all of it would play a role when the time came.

The wash of emotion that flooded through Ben should have been relief or joy or a wave of confidence that he had been given tools to fight the invading enemy. However, the reality of his obligation to protect Ella and Amos had been enough. Did this mean that he was now obligated to protect the entire planet? It was, in a word, unbelievable. Things like this didn't happen to normal people. Average people. People like Ben. His mind railed against the words of the Other, calling him Singular, and it railed against the crush of the new responsibility. The weight of it nearly sagged him to his knees. What would be required of him and how much pain would he and his newfound family have to suffer? The thought tore at his soul and twisted his stomach into knots.

Ben let his eyes rest for a moment on the young boy who had been dropped into their lap and who he already cared for like his own blood. Amos was still munching on a piece of candy and when he swallowed, Ella smiled over at him. Then, she turned her happy smile on Ben. She was beaming with joy. Ben flicked his eyes down, letting them travel over her body that had become so familiar to him over the past few weeks. His gaze lingered on her breasts. He hadn't noticed how much fuller and softer they were than before. Ella had always enjoyed her candy. That wasn't anything new. But over the past week, her desire for the sugary sweet snacks had become almost like…a craving.

He saw the truth in her eyes the instant before he heard the words in his mind.

"Yes." She nodded silently at Ben. "And I'm sure it will be a boy."

TWENTY-ONE

Knowing he was going to be a father soon should have frightened Ben. It was definitely one more responsibility added to all the other new responsibilities he had accumulated over the past couple of months. Together, he and Ella had piloted their way through dealing with the fires in the sky, all the way to watching the startling and painful transformations of the townspeople of Morgan Valley. They had seen things that he had only read about in science fiction novels. But this was a completely new thing. Being a father to a child of his own was a lifelong commitment that he had never planned on.

With thoughts of Ella's pregnancy and the eventual delivery of the baby weighing heavy on his mind, Ben walked slowly behind Amos and Ella. With the skies cleared of smoke, they had decided that some fresh air was needed. A trail wound from the back steps, leading them toward the dense woods just behind the cabin. At first, Amos had hesitated. His experience with the Other was still fresh in his mind and he had been resistant about going outside at all. But Ella had tapped him on the nose with a finger and pulled gently on his hand. He had lifted his chin bravely; he never wanted to disappoint Ella who had been itching to get out of the cabin for the past few days. Ben carried both loaded guns and kept an eye out for anything out of the ordinary. Although he wasn't exactly sure he could define what ordinary was any more.

He watched as Amos took one step and then hopped forward with both feet, repeating the pattern with each new step. His blue tennis shoes bulged as his feet pressed into the soft ground, preparing for the next jump. The shoes would be too small for him soon and they would need to get him a new pair. Caring for Amos was getting easier for Ben. But unlike the newborn to come, Amos wasn't a baby who needed constant care and attention. At nine years old, he was just over four feet tall and seemed to be in fairly good health. His bare arms in his blue t-shirt, emblazoned with the bright red and yellow Superman logo, were slim but not too thin and he continued to have a good appetite. And that reminded Ben…

"Don't touch anything you find on the ground or on any bushes. We don't know what that rain or the clouds have done to all the plants." He called out.

"We won't." Ella sang back her reply.

The sun was warm and Ben lifted his face up to the sky. The trees were dense but the canopy at the top was thin, letting the bright light filter all the way to the ground.

"But what if we find berries?" Ella swung around to smile at Ben and as she did, her swelling belly came into view. It seemed much rounder and larger than just a few nights ago. But that couldn't be possible. Ben shook his head. He must not have been paying attention and she was farther along than he had thought.

"Don't touch anything meanssss…?" He drew out the word and lifted his eyebrows at her, waiting for her to finish his sentence.

But before she could respond, Amos hopped again, landing on both feet and threw up his arms and said loudly, "Don't touch anything means DON'T TOUCH ANYTHING!"

"Exactly!" Ben said loudly and gave Amos a beaming smile.

At the rare full smile, Amos nearly tripped over himself as he raced over to Ben, flinging his small body at him and his arms around him so forcefully that Ben staggered back a foot.

"Heyyyy…" Ben rested his hands on the boy's head and looked quizzically over at Ella.

"He likes your smile, I guess." She laughed and the sound floated up through the trees like soft smoke.

Ben slowly pulled Amos' tight grip away from his hips and looked down into the boy's face. A fluttering in his gut that was a not unpleasant jumble of both fear and love clutched at Ben.

"I like your smile, too." Ben said softly and kneeled down to gather the boy in a quick hug.

Ella stood watching her two men, her head cocked slightly to one side and her hands softly caressed her swelling stomach. She knew the baby was growing fast and he would wriggle his way into the world long before nine months. She knew that with a certainty and she sent that thought to Ben.

"It won't be long now." She smiled.

"I know." He smiled back and rose to his feet.

"What will we do for food when all the grocery stores are empty?" Ella asked at the same time her stomach growled fiercely.

"We'll think of something." Ben hoped his words were true.

"Wow! Pretty!" Amos suddenly yelled and lunged toward a group of brightly colored flowers near the base of a tall pine tree.

"No! Wait!" Ben yelled and dove forward, already knowing he was too slow and it was too late.

Ben was dimly aware of Ella screaming Amos' name and her mouth was a wide circle that seemed to swallow her entire face. Ben's feet were moving but it felt like he was running in a hot sludge of tar, way too sticky and pulling him backwards with every step forward.

Amos' hands were already blistered and puffy in the mere seconds it took for Ben to reach him.

"Stay back!" Ben yelled at Ella. He was so scared she wouldn't obey. But she did. She stopped and stood stiff as a board and her eyes and her mouth were still wide and round. But she stood still and watched.

Amos didn't make a sound but the tears streaming from his eyes told the depth of his pain. The blisters were red now. The skin was already peeling and raw and Ben saw the beginnings of the bright red blood welling up under the ravaged skin.

Ben didn't need anyone to tell him that the flowers had been too bright, too colorful, too enticing. Just the thing that anyone walking through the forest of deep subdued greens and browns would be drawn to. And he also didn't need anyone to tell him that these flowers were the work of the same alien group who created the mouse and the tree in the road. All were designed to snare any unsuspecting humans or animals and leave them weak and powerless to defend themselves.

But Ben had an ability he was sure the alien enemy didn't count on. Grabbing Amos' now bleeding hands, Ben ignored the boy's anguished screams as the seared flesh was pressed tight between Ben's palms. It wouldn't take very long. The burns were still surface and the healing would come quickly. Ben had no concerns about his own safety. He was certain that whatever caused the burns on Amos would have no effect on him.

As he held Amos' hands between his, Ben smiled a reassuring smile. "It won't take long. Then you'll be fine." He nodded his head as he spoke and waited for the tingling and the heat that would restore Amos' damaged skin.

But as the minutes ticked by, Ben was confused. He felt nothing. No heat, no tingling. Nothing at all except the wetness of the boy's blood as it seeped from his wounds into Ben's palms. Ben stared over at Ella, unable to comprehend.

"Why isn't it working?" He sent the thought to Ella and almost immediately her thought returned, *"I don't know."*

For several more long minutes Ben held Amos' hands tightly as the little boy squirmed and the tears fell from his eyes.

"Why isn't it working?" He sent the thought again, not really realizing it. But when the thought from Ella returned, this time there was another thought along with it. An unfamiliar voice but familiar at the same time.

"The gift is not yours alone..."

Both Ben and Ella dropped dumfounded eyes down to Ella's belly, already soft and rounded to carry their child. They both blinked in surprise as the voice came again.

"The gift is not yours alone..."

TWENTY-TWO

And there arose another phenomenon that simply wasn't possible. There was no way the child Ella was carrying should have been able to communicate with them the way it appeared to be happening. Sure, it was known that babies could hear and learn and even react to outside stimulus while in utero. But that wasn't even close to what Ben and Ella were experiencing. How could a fetus, only a few weeks old at the most, communicate a concept as complex as why the healing of Amos wasn't working?

Ben and Ella stared quizzically at each other and their minds scrambled to try to understand what it all meant. Was Ben only able to heal Ella with the help of their unborn baby? The healing of Ella was crucial to the survival of the baby so that did make a certain kind of sense. And Ben had finally accepted that there was something about him that made him special. Singular. So was it truly beyond the realm of possibility that his child might have some type of special abilities as well?

As Ben and Ella continued to ponder what may be a new and unsettling truth for them, they weren't aware of the change in Amos' demeanor. His tears had finally subsided and he was quiet but they hadn't registered the new look in his eyes. Amos' eyes had begun to narrow as Ben and Ella drew to stand closer together. Their attention was focused only on each other and the throbbing in his burned hands caused him less pain than the worry that started to build in his heart like a volcano.

The alien voice that pushed itself into his mind wasn't a scream this time. It was a whisper. Amos was too young to realize that the enemy was expert at forcing their way into his thoughts when his guard was down or his emotions were high. And right then, he was experiencing both. His body stiffened as the cold thoughts assaulted him with the new fear that Ben and Ella were pulling away from him. Abandoning him for their own child. They hadn't said the words, but Amos knew. And the voice whispering like a wraith in his mind told him with a certainty that as soon as their baby came, they would find a way to get rid of him.

"You don't want me!" Amos suddenly screamed at the couple and a loud sob flew from his lips. "You could fix my hands if you wanted to, but you don't want to! You have your own baby coming now and you want me to die so you don't have to be bothered with me anymore!"

When Amos turned and darted into the dense undergrowth and into the woods, Ben and Ella stood frozen where they were, literally stunned into silence. Neither of them would ever have imagined that thought was in Amos' mind. And they would have been right.

"Amos!" Ben finally found his voice and called after him as the boy ran deeper into the woods.

"We have to find him!" Ella's voice was high pitched and strangled with emotion. "We don't know what else is in those woods. He could get hurt or…"

The anguish on her face was etched like a deep scar and Ben struggled to keep the same feelings from taking him over. Amos wasn't his son by blood but he may as well have been. He had become a part of his life and his heart in only a few days.

Ben grabbed for Ella's hand and they turned toward the woods, racing after Amos. Ella held tight to his fingers and scrambled after him and Ben had to trust that she would be able to keep up. Ben thrust one hand out in front of him to slam the low hanging branches out the way as they flew past the trees. As they ran deeper into the dense forest, the ground was thick and spongy with moss. Fallen trees and vining roots threatened to wrap around their feet at every step.

"Amos!" Ben yelled again and tried to make his voice sound as stern as possible. Amos wouldn't want to stop running but perhaps hearing a command from Ben might make him hesitate. At least long enough for them to catch up with him.

Thundering through the trees, Ben picked up speed and released Ella's hand. He risked a glance back at her and saw the determined look on her face as she kept up her stride about two feet behind him.

Swinging his head back around, Ben heard Amos' crashing footsteps only a few yards ahead. There was no way to know what dangers Amos might come upon as he ran through the woods. He was sure the Others had many other traps set for humans who hadn't been killed or transformed. His mind swirled with the understanding that any healing he might perform on Amos had to be done through his connection to the baby and through Ella. The interconnectedness of it all made his head pound and his mouth go dry with fear. What if tried to help Amos and wound up hurting Ella or the baby?

"We do what we need to do and I'll tell you if the baby even flinches." Out of breath, Ella answered the question Ben hadn't asked out loud.

"Hey! Lemme go!" The sound of Amos' startled yelp pierced the air and caused Ella's heart to leap into her throat.

"Not again. Please, not again." Ella pleaded into the air.

Remembering the first time an Other had caught Amos alone, her stomach clenched with anguish and fear. One hand flew to her belly as if to protect the baby inside from her raging emotions. Even as their feet flew over the soft ground toward whatever lay ahead, Ella was preparing herself for the worst.

Before she met Ben, Ella hadn't given a single thought about being a mother. It wasn't that she didn't want children, it just wasn't anything she had ever thought about. And when she met Ben, the fires in the sky and getting away from the choking smoke had been the only thought in their minds for days. And then the Others came and thoughts of anything other than survival were swept from her mind.

Ben came upon them first. He stopped suddenly and threw a hand behind him to stop Ella. She clutched at his arm with both hands and worked to slow her rapid breathing as she looked at them.

In a clearing, a group of about six adults stood facing them. The site had recently been cut, and sawdust still lingered on several freshly cut stumps at the edge of the tree line.

Amos swayed a little on his feet as a tall, sandy haired man kept a firm grip on his bare forearm. Taking in the scene and the forceful grip the man had on Amos' arm, Ben clamped his jaw down tight. His anger shot to the surface and he readied himself to leap at the group and snatch Amos from them by force or any other means. Then, a realization dawned on him. The group was mixed with both men and women. Their eyes shifted from Ben and Ella, then back to stare at the sandy haired man who was clutching Amos. Ben registered the fear and wariness in each pair of eyes at the same time his instincts kicked in. This group was all human.

Glancing back at Ella, he ignored the distress on her face and sent the thought into her mind.

"They're real. They're not Others."

She should have been relieved. They both should have been glad that there were other humans who hadn't been transformed or killed. But as Ben slid his eyes away from Ella and back to Amos, caught in that painful grip, he had to admit that relief was the last feeling surging through him. The sudden silence in the woods was unnerving as the group watched Ben and Ella. The stalemate continued as Ben and Ella stared warily back at them.

"Give him to us." Ben finally spoke. He said the words with an authority in his voice that caused every member of the group to blink and shift their gaze away from him and over to the sandy haired man. But it wasn't enough. The sandy haired man, apparently the leader of the small group, gathered his shoulders back and tightened his grip on Amos' arm even further. Ella gasped as she saw the red marks blooming on Amos' tender flesh, but she said nothing.

"He's staying with us." The sandy haired man spread his feet and set his jaw, ready for a fight. Although Amos' chin quivered a little and light tears sprang to his eyes, he nodded his head in dispirited agreement.

"You don't want me anymore, anyway." Amos said quietly.

It amazed Ben how words spoken so softly could wound so deeply.

"That's not true." Ben said simply. His voice was low and his eyes were trained on Amos. "Things don't work the way we thought. Come back with us and we'll explain." Ben didn't want to say too much in front of the group of strangers, human or not. But he had to try to get Amos to see that he was wrong in how he was thinking and that he needed to come back with him and Ella.

"He was running from you." The sandy haired man spoke up. "That tells me he doesn't want to stay with you. And looking at the two of you, it's clear he's not your son."

"Amos." Ben kept his gaze steady and called the boy's name quietly but firmly. "Come on. Let's go."

Amos was still reeling from the whispered words that had been planted in his mind. He shook his head and dropped his eyes. "No. I'm staying."

Ben had never felt utter helplessness like he felt in that moment. He knew the boy had to come with him. The crushing grasp the sandy haired man held him with, told Ben there was no way this man or this group would treat him right. But Amos was just a boy. How could he know that? Even though they weren't Others, they carried a stink of fear and aggression that made them almost as dangerous. Ben looked back at Ella and frowned, unsure what to do.

The sudden shriek from Ella caused all heads to turn toward her in alarm. She was doubled over, clutching her stomach and her eyes were wide with fright.

"No, no, no, no…" Ben chanted as he caught her sagging body just as her knees buckled, her strength gone.

The low moaning from Ella was like a dull spike that stabbed into Ben's brain and he thought he might go crazy. It was too much. He couldn't lose Amos and Ella and the baby.

"Noooooo!" Amos suddenly squealed and jerked away from the sandy haired man. "No, please no. Don't be sick. Please!" He fell to his knees beside Ella on the thick grass, his arms wrapping tight around her neck. "Please don't be sick. I love you. I want to go with you. I want to go home. Please!" Amos begged loudly and his sobs made his voice thick with his anguish.

Ella shifted herself and moaned again, one arm still cradling her swelling belly and the other wrapping firmly around Amos' back. The group of survivors hadn't moved to help and hadn't tried to pull Amos back. As Ben helped Ella stagger painfully to her feet, one last moan escaped her lips. She lifted her head and looked directly into Ben's face, the torment etched there like lines in a deep river bed.

And then she winked.

TWENTY-THREE

By the time Ben had tugged Ella unsteadily to her feet, the crowd surrounding them had grown suspicious. Amos had fallen for Ella's trick in an instant. It was easy to fool a young boy, but a group of adults weren't so easily misled. It worked on Amos because he loved Ella almost from the minute he saw her. But this crowd didn't know her from Adam and clearly didn't care anything about her.

Ben slipped one arm around Ella's waist. He fought hard for the few inches of her middle he was able to grasp. Amos had enveloped himself around her neck and her middle and his small head was tucked so tightly under her breast that Ben was sure it had to hurt. But she didn't moan and she didn't pull away. If anything, Ella pulled Amos closer to her and the three of them began to back away like some kind of strange, three-headed, six-legged creature.

"Do you really think we're going to let you just walk away?" The sandy haired man stepped menacingly forward and his hands dangling at his sides curled into fists.

"Dan. Let them go. We can't feed another mouth anyway." A petite woman dressed in a plaid shirt at least one size too big for her, spoke up from the group and reached out to lay a restraining hand on his arm. There was an intimacy in the gesture that let Ben know they were a couple but the force with which he slapped her hand away made Ben's brows snap together. He tightened his arm around Ella. It was apparent that Dan was a coward. Only a coward would seek out the smallest woman to make himself seem bigger and use that size difference to control her. Ben's expression dulled as he considered how to handle Dan. Knowing that a coward will always shy away from a real confrontation, it surprised him that Dan would make any kind of threatening move. But Ben had misjudged Dan's craving for power that propelled him well beyond his normal fears.

When the alien ships had first blasted overhead, spewing their thick red clouds behind them, Dan had done what he had always done in his life. He ran. From a lifetime spent hiding and avoiding and never facing anything fully, Dan was perfectly prepared for this response. Hiding out in a dark cave high up in the hills above Morgan Valley, he had survived the darkest of the days on all the canned foods and MREs he had been stashing away for years. If he hadn't been completely alone, chewing sullenly on his hoarded meals, he would have worn out any companion's ears with the words, "I told you so!"

One day, spying an unfamiliar triangle of clear blue sky, Dan had emerged from the narrow opening of the cave. He was as pale as the underbelly of a fish and ten pounds heavier from lack of exercise, but he was alive. Venturing tentatively outside, he had found the first of the survivors within half a day. Skittish at first, a small framed woman had finally understood that he was a survivor just like her. She had been living for days in a tiny, badly made hut crafted from broken sticks and soggy branches.

The woman had sniffed back tears and wiped at her runny nose with a muddy sleeve as she talked. Her face twisted with grief as she explained everything that had happened from the time the clouds filled the sky and began choking out the food supply, to her frenzied dash for safety from a husband transformed into a murderous creature by the strange rain. Flushed and out of words, she had then turned her sorrowful eyes upon Dan, seeking his comfort and guidance. As happy as he was to have companionship – and female companionship was even better – Dan relished the feeling that stirred deep inside him as she looked to him for direction. For the first time in his life, someone had seen him as a leader and not a follower. And as the two of them came across more survivors, Dan found that he greatly enjoyed being the one the group looked to for leadership. He couldn't let it end for him so soon.

When Dan suddenly stretched one arm behind his back, Ben could have stopped him. The reach behind him was slow and awkward and revealed a man not as expert with guns as he would have everyone believe. But Ben didn't want to loosen his grip on Ella, so he let the scene play out and let the man have his moment. Swinging his arm around to the front, Dan brought the barrel of a six and a half inch baby Glock level with Ben's chest.

A harsh laugh at the tiny size of the gun burst out of Ben before he could stop it.

"What's so funny?" Dan growled, his pale brow creasing into a scowl.

Ben's laugh died abruptly. "Nothing." His dark eyes bored into Dan's with a coldness that sent an involuntary shiver through the sandy haired man. "Nothing is funny about this at all."

A lone sparrow chirped overhead, and for Ben, the brightness of its call brought with it a feeling of nostalgia and loss that was nearly overwhelming. He was tired.

"This will end badly for everyone if you don't put down the gun and let us walk away." Ben spoke softly with a twinge of sadness in his voice. He didn't want anyone to get hurt. If Dan could have his moment of false bravery, and choose to let them go, he could still keep his position of man-on-top well after Ben and Ella were gone.

"It will only end badly for you if you don't give us back the boy." Dan laced his voice with as much venom as he could muster.

Ben drew in a long breath and strained to maintain control. There was no value in the standoff. Dan didn't really want Amos and as the woman said, they could barely feed the people who were already there. It was a power play pure and simple.

The light of the early afternoon sun slanted across Ben's face and he deliberately shifted his gaze away from the gun pointed at him. He peered up at the blue sky, suddenly so weary he could barely stand. Ben's shoulders slumped and in an instant, before he could think to throw up a block in his mind, the alien words slammed into his brain with a fury.

"YOU ARE TOO WEAK TO WIN!"

Ben immediately realized his mistake. Letting the weariness overtake him had opened the way for the aliens to invade his mind. The attack was stronger than before and it felt as if there were millions of malevolent fingers jabbing into his thoughts, trying to turn him into someone else. Trying to turn him into someone whose sole aim was to abandon Amos and destroy Ella and his unborn child.

"GET OUT!" The angry explosion of thought in Ben's mind was hurled at the alien voice with the rage and force of a thousand suns. Ben felt Ella shrink forcefully away from him as the words echoed in his mind. His eyes snapped downward and then trained on the crowd. As furious as Ben was, he was still stunned to see their eyes widened and fear stamped on every face. He hadn't yelled the words out loud. What had they heard?

Ben's confusion lasted only a second before he flicked his eyes downward and realized he was holding both of his guns in his hands, arms outstretched, his fingers on the triggers. He had no memory of unsnapping the holsters and yanking out the guns, but there they were, held stiffly at the ends of his arms like two gleaming silver weights. Ben shifted the guns higher, his hands moving slowly left and right to encompass the crowd. There was a sound behind him, a small grunt he was sure came from Ella. But he didn't turn around.

His head felt way too hot and his heart pounded like a hammer in his chest. But he gripped the guns tightly and tried his best to keep his voice steady.

"We're going to walk away." Fire still blazed in his eyes as he stared directly at Dan.

"You won't get far." Dan said boldly, but a slight tremor in his voice gave him away and the Glock in his hand wavered.

They were all afraid. It was hard to tell if they were afraid of Ben or the guns or the way they seemed to miraculously appear in his hands. Maybe it was all of it. Maybe it was none of it. Maybe it was because he was the Singular. Did they know? Could they tell? An idea flickered in Ben's brain.

"Do you know who I am?" Ben's eyes narrowed as he challenged them and waited for an answer.

The confused looks and glances that leapt from once face to another told Ben all he needed to know. They saw him as a man who could perform a fancy trick with his guns, but nothing more. They didn't see anything else special about him and they certainly didn't see him as Singular. The disappointment that fanned his soul was almost a physical sensation. The Others knew who he was and so far, he hadn't been able to hide from them. Ben had dared to hope that someone in this small group might see that he was different. If they saw anything special about him, maybe he could count on at least a few of them to help him fight. But they didn't see anything except a man with guns fighting to save his family. This time, when the crushing frustration and exhaustion began to overtake Ben, he drove the emotions viciously from his mind, closing the gap that the alien force would certainly try to exploit.

"Turn around!" He shouted to the crowd. He felt Ella's hand creep around his waist and he drew strength from her touch.

He watched as several tense faces turned to stare uneasily at Dan, unsure what to do. The sandy haired man struggled with his pride and considered his options. If he let Ben and Ella go, taking Amos with them, the group might think he was weak. Control was too important to Dan. He was a man who had never before wielded any kind of power and he wasn't going to give it up easily.

Dan's Glock was still pointed at Ben's gut. Dan calculated he could at get off at least one shot before Ben could react and fire a return shot. In that instant of time, Dan cockily figured he could leap to one side or drop to the ground. Someone else in the group might get the bullet that was intended for him but he decided that was a small price for someone else to pay to insure his life was spared. He was their leader after all. They needed him. He stared Ben in the eye and Dan's finger tightened on the trigger.

They say that in moments like those, everything happens in slow motion. But for Dan, it was as if everything happened in two blinks of an eye. One blink and he was holding the gun in his outstretched hand, sighting on the midsection of the dark-haired man. The next blink and Dan was howling, clutching his bleeding hand as his useless gun skittered away from him along the damp ground. Without a word, Amos darted out and scooped up the Glock and then trotted quickly back to his place tight against Ella.

"I said, turn around. All of you." Ben commanded again and shifted the muzzle of his gun up and over to point straight into Dan's left eye.

Ben thought at first that Dan might stand his ground and be willing to die to maintain his unfounded reputation as a badass. The struggle inside him was real and tormenting and Ben could see he was quickly weighing his options. Then his eyelids dropped and he muttered darkly under his breath, "We don't need you here anyway. Just go." His words were empty of any power and they both knew it. Dan waved a hand vaguely to signal everyone to turn their back on the trio.

Ben wrapped his arms around his family and turned to make their way back to the cabin.

TWENTY-FOUR

Their footfalls made little noise in the stillness of the woods as they made their way single file back to the cabin. Amos was in the lead, his blue sneakers thudding softly on the dark ground. His head hung low with shame and hurt over his part in what had just transpired. He still didn't understand that the thoughts that made him race blindly from Ella and Ben weren't really his thoughts. Amos' mind remained stuck in a web of grief that weighed on his small neck like a millstone. Ella trailed only a foot behind him, her eyes never leaving the back of his bowed head and her hand resting firmly on his shoulder.

Ben took up the rear, his eyes darting left and right, his hands restless on the grips of his guns. He refused to look behind him. A feeling deep in his bones pressed him forward, one that convinced him if he looked back, if he doubted for an instant that they would get away safely, that they would all turn instantly into a pillar of salt like the Biblical Lot's wife.

"Where do we go now?" Ella questioned him without taking her eyes off the grassy path and without taking her hand off of Amos' shoulder.

"I don't know," Ben answered. "But I don't think they will come after us right away. So we should have time to pack the car and get down the road a few miles before they get up their nerve to make a move on us."

Ben said this with more confidence than he really felt, but when he chuckled a little, Ella turned and lifted an eyebrow questioningly at him.

"You ok?" Her smile was twisted slightly. She knew his sense of humor was odd and she was prepared to hear anything.

"I was thinking." Ben holstered one of his guns and slid a hand gently but tantalizingly down her back, his touch causing a familiar tingle through her.

"Thinking is good…" She joked and tried to still the slight racing of her heart. His touch always did that to her.

"I was thinking that we need to teach Amos how to use the guns."

At the sound of his name, Amos looked up at Ben, his eyes wide with apprehension. Ella took in a deep breath and held it. Her fear was well-founded, but she also knew they all needed to be able to protect themselves.

"Su-u-ure." She drew out the word and tried to ignore the slight tightening of worry in her belly.

Amos was still a boy, after all. He was her boy now. She hadn't given birth to him, but the way Ella loved him, she may as well have squeezed him out of her own body. Her hand tightened on his shoulder protectively.

"I don't have to tell you to be careful. I know you will. But I'm going to say it anyway just for the record." Ella said and looked around at Ben. "Please be careful."

"Of course. But in case you haven't noticed, things are changing so fast, he's going to have to grow up fast if we're going to make it."

"I know." Ella agreed, even though it strained her heart to have to admit it. She still held onto a small hope that this wasn't Ben's fight. Even though everything inside and outside of her was telling her differently, her soul still clung fiercely to that hopefulness. There were days when it felt as if hope was all she had.

Ben had felt the change in Ella over the past few days. The fierce protectiveness, the wariness in her eyes as she cradled her swelling belly or as she gazed at Amos. He knew she was frightened and he couldn't blame her. He had no idea what might be around the next bend for them or when the next confrontation might come. Being Singular wasn't something he asked for or even understood. But he wouldn't run from it. If it were up to him to do something, he had to do it. Otherwise, he wouldn't be able to live with himself or ever look anyone - himself - in the eye again.

"For the record." Ben's voice was calm. "Yes. I'll be careful."

Amos had been listening to the exchange between Ben and Ella breathlessly. Learning to hold and fire a gun was something he had been longing to do. His dad had planned to teach him before… "No." Amos shook his head, dispelling the miserable memory. It wouldn't do him any good to think about his dad, or his mom, or his life before…

Ella squeaked out a whimper as her stomach tightened down again into a hot, painful ball.

"Nooooo." She bent awkwardly forward and steeled herself for the next spasm.

She knew it was too soon. It was far too soon for contractions and it was far too soon for the baby to be ready to make his appearance in the world. But nothing about her pregnancy had been normal. Her hips ached with each step forward and she prayed she would make it to the cabin in time. No matter how fast things were happening, she refused to give birth to her son on the muddy ground in the dampness of those woods.

Ben heard the change in Ella's breathing. Her breath came quicker and shallower as she forced her feet onward.

"We're almost there." Ben pressed himself closer to her. He slipped an arm around her waist that seemed to have grown three sizes within the past fifteen minutes. Despite the heaviness of the baby inside her and the pressure she felt to push him out, the small family moved quickly through the woods toward the cabin. For the conversation to come, Ella took in a deep breath and sent her thought directly to Ben.

"We can't let anyone find out the baby is coming tonight. If the Others come while I'm in the middle of giving birth, there's no way we could fight them." Her brow was creased with concentration.

"What about Amos?" Ben sent the thought that Ella feared to give voice to.

Amos wasn't part of their small "thought circle" that included Ella, Ben and the baby. And with the young boy's fears and emotions over what he believed was his uncertain role in their lives, how could they stop him from becoming overly agitated and giving the aliens an opportunity to enter his mind and use him again? Given more time, they could convince him that his place in their hearts was secure. However, everything was happening so fast. Too fast for a little boy to grasp all at once. Trekking through the woods, dashing away from a confrontation with a group of hostile humans, and slowed down by a very pregnant woman likely only minutes away giving birth was the worst possible time to have a serious discussion. Yet, it was going to happen.

"Hey, Amos?" Ben called out.

Amos looked back doubtfully at Ben then swung his head back around to face the path once more. "Yeah?"

"Do you know why you got so mad before? Do you know why you ran from us?"

Amos stared down at his shoes, his mind in turmoil. He didn't understand why he got so mad and why he ran like he did. Ben asking him that question was like a knife in his heart and he shook his head back and forth and blinked back fresh tears.

Ella stroked a hand down his back and with only a few words, set him free. "Do you know it wasn't your fault? Do you understand that those thoughts you had weren't really yours?"

Amos stopped abruptly and turned incredulous eyes up to her. "Was it...*them*?" He breathed out the word "them" in a low voice as if it were a curse, spoken only in hushed undertones behind closed doors.

"Yes, baby. It was them. So we have to be careful. We have to guard our minds all the time."

The wind gusted right then and the breeze lifted the collar of Amos shirt. And on that flurry of mountain air, Amos' shame and guilt blew off his shoulders and toward the west and dissipated like a thin cloud.

"I won't get mad about the baby." Amos opened his eyes wide and looked from one to the other. "I promise." His eyes pleaded for them to believe him.

The sunlight caught the tears that shone in his pale eyes. Amos' countenance wore signs of weariness and stress that caused a painful pinch in Ben's heart. The past few days had been hard on them all, but Ben hadn't stopped to realize just how much of a toll things were taking on the young boy.

"We believe you, Sweetheart." Ella reached out a hand and drew him to her.

Just as Amos' head nestled against her full breast, another contraction hit and Ella sucked in a breath against the pain.

"I felt that!" Amos exclaimed in a whisper that was full of awe.

"Yes. He's coming fast." Ella said out loud and looked directly into Ben's dark eyes. "We need to get to the cabin now."

****

Amos frowned down at the jigsaw puzzle pieces laid out before him. He would have preferred a video game to distract him from the sounds coming from the bedroom. But it was all he could find. Ben had insisted Amos keep his mind occupied and free from stress and anxiety. The boy had to admit, trying to figure out where to place the stiff cardboard pieces was definitely keeping his mind fully occupied. Besides, he didn't really want to hear the moans from Ella as the baby squirmed and pressed his way out of her body. He scratched at a small bump on his neck, not wanting to think about Ella being in pain.

"Is that a piece of tree?" Amos suddenly held up a small puzzle piece with green on the top and yellow on the bottom. Squinting at the lid of the box for reference, he began nodding his head. "Yep. That's a piece of tree." After a second, he decided he liked the feel of his head bobbing up and down. The repetitive movement was calming and in his mind, a snippet of a song echoed through and he softly sang the words out loud.

"Take my hand, baby. Take my hand. We can go on like this forever if you take my hand..."

"What's he doing?" Hearing the sounds of the soft singing coming from the other room, Ben cocked his head as Ella sucked in a harsh breath. The pain in her abdomen was excruciating, but the worst agony was the low pressure that felt as if someone was bending her in half, trying to break her lower back.

"Why are you worried about him, Ben? He's fine." She panted and her forehead furrowed with irritation. "You need to focus on what you're doing here."

Ben's dark hair was wet from sweat. With no time for detailed education on what to expect from childbirth, the mood in the small bedroom was anything but pleasant. All they had to draw on was Ben's rudimentary emergency first aid training he had received as his work shift's health representative. Ella tried her best to be as patient as she could amid the waves of crushing contractions. But her patience finally snapped when in his distraction, Ben pressed down too hard on her swollen fingers.

"Let go of me." She hissed through gritted teeth and yanked her hand free of his grip.

"Sorry…" He mumbled absently. He couldn't stop wondering why the song Amos was singing was making the hairs on the back of his neck stand at attention.

"Go away." Ella flapped a hand at Ben and let her head collapse back on the pillows. "Go see what's up with Amos."

Without waiting even a second, Ben pushed up from the hard chair he had pulled up to the side of the bed. His long legs carried him to the bedroom door in only two strides. Poking his head out into the main room, he spied Amos bobbing his head and slightly swaying to some internal melody that only he could hear. A puzzle piece was clutched between his small fingers and he waved it back and forth in time to the beat. After a second, Amos found the place for the puzzle piece and snapped it into place. His head bobbed even deeper and a smile wove across his features as he reached for another piece, singing along to the melody playing in his head.

"Life isn't like you think…Life isn't for the weak. Take my hand, baby. Take my hand. We can go on like this forever if you take my hand…"

Ben stood so still that he could hear his stunned heart drubbing out a thick beat in his chest. The melody wasn't exactly right, but the words Amos was mouthing were so familiar that Ben could still see each letter of each word written in blocky script on the blue lined paper. It was his song. He had written it when he was fifteen years old and in love with a girl he knew he would never have.

"Life isn't like you think...Life isn't for the weak. Take my hand, baby. Take my hand. We can go on like this forever if you take my hand..."

TWENTY-FIVE

There were no words to describe the feeling in Ben's heart as he watched his son thrust his way into the world and into his waiting, trembling hands.

"Are we done?" Ella gasped with exhaustion and Ben hated to say the next words.

"Not yet. We need to get the afterbirth out and do a little clean up to make sure you don't get an infection. It might sting a bit." He said the words quickly and then turned away with the quiet, wiggling baby in his hands.

"Oh. Please…" Her groan was long and drawn out but her voice was strong. Ella would be fine.

Ben quickly wiped the sticky fluids off the small infant's chest and back and used his fingers to pull the thick liquid from his mouth.

"Come on, baby. Cry for me."

Ben tickled the bottom of the quiet baby's feet and then gave him a little shake as if he might drop him. At the startling motion, the dark haired baby tensed his body and sucked in a huge breath, expelling it quickly as a deep wet cough. Squinting with a slightly hurt expression into Ben's eyes, the baby began to cry, and within seconds, Amos rushed into the room. His normally almond shaped eyes were round with excitement and his mouth was stretched into a huge grin.

"Did you wash your hands?" Ben tossed the question over his shoulder at the smiling boy as he laid a clean sheet over Ella's legs, hiding the messy sight from his view.

"Twice!" He said excitedly, and held his damp hands up for Ben to see. He twisted his palms back and forth, front to back. "See?"

"Alright. Come up here." Ben wrapped the shivering and crying baby in two warm blankets and led Amos to stand close to Ella's side.

"Oh, look at you…" Ella breathed as she took the baby and nestled him tight to her chest. "You are so beautiful. But you hurt me so much. Why did you try to kill me?" She whispered the words softly as she smiled and was rewarded by a laugh from Amos and a small coo of contentment from the baby.

"What's his name?" Amos asked quickly without taking his eyes off the infant's tiny face.

As Ben worked carefully between Ella's legs, his face partially hidden from view, he was aware of the slight hesitation before she answered. They had discussed names several times over the past few days and Ben was sure they had come to an agreement. It wasn't a question of her not wanting to name their son after Ben's father. She hadn't batted an eye when he had suggested it as a first name. Their disagreement was with the choice of a middle name.

"Benjamin." Ella had stated it as a fact, her dark eyes soft but unyielding.

"That's my name." Ben had argued weakly, realizing he had already lost. "He needs to have his own name. Be his own individual person."

"He will share your name *and* he will be his own individual person." She countered.

If he had been completely honest, Ben would have told her he was simply afraid. He was afraid that if his son shared more than just his last name, then he might also share some of Ben's fate. Without knowing where the Singular path would take him, Ben had hoped to spare his son from even the possibility of walking in his footsteps.

Ella had smiled and written down the baby's name on a piece of paper and handed it to Ben.

"I've already lost this fight, haven't I?" Ben had asked and when Ella nodded, Ben had kissed her softly and tried to still his suddenly pounding heart.

There was a smell of dust in the air of the small cabin that did nothing to mask the pungent smell of childbirth. As Ben waited for her to answer Amos, he lifted his head a little to take a deep breath before leaning back down to his task. He saw Ella's eyes meet Amos' and she gave the now warmed up baby a slight squeeze.

"His name is Ethan Benjamin Richardson."

Ben sighed out a breath and dipped his head again. His heart was pounding but he didn't say a word.

"Nice name." Amos grinned and reached a finger to stroke Ethan's cheek. "Hi, Ethan." He spoke quietly to the baby who blinked sleepily at him and opened his tiny mouth in a round 'O' of a yawn.

"We're going to count your fingers and toes while you sleep, ok?"

Ella nodded her head and as the baby's eyes slipped closed, she carefully unwound a part of his blanket and began her examination. When Ella and Amos were satisfied that Ethan had all the parts he needed, he was swaddled again in his blanket and rested comfortably on Ella's chest. Ben had completed his careful cleanup and had gingerly eased Ella's knees down flat on the bed. He held out his hand and gestured for Amos to follow him. "It's time for her to get a little rest, too."

"Okay." Amos nearly sang, he was so happy.

A coldness settled into Ben's chest as he led Amos into the living room. The jigsaw puzzle on the table was a third finished. He hated to steal the boy's joy. The baby was healthy as far as they could tell and Amos was as far from jealous as was possible. But there was something they needed to discuss. Something Ben needed to find out before anything else happened. Since the fires in the sky and the appearance of the Others, Ben hadn't had the luxury to see anything as a coincidence. So when he heard Amos singing a song he had penned years ago and had never published, Ben knew there had to be more to it than mere happenstance.

Sometimes in the night, Ben cursed his fate. Ella. Amos. The baby. But in the light of day with her hand soft and comforting on his shoulder, Ben knew he could never live without her. And even though he had never considered having a wife or children, Ben recognized that they were all in his life for a reason. There had been so many blank spaces in his life he had tried to fill with so many other things; cigarettes, alcohol, sex. Now he had turned his back on all those things – well, two out of three at least. Ben realized his life was so full that he no longer had the intense craving for the cigarettes or alcohol. He no longer wanted to tip back a bottle of anything 70-proof or more to silence the nightmares or satisfy the empty places in his soul. The addiction to the nicotine still fought for dominance from time to time, but the cravings were getting less frequent and less strong with each new day.

At that moment, with his woman and son resting peacefully in the other room, and his near-son peering expectantly up at him, Ben hated to disturb the delicate balance they had created as a family. He was never a man of many words, but even those few words failed to materialize as he dropped a hand softly onto Amos' head. He couldn't stall forever. Amos was waiting and would soon start to worry if Ben didn't start to talk. And that worry could lead to him losing focus and being vulnerable to being used by the aliens.

"Tell me about the song." Ben sat in the hard wooden chair and gestured for Amos to sit in the other.

"Oh, was I singing too loud?" He sounded more embarrassed than hurt.

"No," Ben held up a calming hand. "I just want to know where you heard it from."

Amos' smile returned and he scratched at the side of his tangled hair. He needed a haircut but there simply hadn't been time.

"My mom used to sing it to me when I was little." He smiled more broadly at his own words. "When I was "little-er." He laughed and Ben couldn't help but laugh with him.

"Ok." Ben glanced away, and then back. He would tell Amos the truth and see how it went. He could feel in his gut they were running out of time and he knew everything was connected somehow. Even this. So he took a deep breath and continued. "The reason I'm asking is because… I wrote that song when I was just a few years older than you. I never showed it to anyone. Ever. And now you're telling me your mom sang that song to you when you were 'little-er'?"

The look on Amos' face shifted and changed and the smile fell so quickly that Ben could almost imagine it had never been there.

"I don't understand." His voice rose a little at the end and Ben knew the boy was getting anxious.

It was important to keep him as calm as possible so the aliens couldn't probe into his mind and manipulate his thoughts. But it was also important for Ben to know where he had heard that song. Ben felt that once he had opened the door with the question, he needed to follow through. He would do his best to keep the boy calm, but he had to know. He had to.

"I'm not mad at you." Ben reached out a hand and laid it on Amos' arm. He was silently relieved that Amos didn't pull back from his touch. "I just need to know how your mom could have heard that song when I never sang it to anyone."

Amos' eyes darkened a shade as he stared at Ben. He wasn't mad that Ben was accusing him of something, but he was getting pretty mad that Ben was accusing his mom of something. "My mom didn't steal your song." His voice was rising and Ben could feel the start of the anger he had been trying to avoid.

"I'm not saying she did. I'm just trying to figure this out." Ben answered quietly and honestly and hoped Amos could control his anger for all their sakes. They didn't need the any outside interference right then. They weren't prepared for that.

But it was already too late. Amos shot to his feet as if a marionette string was jerking him upward. Ben startled backwards, then quickly moved forward and tried to reach out for him. The boy slapped at Ben's hands like they were pesky mosquitoes and his head shook back and forth.

"No!" Both hands wrapped around his thin chest to keep them away from Ben and he danced back, his head still shaking "She didn't steal your song! She wouldn't do something like that. You didn't even know her!"

Ben stood slowly and tried to ignore a light pounding in his head. It wasn't a headache exactly. Just a dull ache of tiredness that made him want to press the heels of his hands to his temple and squeeze his eyes shut. But he didn't. He kept his hands at his sides and waited. He needed Amos to calm down and he wasn't sure how to do it. And to his distress, Amos seemed to be working himself up more and more.

"You're never going to like me, are you?!" His small face wrinkled into a mask of hurt and rage. "You're never going to trust me!"

144

As Amos' voice rose with each syllable, the newborn baby stirred on his mother's chest. Ben felt the dull ache in his head again and added to that now was a mounting tension that made his stomach tighten and his balls shrink against his body. His fear was that the aliens were soon going to make their way into Amos' anguished mind and he steeled himself for the onslaught to come.

When the first shriek from his newborn son pierced the air, Ben almost didn't register what he was hearing. The wail was a sound so new and so foreign that it took a second for him to place it. But Amos immediately recognized the sound for what it was. His small hands dropped abruptly from his chest and the anger fled from him like a skittish rabbit.

"Ethan." Amos whispered and rushed past Ben into the bedroom.

Ben stood still and tried to pretend there was no connection between the two things that happened when Ethan cried out. In the wake of his son's wail, Amos' anger completely dissipated. And at the same time, the dull throbbing in Ben's head and the feeling of apprehension, also disappeared. He tried to convince himself that his son couldn't know that the aliens needed a mind that was weak from stress or emotion to enter and that Ben was struggling to keep Amos calm as he questioned him about the song. But just as he was working his mind furiously to convince himself it was all a coincidence, he heard Ethan's tiny baby giggle from the other room.

Amos was calm and Ethan was happy again.

TWENTY-SIX

The small family drove south on the narrow gravel road leading them away from the woods and from the cabin. It was still early and the yellow rays of sunlight slanted through the glass of the car windows.

Ben had spent the past two days listening closely to his intuition, waiting for the sign that told him it was time to move on. He knew they would have to leave the cabin sooner or later and he had hoped to allow Ella some time to rest before they needed to pack up and go. Even with Amos eagerly waiting on Ella hand and foot, caring for a newborn was hard work. Their concerns about Amos being jealous of Ethan proved to be so unfounded as to be laughable. There wasn't a moment that passed when Amos wasn't watching Ethan or touching his tiny foot or begging to hold him or feed him. For Ethan, the double attention was a baby's dream and when he wasn't snuggled up in Ella's arms, his wide eyes were searching for Amos. If Ben wasn't so preoccupied with keeping his senses attuned to any possible threats around the cabin and teaching Amos some rudimentary skills in handling a gun, Ben might have been jealous of Ethan himself.

But in the early morning hours of the second day of Ethan's life, Ben awoke with a stirring like a restless storm of bees in his mind. It was a pressing urgency that refused to let him wait any longer.

"Time to go." Ben announced an hour later while the taste of their breakfast still lingered in their mouths.

All eyes had regarded him thoughtfully but there were no arguments. They accepted that it was time and they packed up their few belongings and trudged resolutely to the waiting car.

Driving too fast down the steep hill, Ben took a hard turn with a spray of gravel and a soft grunt pushed from his throat. Ella snuck a sideways look at his profile from where she sat buckled in the passenger seat.

"You know we aren't using a car seat." She stated the obvious, then glanced down at the tiny bundle held tightly in her arms. "If you hit a tree, we're all dead." Lowering her voice to a whisper on the word 'dead', she threw a glance over her shoulder to where Amos sat safely strapped in the back seat.

Over the weeks, Ben had learned to recognize the subtle changes in Ella's tone of voice. This tone however, wasn't subtle at all. It caused him to immediately lift his foot from the accelerator and slow his speed to something more to her liking.

"Sorry." He mumbled and shifted his hips on the cloth seat, flicking his eyes to the rear-view mirror.

The tall mountain trees flew by on the right hand side as the car wound its way down the pass heading toward the valley. Ben smiled to himself as he thought of Ella's temper and how her words could affect him more deeply than even the words of the aliens when they tried to bombard his mind. Since the fires in the sky had begun and ended, she was more and more intertwined with his life and his mind and he knew that in the days to come that might work for him or against him. His fear was that the enemy would use his love for her as leverage and he wouldn't be able to do what he knew he had to do.

It was a simple thought that entered his head then. *He was Singular and he would win.* It was a comfort to him in a way to finally accept that he was born for this time and this task. It made a crazy sort of sense to know that all he had endured and experienced in his life had led him to this place with Ella, and his son and with Amos. Ben would probably never understand why he was chosen for this task or why he was Singular. But as he and his family bore down on the next valley town, he felt more at peace with himself than he had since the alien ships had first appeared in the sky.

In the backseat, Amos once again hummed the familiar tune from his childhood. Ben ran a hand through this hair and wondered when the time would come again for them to talk about the song. He hadn't tried to talk to Amos since that first night and frankly, he hadn't wanted to bring it up. Amos had been ecstatic to be taking care of Ella and Ethan and it seemed his joy and energy was endless. Ben hated to be the one to bring an end to that blissful state, but he knew at some point, he would have to broach the subject one more time. For a while though, he would let the subject lie. They would reach the town soon and their main mission was to stock up on food and supplies. The talking would come later.

Reaching the valley below, Ben drove directly to the first grocery store they came to, not even stopping to fill up on gas. Standing in front of the wide double doors to the store, Ben took a quick look around. Seeing no one, human or Other, he wedged his fingers behind the thick black rubber trim of the door and gave it a quick yank. The electricity to power the door had long since stopped working and he had to throw his back into it and give the door a second hard yank to pry it open.

Once the heavy sheet of glass cracked open with a loud 'pop!' the smell of rotting meat and vegetables seemed to leap out of the opening and assault his nostrils. Ben slapped a hand over his nose and motioned to Amos and Ella to follow him inside.

"Pew! No!" Amos screeched and swung around so fast he nearly tripped on his own feet.

Ben paid no attention and held the door open for Ella. She carried Ethan cozily close to her body, held in place by a babywearing shirt she fashioned out of one of Ben's undershirts.

"Whoah!" Ella dipped her head and snuggled her nose next to Ethan's face, preferring his sweet baby smell over the rancid odor coming from inside the abandoned store.

"We'll go through fast." Ben said as he snagged Amos by the back of the shirt and began to drag him along behind him.

"It smells so bad!" Amos wailed and pulled up the neck of his t-shirt to cover his nose.

"Yeah. It's bad." Ben agreed.

He wasn't paying that much attention to the smell of rotting food. There was an undertone of something else, something oiler than just food that had been left to spoil. The stink of the other smell slid into Ben's nostrils and he snorted out, hoping to dispel it from his nose.

"We need to hurry." He called out as the three of them fanned out to get as many of the items on their list as they could find.

Picking out the baby car seat was Ella's first priority and she hustled her way toward the middle of the store, stopping only to tug a silvery shopping cart from the rack. The cart's companions, upset at losing one of their own, screeched mightily, resisted her pull for a moment, and then with a final high pitched scrape of metal on metal, obliged.

"I don't think anyone is here now," Ben kept his eye on the front door and the car parked outside. "But they could be anywhere watching us and I don't want them to trap us inside."

Ella had unstrapped Ethan and propped him on a small pile of shirts in the front basket of the squeaky-wheeled shopping cart. Ethan's contentment was evident by the bubbling and gurgling emanating from his tiny mouth. Amos ranged wide, already munching on a bright red Twizzler candy as he scooped up toothpaste from one aisle, then ran to the next aisle for soap. Ben stayed near the exit, his eye occasionally distracted by the ravaged piles of impulse items near the registers. A look of unmistakable relief washed over Ben's face when Amos and Ella finally made their way to the front of the store.

Ben knew it was vital to have enough food and supplies on hand to last a while. Still, he lifted an eyebrow in surprise at what he spied in Ella's cart. The pile of much-needed diapers and wet wipes were surrounding by numerous brightly colored packages of crackers and cereals along with nearly two dozen tins of canned chicken and beef and tuna.

"Did you make sure to get a can opener?" Ben asked dryly.

Amos chuckled a little around his sticky red candy and looked up slyly at Ella.

"We got five." She announced proudly and pointed to a bulging plastic bag hanging on the side of the cart. "And we got waters and some fake juice and some peanut butter and jelly and trail mix and…"

"What? No cheese?" Ben interrupted with another quick look toward the car.

"Did you just meet me?" The corners of Ella's lips tipped up in a smile. She pointed to another sack hanging on the opposite side of the cart that was bulging with yeasty smelling packets of shrink-wrapped cheese. Ben cupped Ella's face in his hands and deposited a soft kiss on her lips which tasted faintly like salt and parmesan. "They're all dry, hard aged cheeses." She licked her lips. "That should last us a little while."

There was a moment when Ben almost turned and led them out of the rank smelling grocery store out into the bright sunlight. His main concern was to get them out and back in the car before anyone found them inside.

"Wait. I need to check." He said with a light sigh, and then more forcefully, "I need to check everything."

"Why?" Ella protested as she began wrapping Ethan back into the snug t-shirt carrier. "I checked all the food. None of it is spoiled."

"I'm not checking for spoilage." Ben replied. "I'm checking to make sure it's all…real."

Standing in the front of the store that looked so real, Ben and Ella looked at each other and their eyes spoke what their minds were just beginning to grasp.

"Can they do that, too?" Amos spoke up, a puzzled look on his sticky face.

"Yeah." Ben answered and said nothing more.

For the next five minutes, Ben lifted and examined every item in Ella's cart and Amos' basket. Amos stood nervously off to one side, afraid Ben might fuss about all the candy he had snuck in along with the shampoo and extra toothbrushes. At another time, that many sweets may have been a concern for him, but Ben had another agenda and his mind was completely occupied with that one thing. Knowing that the aliens could create almost anything with the black, wispy shapes, it wasn't a question of if they would try to trick them again, it was a matter of when and how. Leaning his head to one side so as to better feel what they were made of rather than rely on his eyes, Ben strained his mind to detect even the smallest evidence of 'otherness' in each item he turned over in his fingers.

"We're good. Let's go." He announced after checking the last item of clothing.

Amos grabbed eagerly at his basket, his eyes already selecting the next treat he would sample.

****

It came as an honest surprise to Ben that everything fit in the trunk of the car with the exception of the diapers. Those would have to ride in the back seat. Once everything was positioned, the mound of plastic packages filled the floorboard of the car on the side where Ethan's backward facing car seat was installed.

With the baby and Ella safely settled in the back, Amos hopped happily into the passenger seat beside Ben. He had been reluctant at first to be so far away from Ethan for the ride to the next town, but when Ella referred to his passenger seat position as 'riding shotgun', his eyes lit up and his grin exploded onto his face as he nodded.

"It's a big responsibility, okay?" Ben peered seriously down at Amos and tried to suppress a smile at the boy's enthusiasm.

"Yeah. I know." He answered quickly and yanked off another chew of his Twizzler.

"I mean you may actually have to use the gun while I'm driving."

"I know. I'm ready." Amos' eyes grew wide but he continued nodding. "I'm ready."

And the truth was in his eyes. Amos was ready. He was ready to protect Ella and Ethan and if it came to it, Ben was sure he would protect him too. Their relationship hadn't been an easy one but since Ethan was born, Amos had come to find his place in the family. And that place was right beside Ethan, day and night. The connection between the two boys was stronger than they could have ever imagined. During those difficult times when Ella couldn't do anything to calm down the fussy infant, Amos would bring his face close to Ethan's and whisper, "Settle pettle, buddy." Ethan's struggles would immediately lessen and his dark eyes would lock onto Ethan's gray ones. "Settle pettle, buddy." Amos would chant softly until Ethan was still and content in his mother's arms.

Ben gave a slight nod toward the glove box. "It's loaded. Just thumb off the safety, aim and shoot just like we practiced."

"Yeah…" Amos breathed in and out and his candied breath was a sweet balm of innocence and a memory of childlike things Ben had long forgotten.

Maneuvering his way out of the parking lot back onto the main road, Ben glanced down at the gas gauge. His eyes flicked up to the rear view mirror and Ella caught his eye. "We need gas?" A head nod from Ben brought a frown to her features and she laid a hand defensively on the sleeping baby beside her. "Another stop?"

She wasn't as concerned about having to make a second stop as about where it was they needed to stop. The memory of the two Others Ben had shot without hesitation in the gas station in the other town was still fresh in her mind. It was the first time she had seen him kill anyone. True, they weren't actually human, but they had looked enough like humans to make her blood run cold at the sight. The emotionless way he had pumped two bullets into each body still played in her mind like a rerun of a bad movie.

"It will be fine." Ben murmured and dropped his eyes back to the road ahead.

At first Ben thought Amos had traded in his sweet smelling Twizzler candy for some new noxious scented treat. But as the sickly smell of ozone and sulfur tingled its way into his nostrils, Ben's hands tightened on the steering wheel.

"Do you smell it?" Ella eyebrows furrowed and her left hand pressed down on Ethan's stomach, causing a small burp of milky air to escape his lips.

"I smell it." His voice was tense and Ella saw his shoulders push back against the driver's seat as he steeled himself. "Amos, grab the gun."

When Amos looked up and met Ben's eye briefly, the boy gulped down the last bite of his bright red candy and reached for the glove box.

"Do you smell that?" Ben asked Amos.

"Yeah, it stinks."

"Don't ever forget that smell."

"Is that them?"

"Yeah. It's them. You need to understand how they can make things. Things to try and trick us."

"OK." Amos' hands shook only slightly as he hefted the heavy gun and held it in both hands. His head bobbed up and down as he shifted his butt on the seat and scooched himself up higher.

"But they aren't as smart as we are and there's always a way you can tell it's something they created. There's the smell of course, and if you look closely and watch carefully, there's something not quite right about the things they create. They…" Ben hesitated, searching for the right word. "The things they make aren't perfect and they certainly aren't natural. They…"

"They shimmer." Ella piped up from the backseat and Ben nodded his agreement with her choice of words. "They wiggle around the edges like they are being held together with something that's not really solid."

That was the perfect way to describe it, Ben decided. Amos nodded his head in understanding and clicked off the safety on the gun. He was ready.

As the loaded down sedan carrying the family rolled down the deserted asphalt road, everyone in the car held their breath. The landscape of the town had changed and the area held a musty air of disuse.

On both sides of the road were industrial buildings and the low gray structures were set back from the road to allow for the delivery trucks to offload their wares without having to navigate around to the rear of the buildings. On the right, a set of four silvery tower silos rose into the cloudless sky and cast long shadows across the road. The stink of ozone in the car grew stronger, and Ben and Ella both realized with the smell that strong, the alien illusion would be bigger than any others they had seen before. The odor permeated the car like a fog and Ella pulled the light blanket higher up over Ethan's face to try and protect him from the overpowering smell.

"Don't they know they stink?" Amos rubbed the back of his hand under his nose.

Ben snorted out a short laugh. "Maybe they don't know. Or maybe they think we are so stupid that we would never connect the two."

Amos' question pricked at Ben's brain, though. Why didn't they even try to disguise the smell? He had wondered about that very thing before but with so many other things to consider, the question had been pushed to the back of his mind.

The road curved to the right and when the red white and blue logos of the Chevron gas station came into view, Ella's sigh of relief was deep and loud.

"Finally." She breathed and settled back against the cushions of her seat.

It was only when Ben had taken his foot off the gas to begin his turn that Amos called out. "Wait!"

Ben switched his foot to the brake and brought the car to an easy stop.

"It…shimmered." Amos was already rolling down the passenger side window when he felt Ella's hand on his shoulder.

"Are you sure?" Her voice was soft with only a hint of a quaver.

Amos glanced over at Ben who answered his look with a tilt of his head. "I'm sure." Amos answered confidently and twisted back around to face the window.

"Aim for the pumps." Ben maneuvered the car to the other side of the road and backed into position to give Amos the clearest shot. If the pumps turned out to be real, they would only have a few seconds to pull away before the entire station exploded in searing hot flames. If the pumps weren't real, then he wanted the car to be far enough away that the alien black filaments weren't hurled back on them and into the car.

Amos' pulse raced. He lifted the gun and rested the heavy barrel on the open window. Ben had showed him how to sight and aim during their practice sessions. He took in a deep breath and held it and let his eyes flick down one more time to make sure the safety was off.

"Do it now, Amos." Ben said softly and Ella laid her hands on both side of Ethan's head, protecting his ears from the blast to come.

To say the gunshot was loud was an understatement. The thunderous boom reverberated through the air and all four inhabitants of the car jerked in its wake. Ethan's eyes flew open wide and his lips snapped apart with a soft pop. In the split second it took for Ben to switch his foot back from brake to gas, three things happened at once.

Amos pushed the gun into the still open glove box like it was a serpent coiled to bite and yanked up on the button to raise his window.

The impact of the bullet tore a quarter-sized hole in the gas pump in the silvery space between the tag that labeled the 91 and 89 octane pumps.

And third, with a hissing sound exactly like air escaping from a punctured tire, the entire bank of pumps wavered in the waning sunlight and then exploded in a greasy mass of black ropy filaments.

TWENTY-SEVEN

That Amos had recognized the gas station was a fake gave Ben a sense of comfort in the deepest parts of his soul. It pained him to even acknowledge it, but he had been struggling not to see Amos as a liability and a burden. The disloyal thought always snuck its way in late at night when he wrestled with his dreams. It was relentless proof to him that he wasn't the kind of father he would like to be and surely not the caliber of man Ella seemed to think he was. In some ways, the mistrust and doubts about Amos were more painful, more disturbing than any the aliens could thrust into his mind. Ben knew his reservations were homegrown, cultivated over the years by his own worries and insecurities.

The minutes ticked by with Ben staring out the windshield at the deserted street beyond. So lost in his thoughts, he didn't realize Amos had been calling out to him, trying to get his attention.

"Maybe he's asleep." Ben finally heard Amos' voice as if through a thick fog, and he shook himself free of his musings.

"No, not asleep." Ella said with a note of concern, never taking her eyes off of Ethan's face. "But maybe dreaming?"

Ben knew why she was concerned. His earlier vision had been so unsettling to her. If he was having another one, she could only worry what witnessing that might do to young Amos.

"No." Ben shook his head and caught her eye in the rear view mirror. "Just thinking."

"About what?" Ella replied a little too quickly.

Ben's face closed in a little on itself. There was no way he would tell her what he was really thinking. Not right there in front of Amos. So he brought to the front of his mind a question that had only been a tiny nagging one, although he realized with a jolt of alarm that it should have been the main question.

"Why fake an entire gas station?" Ben asked.

Amos shrugged and turned again to look out the passenger side window. There was nothing left of the gas station that had previously occupied a space at least 50 feet square.

Ella shook her head miserably. "I think you know the answer to that, Ben."

"They knew we would have to stop for gas sometime."

"Right."

"And in these little towns there are usually only one or two stations so the odds were in their favor that we'd stop at one of their traps."

"Right." Ella said again and let her eyes also wander over to the now empty lot.

Did this mean they had to assume all the gas stations were fake? That was a scenario too disturbing for Ben to fully consider. Once they were out of gas and without a car, they would be forced to travel by foot. If that happened, Ben didn't know how they would be able to stay ahead of the Others or the survivors who they now knew could be just as dangerous. And while he knew there was going to come a time when he had to face his adversary, Ben still hadn't figured out how he would fight them. Time. That's what they needed. More time. But it was beginning to look like time wasn't something they had a deep supply of.

Ben's eyes hooded again in deep thought and he drummed his thumbs broodingly on the steering wheel.

"Ahem." Amos said and pressed his index finger into the soft flesh just under Ben's armpit.

When Ben jerked in surprise and turned to stare at the boy, Amos pointed two fingers at Ben's eyes and then turned his hand to point one finger out the window. In another time and another place, the sarcasm behind the gesture might have irritated Ben into hot anger. Instead, he tamped down his emotions and let his eyes follow the boy's narrow finger to its tip. His small finger tap-tap-tapped on the glass of the window. It had been several minutes since the false gas station had exploded from Amos' gunshots and the full service Chevron station had dissipated into nothing. Not even the smell of sulfur and ozone was left. Or so it seemed at first glance.

"Can you see it?" Amos craned his neck around to peer at Ben who silently cursed himself.

If he hadn't been so engrossed with his thoughts, allowing the old insecurities to push through to the surface, he might have almost overlooked what turned out to be the biggest piece of the puzzle so far.

Through the tempered glass of the car window, the array of silvery flakes scattered on the weed-filled asphalt glittered in the late afternoon sun. Each piece appeared to be about the size of a sheet of paper but the pieces looked much thicker, with sharp, jagged edges. His mind automatically began counting the number of the flakes and when he got to fifty, he realized there was no point in continuing. He had his answer. He closed one eye against a light throbbing headache and tried to remember. Had there been anything like that with the mouse in the backpack or the tree in the road? He closed his other eye for a second, concentrating on the memory.

"It was too big." The revelation hit him all at once and Ben was already reaching for the door handle as he spoke.

"What?" Ella and Amos said in unison.

"The gas station was too big to create with only their black threads. They needed something more to make this illusion work."

He could hear Ella calling his name, calling him back, but softly. She didn't want to alarm Amos or the baby and he felt her conflict, but he didn't stop to explain. His long legs ate up the distance from one side of the road to the other in only nine steps and then he was standing, looking down at the first silvery flake he came to.

Reluctant to touch the metal, unsure it really was metal, Ben cast around for something he could use as a tool. His eye fell on a six-inch length of wood, bleached and dry, lying close to his left heel. He sniffed the air lightly and watched the piece of wood for a moment. It didn't wiggle; it didn't shimmer. It was real wood. Using the stick as a lever, Ben tucked it under a bent corner of the metal sheet. Flipping it over quickly, Ben stepped back as it tumbled twice and landed with the opposite side up. No black filaments wiggled underneath and no boogey-man jumped out to scare him. Although with all they had been through with the Others and the transformations and the attacks on their minds, maybe a boogey-man might have been easier to deal with than this new truth.

As he stared hard at the silver flake on the ground, Ben suddenly recoiled as he saw the edges of the metal begin to shimmer. His fists tightened and he had almost turned and raced back to the car, but then he realized. He was staring at them too hard in the bright sunlight. The dots of light were coming from his own eyes and not from the metal. Ben blinked and cleared his mind.

Painted on the metal with what looked like a standard bristle paintbrush, was part of a logo. Even though he couldn't see the entire logo, Ben's mind easily filled in the blanks. He had seen that logo before, long ago. The image had stayed with him since he was nine years old and standing in a place he had no right to be standing. On that rare occasion, his father had wakened him early and whispered for him to quickly get dressed and follow him. The boy had obeyed his father without question. Father and son rode quietly side by side in the old maroon Ford Fiesta, passing darkened stores and shadowy motels until they reached the outskirts of town. When they finally reached the entrance gate to the military base, his dad had slowed, flipped his ID card out to the gate guard and tossed a nod in his direction.

"My son." The pride in his dad's voice was evident as he jerked a thumb toward Ben and the gate guard snapped an indulgent salute as he waved them through.

Once inside the immense metal airplane hangar where his dad worked, his father had turned to him with an expression that was hard to read.

"You're not supposed to be here, ok?" The boy's eyes were round at the secrecy and he bobbed his head up and down. "If anyone asks, you snuck into the car and I didn't know you were there until it was too late, okay?"

Ben had nodded and gaped in awe at the sleek silvery aircraft. "It's a fighter jet." His dad whispered with more than a hint of pride in his voice. "The F-16 Fighting Falcon." Ben had stared at the red, white, and blue star logo on the side of the jet so long that the shape and color of it had burned into his memory as if it had been branded there with a hot poker.

Now, years later, staring down at the metal flake that was all that was left of the alien's grand illusion, a portion of that same logo stared back up at him.

In the car, Ella was suddenly overwhelmed with an uneasiness that left her breathless and lightheaded. To say her mind was a blur was an understatement. As she kept her eyes on Ben's back, her left hand still absently petted her baby's tummy. Her thoughts had raced beyond a blur to a pure white of terror. Where was that fear coming from? She knew Ben had found something in the wreckage of the alien illusion. Shouldn't she have been glad that they were getting some answers? With her fear mounting over what he may have discovered, Ella felt a slight tickle in the back of her brain as if small fingers were gently probing her mind, massaging her thoughts. Her eyes squeezed shut as the whispery fingers quickly altered and became harsh and invasive.

"No, no, no, no, no…" She chanted out loud as she realized how close she had come to giving space for the alien thoughts to invade her mind.

"No, no, no, no, no…" Ethan's baby voice hummed and mimicked her chant and both Ella and Amos turned to stare.

That was the way things were. Everything was startling but not really unexpected. They were sitting in a car in the middle of a dead town and her three-day-old baby boy was warning her to keep her mind sharp and focused. Ella was aware of Amos' eyes on her and an undercurrent of astonishment blinked between them.

The moment might have stretched out forever, but just then Ben yanked open the car door and a wave of hot wind rushed in. Ella idly wondered if it wouldn't have been so bad if the moment had stretched out forever. If time simply stopped and everything and everyone stayed right where they were, would that be so awful? Ethan would stay her sweet baby. Amos would stay safe and not handle guns anymore, and Ben? Her dear Ben would forever be alive and hers and standing no more than two feet away from her.

"Hey." He slid easily into the seat and positioned his hands on the steering wheel in the 10 and 2 o'clock position.

"Hey." Ella replied and found herself halfway listening for Ethan to say the same, but the baby had closed his eyes and was quietly sucking on his bottom lip.

Ben's expression was wasn't one Ella often on his features. But there was no mistaking the gleeful glint in his eyes as he said,

"I know where they are."

TWENTY-EIGHT

The drive from the site of the counterfeit gas station to the closest genuine gas station didn't take long. Ben had insisted they try again. Not only because they were dangerously low on gas, but because he was sure the aliens wouldn't take the time and effort to make more than one huge decoy station. There was nothing especially logical about his decision. It simply *felt* right. His instincts led him down the road about two miles to an older station with only two late model gas pumps under a faded metal awning. The long squat building attached to the awning gleamed a dingy white and the windows of the attached garage had long been boarded over with pieces of plywood.

Pulling the car over to a stop on the far side of the road, Ben and Amos waited, staring until their eyes burned with the desire to blink. Nothing shimmered, nothing wavered, and as a matter of fact, nothing moved at all. The gas station was real and as they soon discovered, the pumps were still operational.

Feeling too antsy to hang around the station after filling up the car, Ben continued a few miles down the road to a small park next to a sluggishly moving creek. Ben and Ella sat side by side on the wooden seat of the picnic table, watching as the late afternoon sun slid its way behind the tallest trees toward the darkening horizon. Amos sat behind them on the tabletop, his long legs straddling Ethan's car seat, his hands firmly locked around the bottle held in the baby's mouth.

"Gonna need to breastfeed soon." Ella whispered. With both palms, she pushed at her breasts, heavy with milk. Ben peered down at her swelling bosom, smiled and waggled his eyebrows seductively at her. "Oh, please." Her eyes rolled and her grin widened. "Try and touch them now and it'll only get you a poke in the eye."

They hadn't had much time to be alone together in the past couple of weeks. So much had happened so quickly, the least of which was Ethan's accelerated gestation and birth. Neither of them had brought up the speed of her pregnancy and why their full term baby boy was born completely healthy after only four weeks. Yet, what Ella had discussed at length was the physical toll the rapid swelling had taken on her body. "These stretch marks will never go away." She had cried as she slathered the warmed cocoa butter oil over the light pale marks on her stomach.

"They are marks of our love for each other." Ben deadpanned and tried not to look her in the eye as he said it.

"You have lost your freaking mind." She had laughed and pushed hard at his shoulder, nearly toppling him over the side of the bed.

He hadn't lost his mind and he knew there was truth in what he had said. Although it wasn't the stretchmarks. It was Ethan who was the result of their love for each other. The baby wasn't planned and he wasn't expected, but from the minute he took his first breath, Ben couldn't comprehend their lives without him. Or without Amos.

Ben twisted around to watch as the older boy laid the empty bottle to the side and began playing a game of keep-away with Ethan and his pacifier. He would let Ethan give the plastic nipple a few good sucks and then he would gently pull it free with a loud 'pop'. And with each 'pop', both Ethan and Amos would laugh out loud and Ethan would wave his chubby hands in the air. Then opening his mouth wide, Ethan would prepare for the next entertaining repetition of the game.

Turning his head back to Ella, Ben's eyes darkened a shade, making them appear almost black. In a distant part of her mind, Ella could hear warning bells clanging, but she shut out the sound and drew in a deep breath.

"Tell me what you want to tell me."

Ben dipped his head away from Ella and stole one more glance at Amos, glad he was so preoccupied with Ethan.

"I need to go alone." Ben kept his head down as if searching for something on the ground.

Ella brushed a stray hair away from her forehead, the gesture slow and deliberate. "Okay. And what will you do when you come face to face with them?"

It was a fair question and the most obvious question, yet it still rankled that she could possibly think he hadn't gone over in his mind a hundred times what he might do in that meeting. It was all he could think of from the minute he recognized where the silver metal flake had come from. The military base and the airplane hangars weren't more than five miles from where they sat. His dream of the silver room and the bright red laser swam into view and the pain from that burning cut was as vivid in his mind as it had been in the dream.

"So you walk in, they kill you and it's over." Ella gave a shrug, as if she didn't expect anything other than that to happen.

"Your confidence in me is staggering." He replied sarcastically.

"So tell me. What will you do?"

"I don't know." He said it simply and in that moment he almost gave up. He almost stood to his feet and walked down to the edge of the creek and kept walking. Walking until the water was over his head and pouring into his mouth. Walking until there was no more air in his lungs; only water filling all the pockets and suffocating him until there was nothing but blackness and release.

Ella shifted closer and laid a soft hand on his knee. "They want you dead. They want us all dead. Dead or transformed to do – I don't know what. But they clearly don't want us alive and running around on our own. And as far as killing us, it's not even a question of if they can do it. We know they can." She looked closely into his face as she spoke. "We know you're different and so do they. You have some kind of...*power* that they can't fight just yet, but you're not immortal."

He held her gaze and spoke quietly. "That's why I have to go now and go alone. They don't know what I am or what I can do. Hell, I don't even know what I am. But I do know that I need to go to that hangar and try to find a way to stop them and reverse what's been done to the world before they find a way to stop me. What else can I do? If I don't go, what happens to you?" He stroked a hand down her cheek as he spoke and tears sprung to her eyes. "And what happens to them?" He jerked his head toward the table where the boys sat. Ethan giggled loudly at some silly thing Amos was doing and Ben's heart nearly exploded with love for them both.

Said that way, in that simple direct way, it sounded like a thing that could be done with no muss and no fuss. He would go in, fight them, win and then walk out. And they would be safe. And their world would heal. But of course nothing in his life had ever been simple and he was sure this wouldn't be simple either. Three complications to his simple plan sat calmly around him, their lives intertwined by events none of them could have ever predicted.

Ben pushed to his feet and pulled Ella up. They stared out at the slowly moving water in the wide creek. Their eyes were drawn to the banks where the high water mark extended a good five feet from where the water now flowed. The blades of grass that lined the edge of the creek were yellowed and had long since given up hope. With weeks of no rain and the creek quickly receding, there was nothing to keep them rooted. The ground gave them nothing. The creek gave them nothing. The sky gave them nothing. Nothing unless you counted the strange rain that had transformed the world into mindless clones controlled by invisible aliens. And Ben was pretty sure that loathsome rain carried no nourishment for the creeks and farms and the dry parched areas that so badly needed moisture.

At last Ella turned to wrap herself around Ben, stomach to stomach, and her sigh was long and deep.

"Please come back to us." She pleaded with her eyes and her words. "Promise me that. Even if it's a lie, promise me anyway."

"I won't lie to you." Ben's fingers rose and fell as he tapped her gently on the back.

"Why not? What's wrong with you? All men lie."

He looked down at her, her eyes were closed and her head was pressed tight to his shoulder.

"I don't want to ever lie to you."

"Just this once." Ella begged and finally, Ben relented but prayed his words held some small grain of truth.

"I'll come back to you." His promised as his chin rested in her hair and his dark eyes stared out at the horizon.

Ben glanced around at Amos and Ethan and felt a hard tightening in his stomach. He had to go face this enemy on his own and that meant leaving them all behind. Whatever power he had as the Singular was what kept them safe as long as he was with them. Smiling over at Ethan, Ben was grateful that it seemed like his son also manifested some kind of powers.

He had no way of knowing exactly what Ethan could do at his age with his tiny body. Why he thought having Ethan with them would make that much of a difference, but it was how he felt. With Ethan they at least had a chance, even though the chance, like three-day-old Ethan, was much smaller than he would have liked. Ella was a fighter and Amos was a survivor. They had to make it without him. There wasn't any other choice.

"I'll go tonight." He said.

"Why at night?" She frowned. "You don't know what they look like or what they can do. At least in the daytime you'd be able to see better what you're walking into."

"The dark doesn't bother me. I've wandered around in the dark so many nights when I couldn't sleep. I'll actually do better in the dark."

"Ben…" Ella started. Ben silenced her with a shake of his head.

"Tonight." He said again and the decision was made.

TWENTY-NINE

Ben walked boldly through the main gate of the deserted Rexton Air Base. No gate guard met him at the guard shack or sketched a salute for his entry this time. Abandoned for years, bored local teens had long since overtaken the remaining empty structures, transforming the blank, corrugated metal walls into rippling multicolored murals. Even in the dark, the full moon gave enough light for Ben to see the mostly undecipherable graffiti tags that adorned the outside walls up to the hundred foot mark from the ground.

Three unused hangars were spread out over the three acre fenced-in area and Ben hesitated a moment, trying to determine which one was the most likely hiding place for the alien craft. There was no doubt when he found the craft, he would find its owner and also, finally, find his fate.

A dim bulb pulsed weak, yellow light above each open hangar door, giving the appearance of a flashlight shining into a gaping mouth. In fact, that was true for only two of the hangars. Two of the hangars were missing their huge sliding doors and Ben was able to quickly see that they were empty of any craft of any kind, alien or manmade. He could immediately see that the third hangar was different. The surprisingly shiny metal doors were tightly closed and fastened together with a square metal box that must have been a lock. The brightness of that gleaming silver door was a stark contrast to the graffiti-covered sides and the top of the front of the hangar. The door had been recently installed. It wasn't a type of lock Ben had ever seen before so there was no point in trying to break in.

Besides, whoever or whatever was inside that hangar knew he was coming. He was sure of it. He could feel it in his chest just as strongly as he felt his heart pounding. Although Ben's mouth was dry and tension tingled from him like electricity, his mind was calm. As he drew closer to the doors of the old hangar, he could feel the alien presence like a dark, dank blanket thrown across his shoulders. It threatened to weigh him down and stop his feet from moving forward. Yet he pressed on and resolutely placed one foot in front of the other, each step bringing him closer to his whatever waited for him inside.

****

Ella chewed a thumbnail as she waited in the front seat of the car. The moonlight gave the empty street an eerie, gray glow that did nothing to help alleviate her fears. She desperately wanted to be in the back where Ethan rested in his car seat and where Amos leaned his head so close to the baby that they looked like some kind of crazy mismatched twins, joined at the cheek. The two of them had bonded so well that Ella could barely remember Amos' jealousy or how he had run from them into the woods. Although, that was how they found out there were still a few unconverted humans left in the small town, so if there was any saving grace to that time, that would be it. Almost losing Amos tugged on her heart in a way she would never have expected. In his short time with her and Ben, he had become their son. There was no other way to say it. Ben and Amos and Ethan were her family now and the thought of losing any of them was unbearable.

Her restless mind ranged back to the surreal moment she had lost one man and found another. Ella could hardly believe how hurt and angry she still was at the way her husband had been taken from her. The familiar ache in her chest began again as her thoughts turned to him. She had never loved anyone before him and as his life and breath deserted his battered body, Ella had been convinced she would never love anyone else. A searing rage and grief over her loss overwhelmed her and her fingers clutched at the steering wheel, pressing round wells into the soft leather cover.

Ella's chin quivered for a moment as she struggled with her emotions. In the early days after the cloud attack, the choking smoke in the air and the dwindling stores of food had made everyone scared and crazy. When the food in the larger towns had run out, desperation had set in and turned people into nothing less than lawless savages. Her husband hadn't wanted to fight them. He tried to talk to them like they were reasonable people. That's how he had always solved things in the past, but the past was gone and no one was reasonable anymore. Every morning when she awoke, Ella wondered if things would have been different if her husband hadn't tried to reason with the group of men who wanted to take all their food. She wondered if things would have gone differently if he had instead, pulled out a gun and shot into the small crowd.

He wasn't a good enough shot to kill them all, but if he had at least showed them that he had a weapon…maybe. Maybe the fist-sized rock that slammed into her husband's head would never have been thrown. They were all cowards and she never saw who threw the deadly projectile.

When her husband had crumpled to the ground with blood pouring out of the jagged gash in his forehead, they had all stared wide eyed for a horrifying, long second. Then, not even being men enough to stay and take what they had so spinelessly won, they had turned and skittered down the darkened street, leaving her to hold his bleeding head in her hands and watch his eyes close and his breathing stop.

*****

Ben angled past the two empty hangars, forcing his breathing to remain normal and his thoughts clear as he approached the third hangar with the large metal door. The closer his feet brought him to that hangar, the more he began to feel a light, maddening itch behind his eyes.

By the time he reached the back side of the hangar, the familiar oily smell was so strong, he lifted a hand and left it pressed under his nose. His fingers resting on his lip shook a little and at first Ben didn't give it a thought, When he was directly behind the old hangar, standing beside a standard size metal door, he realized that both hands were shaking. And they weren't just shaking, they were doing a frantic dance unlike anything he had ever experienced before. He had to settle his anxious thoughts. He wouldn't do anyone any good if he couldn't control it. Balling his twitching hands into fists, Ben sighed a deep breath in and slowly exhaled it out. After a few more deep, calming breaths in and out, he was ready.

Shutting down his mind, Ben concentrated on thinking nothing at all. He shut out the sound of the noisy crickets in the stubbly grass behind the hangar. He shut out loud, *lub dub, lub dub* of his pounding heart. And lastly, he shut out the smell of oil and sulfur. That was the hardest. That took the most time. But slowly, finally, he took control of his mind and body so that he heard nothing and saw nothing and smelled nothing. Then, in a calculated move he hoped would work, he left his mind open as wide as he could. And he waited for the aliens to find him.

****

"He smells funny." Amos sniffed and cocked his head slightly away from Ethan. As the baby's tiny face frowned with exertion, the rich pungent smell filled the air like a funky fog.

Ella jerked awake from her vision and swung around to peer into the back seat.

"Oh, come on man." Amos' nose wrinkled in disgust. "I can't believe you did that."

His task completed, Ethan relaxed contentedly in his car seat and closed his eyes. Ella knew she needed to change him. She hadn't taught Amos how to do more than distract Ethan during the diaper changing time. But she didn't want to get out of the car in the dark and not be in position in the driver's seat in case any Others came. She and Ben had talked at length about that part. Ella was to keep the doors locked, and she needed to be able to drive away quickly if anything seemed out of place or if anyone, human or Other, approached the car. The worst part, and the part that she had fought him on at first, was that it meant she had to drive away even if it meant leaving Ben behind.

Amos had his head down behind the seat, rummaging in the bag for a clean diaper. The smell was stronger in the back seat and Amos couldn't stand it any longer.

"Dude. Seriously." He fumbled with the diaper bag on the floor of the back seat, pulling out the plastic container of wet wipes. "Come on, Mom. Get back here. This guy is so stinky."

Ella smiled a little at Amos calling her Mom. It was the first time he had called her anything. He usually just said 'Hey' when he wanted her attention. He had been through so much in such a short period of time. Even though Amos hadn't been a witness to it, Ella was sure he knew what happened between his mom and dad after his dad was converted. There had been so much death, so much pain for such a little guy. Letting Amos call her mom was fine with her. She had lost so much over the past few months as well, but she had gained so much, too. She had gained a man who loved her like she had always been his, and two sons. Two sons. Ella tried to push back her tears but one slipped past her. Amos looked up just as she was wiping the glistening drop from her check.

"Hey." He leaned forward and laid his small hand on her shoulder. "It's ok. It's just poop. We can clean it up."

"Yeah." She agreed without stopping to explain. "It is just poop."

****

Ben stood staring at the grey metal door set into the side of the hangar. A short bark of a laugh shot out of him and he found himself smiling ruefully. He had been standing there, waiting for the aliens to fling open the door and discover him, when he realized that the door was unlocked. They had known he was coming and they unlocked the door for him. He shook his head in wonder. If his brain didn't work any better than that, did he really have what it took to defeat those guys? If they were indeed guys. Maybe they were women. Ben laughed again and tried to bring his mind back from the silly place it was threatening to go. He took in a deep breath and hastily shot it back out. At the door, the oily smell was overpowering. He reached for the door handle and turned the knob.

****

Ella reached back and found Amos' hand and gave it a pat and a squeeze. "Thanks. I'm sure everything will be fine, kiddo." Her smile was genuine and Amos retuned the smile with such love that Ella nearly broke down again. "Why don't you hand Ethan up here to me. I'll change him and give him back."

Outside, the sound of boots crunching on gravel made Ella swing her head around in alarm. She fumbled for the keys that hung in the ignition, her hand shaking uncontrollably. Before her grasping fingers could make good contact with the key, a sound like a thousand jets screaming overhead assaulted her ears and the interior light flashed on, nearly blinding her with its suddenness. The locked driver's side door was yanked violently open and ripped completely from the hinges.

****

It was what he had come for – what he knew had to happen. Yet the idea of finally coming face to face with the true aliens, the ones behind the damage to the earth from the crafts in the sky and the choking red clouds, caused him to hesitate with his hand fisted around the dented silver knob.

A tight pinch in his heart made Ben think back to his family he had left back in the car, parked on the main road near the entrance to the air base. A quiet whisper of a thought told him that something - he wasn't sure what -but something wasn't going exactly as they planned. The plan was that if anyone or anything even came close to the car, she was to start the engine and drive away. And she was to keep driving until she was down to three-quarters of a tank of gas. And then - and only then - was she to look for a quiet, dark place to wait. They had no cell phones and he didn't know enough about his abilities to be sure if he could push a thought into her head from so far away. But the best they had been able to come up with was for her to drive to that halfway point and wait with the kids until morning. As soon as daylight had completely saturated the sky, she was to drive back to the base entrance and wait for him.

Ben struggled to convince himself that Ella could handle whatever came upon her on the road. He had come this far and he couldn't go back and check on them every time he felt a twinge in his stomach. He had to trust that the three of them together could take care of themselves until Ben was done. Ella would fight until there was no strength left in her body. Ben knew that.

And Amos knew how to use a gun like a pro. And Ethan? Ben didn't know all that Ethan could do, but he was sure Ethan was special in his own way and he hoped Ethan had enough "specialness" about him to help keep them safe until…well…until it was all over.

From behind Ben, one of the dim bulbs over the hangar door across the weed-filled tarmac suddenly flickered once and then went dark. Time was moving on. Ben needed to get moving, too. Giving his wrist a quick yank, the knob turned easily in his hand and he pushed the door inward.

****

There were eight of them. And all of them were Others. Ella didn't have to have special sight to figure that out. Their bodies looked normal but there was a deadness in their eyes that made her squeeze herself back against the seat of the car. Two of them crowded close in the opening and the rank, unwashed smell of them almost made her gag.

"Get out." The hollow coldness in the voice of the Other was chilling. The voice was also familiar and Ella took only a second to place it. It was Dan. The Others must have found their little enclave and transformed them. She didn't want to think of what might have happened to the brave little woman who had tried to stand up to Dan. But right then, she didn't have time to think. She had to act.

Ella's mind scrambled to find a way to turn the key in the ignition, put the car in gear and drive away all before Dan snatched her out of the car or before they ripped the back door off and grabbed Ethan or Amos. There wasn't enough time. They were standing so close. But then again…

Jamming her fingers onto the black plastic fob, she churned the key forward and the engine roared to life. Ella felt her left arm being grabbed roughly by one of the Others and she felt hard fingers digging painfully into her flesh as she yanked the car into gear. Faster than she thought possible, she slammed her foot onto the gas pedal and the small car rocketed forward. But the Other held onto her and in less time than it took for her to yell, "Let go of me!" Ella was yanked forcefully from the moving car and hurled to the pavement. The pain was blistering as her backside slammed into the ground and her hip slid along the loose gravel.

The driverless car lurched once and with no foot to hold down the accelerator, the car jerked once more, then coasted to a pitiful stop only a few yards from where she lay on the pavement.

"Get up." Dan's hollow voice commanded again.

Ella scrambled to her feet and began moving her legs as fast as she could, her intent to get back to the car and back to Amos and Ethan.

"No!" The Other barked and grabbed her arm, yanking her sharply backward as Dan grabbed her other arm.

The rest of the group moved quickly past her to surround the car.

"If you hurt them, I promise I will kill every last one of you!" She screamed her warning.

The Others made no reply and Ella wasn't sure if they had heard her at all. All their attention was focused on the car. When the first Other's hand touched the handle on the back door, Ethan started crying and she could see Amos lean toward him, comforting him. Ella tensed in the grip of the Others holding her and she squirmed without concern for herself as she watched them snatch open the back door and reach in for Ethan's car seat. There was a pause and Ella nearly pulled her arm out of its socket stretching in their grip.

"Leave them alone! I'll get them out. Let me get them!" She shouted at the group.

The hesitation was unexpected. When the group recoiled, trying to get away from the open door, they all seemed to bump into each other like comical Keystone Cops. From her vantage point Ella could see both boys' heads inside the car and her heart thrummed in her chest. She willed tears not to come. She needed to keep her eyes clear to see what was happening.

As the first Other standing near the car swung around and she could see his face, she saw his hand come up to cover his nose. Within seconds, the rest of the group shrank back from the car, hands flying up to their faces. Spinning on their heels, the Others turned their back on Ethan and Amos and faced Ella and her captors.

"Get them out and let's go!" Dan shouted, his authority booming through. It seemed Dan was finally the man in charge, but to Ella it seemed the price he paid for that status was way too high.

Shuffling uncertainly, the group near the car wavered between obeying Dan and a desire to get as far away from Ethan as they could. Ella's brow creased with confusion. These Others could rip a locked car door open and off its hinges, but they were stymied by the smell of baby poop? How was that possible? That was when Ethan began to shriek.

THIRTY

The metal door slammed shut behind Ben with a bang like a gunshot. It closed with such finality that he wondered if it would ever open again. Before he had time to pursue that thought any further, his eyes adjusted to the dim light and his mouth went dry.

Directly in front of him, gleaming dully in the light from a bank of overhead fluorescent bulbs, was a spacecraft that measured about twenty feet long. It squatted low to the floor like the universe's ugliest insect. Several piles of metal sheeting had been pushed into the far corners of the room, leaving a clear perimeter around the craft. The original plan of the hangar included a set of offices at the far end of the building. To Ben's eye, it appeared that all the office spaces had been crushed down, and not gently by the looks of it, to create a space large enough for their ship.

Ben was standing on a large black rubber mat that was intended to be used to make sure employees' feet were free of as much mud and dirt as possible before they stepped onto the clean hangar floor. Ben glanced down at his dark brown hiking boots, heavy with mud from the Creekside. With an arrogance that likely meant nothing to the aliens, but made Ben feel surprisingly good, he stepped deliberately off the mat onto the sparkling clean cement floor.

Sniffing lightly, he could make out the distinctive oily sulfur scent of the aliens. It was strong even in the large expanse of the hangar and he was getting enough of a scent that he knew they must be close. Clearing his mind, he listened for any sound coming from the breadth of the hangar. A slight buzzing sound like a fly trapped in a bottle hummed in the air. Cocking his head, he tried to locate the source of the sound. To his right was the front of the hangar where the huge metal doors were pulled together and securely locked.

To his left was a tall structure that appeared to be a pillar of some type, constructed of a dark metal, similar in color to the metal that made up the construction of the spacecraft. It was taller than him by a head and was about four feet square. Stepping closer, Ben could tell that the box was the source of the faint humming and as leaned toward it, his open mind felt the probing fingers of the aliens and he knew he had found them. Ben spared one more brief thought for Ella and the kids and then returned his focus to the task at hand. As he watched, the box began to change color, just slightly, but enough for him to see that the walls were slowly and steadily becoming more and more transparent.

****

Ethan's shrill whooping wails resounded from the backseat of the car. The sudden din broke the Others from their trance of indecision. Ella held her breath as two Others dipped their heads inside the car, reaching for Ethan as the remaining four trotted to the other side of the car to pull Amos out. Ella cocked her head, a quizzical expression mixing with her fear. Amos hadn't said a word. He hadn't tried to jump out and run or reach for the gun to defend him and Ethan. From what she could see, he had sat there quietly beside Ethan the entire time waiting for the Others to take them.

****

There was a sudden screech of metal on metal as the door behind Ben was yanked open. The door was slammed back against the far wall with a loud crash and Ben turned and dropped into a slight crouch. The bright humming from the alien metal box escalated. Ben's head swung back and forth as he tried to keep his eyes on both the box and whoever was coming through the open door.

Tripping slightly over the raised threshold, Ella ground her teeth as she was shoved roughly through the open door. She held Ethan like a football, tucked face-up under one arm with his tiny head cradled in her palm and his bottom and legs wiggling free. Amos was one step behind Ella, one hand holding on to Ethan's bare foot. He didn't seem to notice Ben at all. He gaped wide eyed at the bug-like spacecraft, his mouth round with wonder.

"I told you to stay in the car." Ben spoke to Ella and took a few steps backward, trying to keep an eye on the alien pillar behind him.

"I got hungry." She quipped.

"Are you serious?"

"No." She rolled her eyes and stared hard at Ben, the sarcasm palpable in her tone. "These guys walked up and ripped the car door off the hinges."

"You didn't see them coming?"

"Stinkbaby distracted us." She shifted Ethan a little, his squishy diaper making a sound disturbingly like someone smacking their lips after a delicious meal.

During that entire exchange, Ben divided his focus between the transforming alien box and the group of Others. Two of them had blocked the doorway completely, which so far was the only way out of the hangar without going through a wall. Standing stiffly shoulder to shoulder, they formed a tight barrier behind his family. Ben swept the scene slowly with his eyes and tried to read the situation, looking for a way to get Ella and the boys away without anyone getting hurt. Ella's gaze remained on Ben and Amos' gaze stayed on the spaceship. The Others… Ben frowned. Was one of the Others Dan? Before he could open his mouth to ask Ella, Ben realized the Others weren't watching their hostages at all. All eyes were staring blankly beyond Ben at the shifting walls of the pillar-shaped box. Ben forced himself to turn and look.

The box was completely transparent. Faint shimmering lines of bright blue delineated the edges of the now structure-less box and the ghostly glow pulsed in and out like a heartbeat. There was a surreal moment as Ben finally laid eyes on the otherworldly aliens who had taken so much from him and were intent on destroying his world.

Five orbs, glowing with yellowish gray light levitated above five jet black pedestals. The tops of the pedestals were indented, rounded like a bowl, clearly designed to accept the perfectly round orbs. The orb closest to the front of the group levitated about a foot higher than the rest. It was a symbol of hierarchy so typically human that Ben had to wonder about this alien species. Human beings, strongly motivated by a pecking order, seek out superiors and inferiors and align themselves among them according to their perceived place in line. Were these aliens just as petty? Were they just as concerned about their status in their world and possibly in the universe? Since they had culled out the weak and the young and converted who they thought were the strongest on earth, it all made sense to Ben. They wanted a race of strong slaves who were hearty enough to do whatever it was they wanted them to do. And whatever it was they wanted the converted humans to do for them, he was certain it wouldn't end well for the planet.

On one level, Ben had to admire the race of aliens who had the intelligence and technology to make it all the way to earth and survive on what to them was a foreign planet. But on the other hand, it was his planet and his family and they had no right to come and take over and destroy everything. An image of his dad's face swam into his mind. Ben's heart clutched as he remembered his dad's final moments and the sad resignation in his eyes when his dad muttered, "I don't need to stay here anyway."

He wasn't altogether surprised when the main ball of light pulsed slightly and a string of thoughts appeared in his mind. Maybe because he was standing so close to them, or maybe they were just being kind for their own reasons, but the thoughts were not slammed into his brain like the other times. The thoughts settled like smoke near the front of his brain, slightly below his eyes. They made no sound and it couldn't even be described as him seeing words in his mind. The idea of what they were communicating to him was simply *there*.

"*Destroying you would be easy.*" The alien thought appeared.

"*Why haven't you done that already?*" Ben let them read his reply in his mind.

"*We want to know why you aren't like the others. Once we learn that, then we will destroy you.*"

Ben laughed. *"You guys really need to work on your negotiation and tact skills. So if you're going to kill me anyway, why should I tell you what you want to know? Why should I give you the satisfaction of knowing anything about me?"*

The reply was swift and cold and showed no mercy.

"Because if you don't tell us we will tear their minds apart to get the answers."

There was no doubt who they were referring to. Ben resisted the urge to turn and look at Ella and the kids. The anger inside was like a growing seed and he felt it pressing against his heart like the pea in the proverbial princess and the pea. It was the straightforward unfairness of it all that galled him. Because these aliens had the power to come to earth and take everything from everyone, they thought they had the right to do that.

Thinking of the implications of what the alien was sharing into his mind was horrific. If he gave them what they wanted, they would kill him and continue with their plan to enslave the world. That world included Ella and the boys. And if Ben didn't give them what they wanted, they would destroy Ella and the boys to get what they wanted and then they would kill him too. It was a no-win situation. But he had to win. There wasn't any other option for him. He just needed more time to think and to plan.

"Let them go and I'll give you want you want." Ben spoke out loud.

"No." The answer slid into his brain without a second of hesitation. *"Give us what we want and you will die but your death will be swift. And as long as she is caring for the young ones, the woman will live."*

Shaking his head at the ridiculousness of it all, Ben realized he had no leverage. He had nothing he could bargain with to try and save himself or his family. His mind threatened to shut down on itself and he considered not making any decision at all. But if he didn't give them what they wanted, they would make them all suffer. And he had no idea what kind of suffering they might inflict on Ella, Amos and Ethan. Ben struggled to keep his mind and his thoughts compartmentalized so the aliens couldn't simply read his mind and push past any plan he could come up with. He began searching for a way to throw up a barrier between his deeper thoughts and the place in the front of his mind where the aliens could access.

Numbers. Rows and rows of numbers began piling up in his mind. Random groups of twos and fours and there was no counting them, just numbers stacked one on top of the other, filling the space, filling his mind…

"Stop." The bright orb pulsed with a glow that was somehow deeper and more menacing.

Ben shrugged his shoulders and spoke. "Sorry. That's just how my mind works."

"Tell us what we want to know. Tell us what makes you Singular." The demand came again.

They weren't going to stop. Ben knew they didn't want anything else except to know why he was the way he was and how he had been able to resist them. It was clear their attempt to convert him had failed and they needed to know why. Ben could only play mind games with them for so long before their patience ended, so he had to think of something fast. One idea had been ghosting around the edges of his thoughts and had the slimmest, although the best chance of working, but he had immediately rejected each time it surfaced. It was too risky and if anything went wrong, then there was no way Ella or Amos would ever forgive him, and there was no way he could ever forgive himself in this world or in the next. Yet, there was nothing else he could do. It was the only way.

"I'll make you a deal." Ben said aloud and though his face was calm, the rapid rise and fall of his chest belied his true emotions. "Let us all go and I will give you the baby."

The scream that bellowed out of Ella was almost unhuman. "NO! You won't! What's wrong with you?!"

Ben kept his face turned toward the orbs and said, "The baby is mine. He's just like me. He knows what I know and can do what I can do. Take him. He's younger and stronger and instead of just knowing why we are Singular, you can cultivate his powers and use them for yourself."

"Why would you make this arrangement?" The orb asked and Ben sensed a small nugget of confusion in the thought.

"Because I know you'll kill the rest of us anyway. At least my baby will live a little while longer."

Ella's fierce curses battered at Ben's soul as he wrested Ethan away from her. Amos still hadn't said a word but tears of anger and hate filled his eyes and his small hands were clenched into tight fists, ready to do damage. Handing the baby to the nearest Other, Ben watched with careful interest as the Other grasped Ethan stiffly under his armpits, holding him away from him, with Ethan's tiny body with the sodden diaper dangling. The baby's dark brown eyes were open wide and moved from face to face and his mouth opened and closed as he looked curiously at the unfolding scene.

"Let me just change him." Ella said with tears pooling in her eyes. "He'll get a rash if I don't."

"No, he'll be fine. They'll figure out what to do." Ben's voice was quiet.

"Then let me just feed him one more time." She grabbed onto Ben's arm and her nails dug into his flesh but he didn't pull away. He deserved the pain.

Amos' mouth was set tight in a line and his body was shaking so hard that he looked like an electrified wire. The Other holding Ethan walked briskly toward the group of alien orbs but was quickly intercepted by the Other who used to be Dan. Pulling the baby roughly away from the Other, Dan moved to within a few inches of the orbs, then stopped and held Ethan out to them. Immediately, the five orbs began to glow. Ben could then see the differences in the colors that he hadn't been able to see before. The main orb was the brightest, almost a blinding white. The two just behind the main orb were pulsing the same yellowish gray as before, although much brighter with a golden tint. And in the back, the final two were pulsing a bright blue, almost the same color as the lines that delineated the orbs' containment space.

There were a few seconds when Ben almost made the decision to stay and watch what they would do with his son. Ethan's face was calm as he looked from the faces of the Others to the faces of his mom, dad and Amos. If the baby was in distress of any kind, he gave no indication. Ben dropped his gaze for a tortured moment, then facing Ella, he jerked his head lightly towards the door. The rage on her face was unmistakable and her eyes bored into his like a knife. But she grabbed onto Amos' trembling shoulder and moved silently with Ben. As they slipped unnoticed through the metal door out into the cooling night air, Ben glanced back into the hangar one last time and met his son's eyes.

THIRTY-ONE

The metal door clicked shut behind them with a quiet finality that made Ella twitch like she had been stung by a bee. With Ben's hand on her shoulder and her hand on Amos' shoulder, the three of them moved quickly away from the hangar toward the main entrance. The full moon had moved across the sky. Had that much time passed?

"We have to hurry." Ben said as Ella slowed down and started to turn.

"I hate you." Her words cut the air and sliced into Ben's heart.

"I know." He replied.

Ben pressed on her resistant shoulder and she guided Amos until they were half the distance to the security shack that marked the entrance to the old air base.

"Here." He turned abruptly and pressed them toward a small manufactured building that had seen better days. It had once been used as an office and a single door with an inset glass window graced the long front. Peering through the dust-covered window, Ben changed trajectory and instead pulled them behind him to the back of the building where another door greeted them. Unlike the one in the front, this one opened inward, so Ben slammed his shoulder into the flimsy door and the lock and frame cracked loudly under the pressure.

Herding Ella and Amos into the dark office, Ben yanked a small flashlight from his pocket and propped it on the windowsill. It wasn't strong enough to flood the room with light, but it was enough to keep them from bumping into the furniture and each other.

The office was larger inside than it looked from the outside. In addition to having a large metal desk at one end, the decades-old furnishings included a long rectangular table with six chairs. Pushed against one wall was a low, cloth covered couch that had long ago succumbed to the dust and disuse and looked as if it might fall into itself with the slightest touch. Ben took stock of the rest of the room and while Amos and Ella simply stood in place and watched him. Three long strides took him to the front door where he flipped the lock, leaving it unlocked. Then he dragged two old metal chairs to the middle of the room and then gestured with his hand.

"Sit." He commanded and turned to drag a third chair to the middle of the room, positioning the three of them away from the confines of the long table.

The hurt that fought with the fury on the faces of Ella and Amos made it difficult for Ben to think clearly. They had been through so much together and seeing the distrust and even hatred for him in their eyes nearly brought him to his knees. He tried his best to calm his breathing and focus his mind on what he had to say.

"We don't have much time." He leaned toward Ella as he spoke. "They'll come looking for us soon."

"You gave them my baby." Ella's voice was cold. "*Our* baby."

"Yes." His words were cool and measured. "I gave them our baby. And I gave us a chance to fight them and win."

Ella's head dropped momentarily and Ben was glad for a chance to avoid the look in her eyes even if it was for a second.

"If they hurt him, I'll never forgive you." Her head lifted again and her dark eyes pierced deep into his soul.

Ben shook his head. "They won't hurt him. Not until they find out what he can do. And that's what will buy us some time. Not much time, but enough."

Ella closed her eyes and sighed and the sound was full of loss and pain. He understood the depth of her pain and he was dying inside right along with her. But underneath it all, Ben was just as sure that she should have trusted him more. Why would she ever think leaving their son with the aliens was easy for him? He struggled within himself at the anger that was building but he shook his head against it. It was selfish of him to think that she would know what was going on in his mind. But ever since Ethan had been conceived, she had been able to know. For half a second he paused to wonder when and why their mind connection had stopped. A sudden chill hit his as he realized it had stopped at the moment he turned Ethan over to the alien orbs. Ben's unfocused eyes retrained on Ella just in time to see her eyes open and settle on him again.

Her right hand flew out before Ben could even blink. The slap on his cheek was loud in the stillness of the room and his head rocked to one side from the force of the blow.

"How dare you gamble with my baby's life." Her face was livid and Ben saw Amos flinch in surprise.

Ben gritted his teeth and worked to hold down his anger. He knew how it looked when he gave Ethan to the aliens and he had hoped Ella would understand. He had hoped she would know he would never do anything to hurt her or the boys. Her maternal instincts were strong and he supposed that was a good thing. It would make her a good mother. But right then he needed her to be less of a mother.

"It's not a gamble. I know what I'm doing."

Ella gave a toss of her head that let him know she was also trying to keep her anger in check. Her thick hair had been pulled back into a high ponytail and she looked part child, part adult and he nearly cried with love for her. "You'd better know what you're doing, Ben. Because if they hurt my son..." Her words choked off at the same time a strangled cry came from Amos who threw himself into her arms and hugged her tight.

"Please." Ben reached out to stroke her hair and was grateful she didn't pull away. "Please trust me."

From where his head was buried in Ella's stomach, a strangled sob escaped Amos' lips. Ben agonized over how much ground he had lost with him. All the time they had spent getting to know each other and coming to trust each other was gone in an instant. Ben rubbed his damp palms along the leg of his jeans and forced himself to tug lightly on Amos' arm. The boy resisted and burrowed his face deeper against Ella, his sobs growing and his shoulders hitching with anguish.

"We don't have much time." Ben repeated and at the sternness in his voice, Amos' cries lessened and Ella gave him a light nudge away from her.

"Let's hear what he has to say." Ella gave Ben a slight nod and tipped up her chin, facing him squarely.

"First, let me ask you. Did you see how the Others seemed to not want to touch Ethan?" Ben asked and they both blinked, their minds not yet ready to move beyond losing Ethan or considering what might be happening to him. "Think." Ben prompted and Ella stared down at the dusty floor while Amos cocked his head and continued to look at Ben.

"In the car." Amos' voice drifted up. "They didn't like the way he smelled."

"That's right." Ella agreed. "I saw them flinch like they had been slapped in the face when they first reached in for Ethan."

Ben blinked with relief. They were both thinking and talking and that would make all the difference when the time came.

Ella nodded and turned a palm up to Ben. "Remember? They didn't seem to want to hold him or touch him even when you said to... take him." Her voice choked on her words but she continued. "They took him because they had to – they didn't have a choice. But you could tell they really didn't want to."

"So much of what the aliens have done involved some type of odor." Ben cocked out his thumb and began to count. "Remember the smell in the basement?" At her nod, he continued. "The smell when we got close to the gas station and how it smelled when it exploded? I think that strong odor reminds the Others of the aliens and the control they have over them. So any strong smell affects them. And I think strong scents must mean something important to the aliens as well and they may have thought Ethan's smell had something to do with him being special. That's why I didn't want you to change Ethan's diaper or clean him up. His strong smell confused them and it's probably why the aliens agreed to my deal."

Amos had finally pulled himself away from Ella and was poking with a finger desolately at his dirty shoelaces. He was still mad at Ben for leaving his little brother with those bad men who tried to hurt them. The conversation about the aliens and the smells was important to Ben and Ella; Amos could see they were excited about it. But his thoughts kept returning to the huge spaceship and his tiny brother in that hangar. Amos pushed to his feet and stepped over to the couch, giving the dusty arm a sound thwack! The amount of dust that flew into the air caused him to hop back and wave a hand in front of his face to clear the air.

"Take it easy there." Ben spoke softly. "I think the only thing holding that couch together is the dust."

Amos' lips began to lift in a smile, but then he remembered he was still mad at Ben so he pressed his lips together and only nodded.

Ella mouthed to Ben, too quietly for Amos to hear. "He'll be fine. He just needs some time."

"I'm sorry." Ben said aloud.

The apology was for so many things that Ben was glad Ella didn't ask him what he was apologizing for. He wasn't sure he would've been able to give her an answer that made any sense. He was sorry for meeting her and falling in love with her and for dragging her into his life. But at the same time, he wasn't sorry for any of that. He wanted her in his life for however much longer that was. It was selfish as hell, but it was the truth.

Ella shifted a little and then moved her chair closer to Ben. He didn't hesitate to encircle her waist with an arm. The feel of her was soft and comforting and Ben never wanted to leave her embrace.

"We need to come up with some kind of a plan." Ben ran a hand wearily through his dark hair.

When Amos moved over and sat tentatively on Ben's knee, the shock of that intimate gesture almost knocked him over. The young boy's breathing was rapid and it was clear he was extremely nervous.

"What's going on? Are you okay?" Ella reached a hand down and laid it on Amos' knee, hoping to still his slight trembling.

"Yeah. I'm okay. But…" He hesitated.

The sound of footsteps approaching the building from the front reached their ears. The steady footfalls were like the ticking of a clock. They were out of time.

Amos jumped up, his eyes fastened on Ben. "Wait. I have an idea."

By the time the footsteps were directly outside, they were ready. Ben stood up and pushed opened the door.

"Let's go." The deep hollow voice of the Other standing on the threshold made the skin on Ella's arms stand on end.

Ben and Ella stepped forward but the Other stayed where he was and didn't move to let them pass. "Where's the boy?"

Ben shook his head. "Gone. We sent him away and told him to run until he couldn't run anymore and not to ever look back."

"We'll find him."

"Maybe." Ben locked eyes with the Other who made no attempt to touch him or pull him forward. It was Dan. Whether the man remembered the confrontation with Ben in the woods or not, it didn't seem to matter. Dan looked at them with cold eyes and Ben could also see that the Other knew there was no need to take them by force. Why should he? Ben and Ella never intended to run.

"Let's go." Dan said again and without another word, stepped back. They walked out of the door and with Ella in the lead, they made their way back to the hangar.

****

When everything was quiet and he thought he might choke to death from breathing in the dry dusty fibers, Amos pushed up the moldy couch cushions. He sneezed twice as he crawled from his musty hiding place and then raced for the back door.

THIRTY-TWO

Once outside, Amos followed a path tight against the side of manufactured building and as close to Ben and Ella as he dared. His eyes darted left and right as he pressed his back against the cool metal of the building. He knew he could outrun the Others if they spied him. But if they grabbed him, he wasn't sure he could fight his way free of them. They had proved to be much stronger than any of them had realized. Amos frowned at the memory of them ripping open the car door and flinging it to the ground like it was nothing more than a kid's toy. A sudden *clang* off to his left made him jump and then hunker down into a tight crouch.

"Stop that." The Other hissed viciously at Ben.

Kicking at rocks and pieces of metal that lay strewn along their path, Ben wanted to make sure Amos knew where they were and how far to keep his distance. It was a lot of responsibility he and Ella had placed on the young boy but when Amos had presented the plan to them, he had begged them to let him do it. Ella had squeezed Amos so tight Ben was afraid she might break one of his ribs. Amos had wriggled free and nodded his head vigorously up and down and looked Ben square in the eye. He would do it and he would do it right. Amos loved his baby brother so much, he would do anything for him, even risk his own life. Ben prayed the plan would work and it would never come to that.

Ella was quiet. She hoped with all her heart that Ethan was fine, but the fear in her gut was eating her alive. If Ethan was hurt or dead… She shook her head vigorously back and forth and Ben caught the motion and reached for her hand. She didn't speak or look at him, but she grasped his fingers tightly and to his incredulous surprise, he heard her begin to sing softly. *"Take my hand, baby. Take my hand. We can go on like this forever if you take my hand…"*

The walk back to the hangar didn't take long. Stepping through the doorway into the dim light of the large open room, Ben heard Ella pull in a sharp breath and his stomach dropped to the floor. The adrenaline pounded through his body and he pulled back on Ella's hand, yanking her behind him.

The glowing orbs were still suspended over the five black pillars and the perimeter box that surrounded them was still translucent. The blue outline still there, but the brightness of it, and the brightness of the orbs seemed lighter, *diminished* somehow. Ben and Ella were both close enough to touch the edges of the barrier but neither of them tried. They stared straight ahead and tried to comprehend what they were seeing.

Their days old baby lay on his back, suspended in the middle of the five orbs. He hovered about five feet above the ground and his baby blue onesie and his dirty diaper had been removed. His body was rotating slowly and gently in a circle and from side to side. There were faint blue lines leading from the orbs to his body; some of which held him up and some of them were certainly probing and scanning his little body and mind. As his back end rotated toward them, they could see dark, crusty stains on his bottom and a slight pinkness on the edges that could be easily identified as the beginnings of diaper rash.

"Couldn't they at least clean him up?" Ella sent the distressed thought into Ben's mind. As soon as her thought entered Ben's mind, Ethan's body jerked and he began twitching, trying to roll his body around to face them. As he struggled, the blue lines of light that held him up grew darker and the lines of light that probed him grew dimmer. When the baby was finally rotated in a position to see Ella and Ben, his dark eyes rounded and his chubby hands reached for his mother. As his tiny mouth opened, they expected to hear him cry out. But they heard nothing even though it was clear he was exerting himself and crying to be heard. The protective box was keeping in all sounds and Ben and Ella could only watch and yearn to hold him.

His arms waved and reached for them, but if he was in any distress, his face didn't show it. Ethan's gummy smile was broad and happy and Ella choked back a sob. She wanted nothing more than to rush beyond the blue rimmed barrier and snatch her child from them and run for the exit and never stop running until she felt safe.

"Don't even think it." Ben's voice wasn't loud in her mind, but it was firm.

Ella's shoulders slumped slightly at his command. But through her disappointment, her eyes never left Ethan's as she blew him kisses with her fingers and gave him her biggest smile.

"What makes you Singular?" The alien's question popped into Ben's head like an oily dark bubble.

"Why don't you know that already?" Ben dodged their question with his own.

He truly had no idea why he was Singular and it did make him wonder why with so much power to do so many things, the aliens hadn't been able to figure that out. He tried his best not to recall memories from his childhood that even then had seemed more than odd to him. He didn't want the aliens to accidently get more information than he wanted to give them. But there were all those experiences he had that his father admonished him to ignore or forget. At the time, Ben hadn't really wanted to remember them so he dutifully pushed the strange thoughts and dreams away and tried to act as if everything in his life and in his mind was okay. But even then, he knew he was different. At times, when Ben was overly upset or angry, his thoughts seemed to push beyond the thin membrane of his mind and his dad would frown over at him and rub a thumb across his forehead as if a headache was forming. Was he pushing thoughts into his dad's mind even then?

"It's not good to be so different." His dad had said after one episode when he had pushed an angry thought out of his mind and into what he had thought was simply the air. "Being a little different is ok. But there is a limit that shouldn't be crossed. You need to make sure you find that line, and once you find it, make sure you never cross it."

Had his dad known something that couldn't be explained to a seven year old?

"The world isn't a forgiving place," He had said and placed a rough hand on his son's cheek. "But you still have to find a way to live in this world until you die."

As Ben tried to keep the aliens from probing too far into his mind to gain this bit of information, he realized that he was getting better at compartmentalizing his thoughts. He smoothly raised a mental wall between the conversation he was having with the aliens and the thoughts circulating in the deeper part of his brain.

"I need to know why you're here." He sent to the aliens. *"If you can help me understand what you want then maybe I can make this easier for both of us."* He bluffed.

Immediately, he felt the aliens snatch greedily at his words and the feeling was a nauseating sort of *sucking*. But he needed to keep them preoccupied for a while longer.

"We are the ones who have come for this time." The answer from the aliens was cryptic but Ben still understood. Their goal was simple. They had come for his planet and his world.

"Well, guys. I think you came here too early." Ben sent this with a slight sneer. *"I'm still alive. Why didn't you wait until I had died of old age? It would have been much easier for you then."*

The question was a silly one when Ben thought about it, but it was the first thing that came to his mind. And since he was only buying time to learn as much as he could from them, the question was as good as any.

Ben glanced over at Ella. She was still smiling and making faces at the wiggling baby. As he looked back at Ethan, Ben noticed that the blue lines of the barrier box became fainter as his parrying with the aliens continued. The effort and power it took to maintain a conversation with Ben was clearly pulling power away from the barrier. With some relief, Ben could see that for now, the blue lines holding Ethan up were still dark and strong. Finally, he was able to see something that he might be able to use. They were more interested in keeping Ethan aloft and trying to get their answers from Ben than they were maintaining their barrier. Ben narrowed his eyes slightly and decided he would try something. He prayed he wouldn't make a mistake that might hurt Ethan or himself. But in his gut he was almost sure of what would happen. Even so, he readied himself for any other possibility. But before he could test out this idea, a new thought popped into his mind.

"There's always a Singular." The alien voice crawled into his brain and Ben recoiled as if had been shot with a rifle.

A dim memory slammed into his mind and nearly doubled Ben over. He should have made the connection before. He should have known. Everything that made him different had shown up only after his mom died. He had thought it was due to missing her or to his deep grief, but with one statement – *there's always a Singular* - he knew that wasn't the truth of it at all.

His mother had been Singular. She had been the one who would have been standing right where he was standing if she hadn't been taken away from them by the cancer. When she had finally taken her last breath and slipped from this world to the next, Ben had become the Singular. His dad must have known something. They had lived as a couple for almost seven years before she died. Ben's eyes were bright with understanding as he realized that was the reason his dad was always trying to get him to keep his anger, which was his power, in check.

"How many ships are there on our planet? How many Others did you make?" Ben threw out more meaningless questions while safely in the back of his mind, he tried to put all the pieces together. Once he was gone, would Ethan become the new Singular? He struggled with the thought that if he could defeat the aliens, here and now, why would there be a need for another Singular?

"We took all the strong ones and destroyed the weak ones." The alien voice was cold and remorseless. *"We have all the ships we need to complete our work here."*

With a boldness that surprised even him, Ben sent the thought, *"What if you don't complete your work on this planet? What if I stop you?"*

"Even if you defeat us, others with come." The answer flew back so quickly that Ben was momentarily stunned silent.

But he had his answer. He knew why the line of Singulars had to remain unbroken. Ben raked a hand through this hair and fought down the anguish. He might fight the battle that day and win, but Ethan may have to face the same enemy in his time.

"Tell us why you are Singular!" That time the thought didn't simply appear in Ben's mind, it blasted its way through with a force that tore painfully at the back of his eyes and nearly knocked him backward.

Ben clamped down with his teeth and his eyes blazed with fire. Before he had a second to think about what he was doing, his mind *shoved* back a wordless curse at the alien invasion reverberating in his skull. The response from the alien orbs was instantaneous as the bright orbs dimmed and all the blue lines – even the ones holding up Ethan – became fainter and weaker. Glancing over at Ella, Ben saw her dark eyebrows lift but she didn't make a move. She stared at Ethan and the faint blue lines and she watched intently as his small wiggling body began to sink slowly toward the floor. In the instant before the baby's body touched the concrete floor, the remaining blue lines that made up the barrier also disappeared. With a quick jump, Ella leaped into the middle of the black pillars, ignoring Ben's grasping hands and ignoring the faintly glowing orbs and grabbed for Ethan.

Just as her son was safely in her arms, his tiny head wedged under her chin, the taller of the two Others - Ben - snatched Ethan roughly from her and Ella reacted in fury.

"Give him back to me, you monster!" She yelled and lunged at the Other and for Ethan.

The second Other grabbed for her arm and his fingertips were just brushing the fabric of her shirt when Ben's anger rushed into him again. Ben darted like a cobra at the creature. He hit him square on the chin and Ben felt an instant of excruciating pain as his fist connected with bone. The snap as the Other's bottom teeth cracked into his top teeth was like the snap of a finger magnified a hundredfold. The creature's head flew back, he staggered a couple of steps and then…stopped. When the Other slowly regained his balance and brought its face level with Ben's, the blank stare in its eyes had been replaced by a red, malevolent rage. Ella shrank back, rubbing at her arm where angry bruises were already forming.

The Other advanced on Ben and he clenched his fists, his nails digging into the flesh of his palms. He couldn't believe how quickly things had turned and he stood locked in position, fists raised as the Other stalked toward him.

"NO."

When Ella blinked and her eyes widened in surprise, Ben knew the alien orbs had spoken the first audible word.

Abruptly, the Other halted and the murderous glow in his eyes puffed out like a candle, replaced once again by the blank stare.

"Come inside with us and we will make the small one safe." The alien thought settled into his mind.

Ben nearly screamed with disappointment. Why had he ever thought he was in control? Could he really have thought he had found a weakness in them? His head pounded with frustration. Ben had known Ethan wasn't the one they wanted and it was clear they were done with him and ready to use their blue probes on him.

"Fine. Let Ella take him and go." Ben said aloud. He reached for Ethan and Ethan reached for him.

"NO. HE WILL REMAIN WITH US UNTIL WE ARE FINISHED." The loud voice emanating from the alien orb was somehow worse than having them inside his head. At least in his head, Ben could spare Ella from his failure. Ben felt Ella's tears drop on his arm and with each drop, Ben's heart sank further and further.

"Okay. Show me where you're taking him. Show me that he'll be safe and then I'll come in and we'll chat." Ben said. He sighed and wrapped an arm around Ella's shoulder, pulling her close. He could see she was fighting back tears of anger and her body was thrumming like a live wire against his chest.

Only one second passed before the Others began walking across the hangar toward the gaping open door of the huge spacecraft. Ben and Ella followed directly behind them. Ethan rested stiffly in Dan's arms and his bright, dark eyes peered back at them over his shoulder. Ella's eyes glistened with tears that she continued to blink back as she kept her wide smile in place. Ben tried not to look at his son. He didn't know what fate he was leading him into and the fear and guilt was a cold knot in his heart.

As Dan's feet stamped up the dark metal ramp that led into the spacecraft, Ethan's head swiveled around to the front and a tiny gurgle escaped his lips as he peered inside. Ben wanted to be happy hearing that familiar sound from his son, but his heart was pounding so hard in his chest he could barely breathe. He knew in an instant what they would see once they got inside the ship.

Everything was gray. The walls were gray, the ceiling was gray, and the floor was gray. No, that wasn't quite right. Everything was silver. There was a light sheen to everything, a reflectiveness that let Ben know that he wasn't looking at gray paint, he was looking at silver metal.

It would be just like in his dream.

They entered the wide door and the temperature dropped five degrees. The sudden chill pebbled Ethan's bare arms and legs and fresh tears leaked from Ella's eyes. She made no move to wipe them away. The wide entryway narrowed to a single doorway set into an eight-foot high metal wall. Stepping through the doorway into the silver room, the Other deposited Ethan gracelessly on the cold floor. Ella huffed loudly and jerked out from under Ben's arm.

"You can't be serious? He's just a baby. You can't just dump him here like that! And he's naked. Where are his clothes?" Ella fussed at the Others like they were small children but their blank eyes registered neither her words nor her emotion.

Seeing that they made no move to do anything in response to her cries, Ella quickly unbuttoned her long sleeved shirt, leaving her in only her fitted, dark tank top. Bunching the shirt in her hands, she laid it on the floor and lifted Ethan onto it, draping the sleeves around his bare hips and tummy. Running her index finger softly along his check, Ethan cooed and stretched out a chubby hand for her. Before she could make another move, Dan quickly latched onto her arm and dragged her up from the floor.

"Quit it!" She growled.

Ella yanked her arm away and dropped back to her knees and grabbed Ethan's face in her hands. Ben took two steps toward the Other whose chin was already sprouting a bright red knot from Ben's punch. The Other took two quick steps backward.

As Ella kissed Ethan's soft skin, she whispered in his ear. "We'll be back for you before you know it, my sweet." Boldly turning her back on her baby, she walked toward the door leading from the silver room.

"Let's go and get this done." She hissed and Ben and the Others trailed behind her.

Taking his place in the midst of the glowing orbs, Ben mouthed the words to Ella. "I'm sorry."

Her chin quivered as she lifted her head and blinked back angry tears. *"Just come back to me."* She sent the thought into his mind and the softness and mercy in her thought bloomed in his heart like a rose.

As the faint blue lines leading from the orbs grew darker and stronger and reached out toward him, Ben tried his best to relax and prepare his mind. He continued to keep the mental barrier intact and he closed his eyes in concentration. His thoughts were still for one brief moment and then he heard a sound filtering through. He cocked his head to one side. It wasn't a thought being pressed into his mind, but a sound. A normal human sound. And it sounded like singing.

****

Outside in the darkness, Amos slipped around the far side of the large hangar. He could hear a sound in his head, a faint humming, a faint tune. He didn't know for sure where it was coming from, but tears sprang to his eyes. It was a song he knew by heart.

"Take my hand, baby. Take my hand. We can go on like this forever if you take my hand..."

THIRTY-THREE

As Ben stood on the hard concrete floor in the middle of the blue lined barrier surrounded by the five glowing orbs, his eyes closed and his head swam with thoughts and visions that were not his own. Although he didn't try to force his eyes open to see her, Ben was aware of Ella staring at him. Her eyes were locked on him and her fingers clutched at her bare arms. He could still hear the faint hum of the song that came from her mind to his, but he shut it out completely as he felt the first fingers of the probes reaching into his mind.

The image they were projecting into his brain was of the silver room where his son lay cold and alone. The room was the same as in his dream of nights before; a large, silver, perfect square. Ben's eyes rolled back and forth behind his eyelids as he finally spied the glowing red dot pulsating from a spot high along one wall. The fear that shot through him was brief before he pushed it down, trying to focus. This time however, different from in the dream, the small square box mounted on the far wall wasn't the only one. In the front part of his brain, Ben felt a dizzying feeling of vertigo as the alien image rotated around like a camera. He could then see that there were boxes with glowing red dots positioned high on each of the four walls and one affixed to the ceiling. The feeling of dark malevolence he had felt so strongly in his dream came over him again and with it came an even more painful realization.

If he didn't give them what they wanted, the red lasers would flash out and slice his son to pieces.

Ben felt a searing phantom pain as the memory of the dream became nearly real to him. He squeezed his eyes tight against the anger and fear of what he had led his family into and just as he thought he might lift his head and shriek out loud, the alien voice blasted into his brain like a firestorm.

"YOU ARE TOO WEAK TO WIN!"

The attack seemed to come from all directions and Ben realized that all five of the alien orbs were forcing their words of defeat into his mind. He couldn't see her or hear her, but he felt the Ella's thoughts competing with the aliens; pushing and singing her sound into his head.

"Take my hand, baby. Take my hand. We can go on like this forever if you take my hand..."

The feeling of being probed and violated by the glowing orbs was getting stronger and soon they would ram past all his weak barriers and know what he knew. They would know he had no idea why he was Singular and no idea what he could do and how he could stop them. Then they would kill him and his family. And there was nothing he could do. The feeling of hopelessness began to spread through him as he felt them coldly jabbing into his brain, sifting his thoughts and searching...searching...

****

Outside the hangar, in the inky darkness, Amos tucked his body into a tight corner where the square metal drainpipe met the wall of the metal building. He didn't know what to do. Ben and Ella had said they would send him a signal of some kind to tell him what to do when the time came. But he hadn't heard anything or seen anything that could be considered a signal. Amos considered simply running inside and doing something. But what? The idea that he might get them killed – get his baby brother Ethan killed – rooted him to the spot with fear. He needed to wait. From the moment Ethan was born, Amos saw him as his brother. He loved Ethan in a way that surprised and frightened him sometimes. He had loved his dad and his mom. But thinking of them and of what his dad had done to his mom chewed at his gut like a thousand tiny knives and his heart and mind constricted with agony. He tried not to let the grief overwhelm him. He had to stay in control like Ben had taught him and not let his thoughts run loose. But he missed them both so much. Amos dropped his head for a split second and let his last happy memory of his mother enter his mind.

****

A blackness like a cloying fog blanketed Ben's mind as the multiple assaults on his consciousness continued. He was sure he was going insane and his mind was whirling frantically trying to stop the aliens from unearthing his secret. And in the midst of all his struggles, Ella was…singing. She was singing his song into his head and for an instant he wanted to hurl back the thought, "*Stop it!*" before he completely lost his mind. His head screamed with pain as he forced himself not to think of Ella or Amos and where he might be.

"*Outside.*" It was a whisper that came and went like a soft wind. Even as soft as it was, Ben's mind clicked with trepidation when the tall Other that he had clipped on the chin suddenly left his place with an abrupt turn. Ella's eyes followed the creature and hugged her arms around her even tighter. The Other was heading for the door on the far side of the hangar. The one partially hidden by the large spacecraft. The one Amos had been keen enough to spy earlier on their way out.

Ben closed his eyes. It was too much. It would only be a matter of minutes before the Other found Amos on the other side of that door. The plan had been so flimsy but it was all they had, and now it was all going to be over and Ben's stomach knotted in fear for Amos. Ben was so weary. He felt as if he were being ceaselessly herded into a hard corner, and he ached for a few seconds of peace. That was all. Just a few seconds. Ben decided to let his mind accept the sound of Ella's sweet melody and the familiar words. He drew a last bit of strength from his song, written all those years ago – the same song Amos had been singing the night before. A sense of calmness and love for Ella overtook Ben at her attempt to comfort him with something from his past. And while one layer of his brain still resisted and tried to repel the alien thoughts, Ben was able to let himself be soothed by the words of the familiar song.

"*Take my hand, baby. Take my hand. We can go into the silver ship, we can go on into the silver room if you take my hand…*"

In the dim recesses of his mind, Ben listened to the song. Something was wrong. The words to the song were close, but they were still…wrong. There had been nothing in his song about a silver ship…

"HAH!" The laugh exploded out of Ben, and as it did, the probing in his brain lessened a little and in that instant, he gathered all the strength he had left and hurled a thought into Amos' mind like a stone.

Ella had no idea at first if her thoughts had made it through to Ben. But then she saw his eyes and his mouth fly open wide. Even though she couldn't hear his words though the alien barrier, it looked to her exactly like a victory yell.

As the force of the word propelled out of his mouth, Ella felt a hot rush of air pushing at her body and it rocked her back on her heels. She stole a glance behind her at Dan and she was amazed to see that he too, was recovering from whatever shockwave had been created by Ben's yell. Ella fought to stay on her feet and fought to keep her mind clear. Amos' plan had to work. It had to. Replaying the tune over and over, she filled her mind with the melody and with Ben's words,

"Take my hand, baby. Take my hand. We can go on like this forever if you take my hand…"

****

The darkness should have been a good cover for Amos in his narrow hiding place beside the drain pipe. He was a small kid and it was a large pipe, but the metal door was squeaking open and he knew even before he saw the figure step outside that it was an Other. Amos held his breath and even tried to still his beating heart. The Other strode through the doorway, its face eerily illuminated by the dim solar powered bulb over the door. Hot tears sprang to Amos' eyes as he mentally kicked himself. If he hadn't given in and opened his mind to think of his mom, the Other would never have known he was there. Ben and Ella were counting on him. It had been his plan and his idea and he couldn't believe he would be the one to ruin it. As the Other shuffled toward the top step of the small landing, Amos let his eyes roll to his left, searching for a place to run if the Other spied him. Just as Amos' eyes shifted back to the right after seeing nothing except a blank wall and dark shadows, two things happened at once.

His mother's song – Ben's song - the one that had soothed him to sleep on so many nights, shot into his mind with the speed of a bullet and the force of it nearly toppled him over. The melody and the words reverberated through his skull and made him so dizzy he thought he might vomit. *"Take my hand, baby. Take my hand. We can go into the silver ship, we can go on into the silver room if you take my hand…"*

At the same instant as the song rocketed into Amos' brain, the Other jerked violently and his body bulged forward as if he had been hit from behind by a cannon ball. The creature pitched forward, snapping over at the waist like he was bowing to an adoring crowd. The Other might have recovered, but as he lurched forward, the left side of his head clipped the edge of the thick metal stair railing. The clang of bone on metal reverberated loudly in the stillness of the night. The Other jerked up reflexively, but then his strength left abruptly and he sagged down, tumbling over the three steps and landing face-first onto the pavement. His head and body hit the solid ground with a meaty thud.

Blinking in stunned surprise, Amos still seized the opportunity and ran from his hiding place, scrambling up the uneven wooden stairs. He ducked his head, trying not to look too closely at the Other splayed on the ground with a widening pool of blood spreading beneath his head. The young boy slipped through the open door and froze in his tracks.

The dark alien spaceship loomed before him much closer and larger than he remembered. His head pivoted from side to side, trying to take in the magnitude and the size of the ship. It seemed even bigger than the hangar itself and his young mind grappled to comprehend the inconsistency. But the familiar song still echoed in his mind and drew him onward to the silver ship. He knew the silver room had to be in there and he knew he would find his brother there. He would find Ethan.

****

The strength of Ben's shout had caught the aliens off guard, but he no longer put any trust in the strength of the blue lines. They had begun to flicker from light to dark like an old fluorescent bulb. Ben had seen Ella and the Others stagger back when he yelled out and at the moment he shoved the song into Amos' head. There was no point wondering if the message had been sent; the looks of confusion on their faces was his proof. Ben also had to trust that he had learned how to target his thoughts well enough that only Amos heard what he had pitched so rudely into his young mind. He hoped Amos would forgive him for slamming the words in so hard, but Ben didn't have time to be gentle.

If the aliens did somehow sense what message Ben sent to Amos, then Amos would be walking into a trap and there was nothing Ben could do. Turning his mind back to the probing that was becoming more insistent, Ben thought he might be able to plant a distraction seed in the front part of his mind. Something the alien orbs might grasp at and give Amos a better chance to finish his task. The blue lines probing his body still flickered and Ben hesitated, waiting to find out what their next move would be. Was it even possible to counter them or outsmart them? He was the Singular after all. Didn't that mean something? To his relief, the mental pressure from the aliens had lessened and he was able to take in a deep breath.

Seconds ticked by and the blue lines flickered as the alien orbs seemed to be trying to regain their balance. A thought clicked into place. Were they afraid now to push too hard at Ben? Was it was possible that they truly didn't have the power to destroy him like they threatened? Lifting his head and locking eyes with Ella, Ben prepared to send a thought into her mind. The feeling of having hurt them in some way was strong and he wanted to communicate that to Ella. To prepare her. Warn her that what he would do next was another gamble. Hopefully calculated to win, but a gamble nonetheless. His plan was to recreate the hard push one more time and find out what his mind really could do. Hope soared in his chest.

"Tell us what makes you Singular."

Was the thought placed in his mind actually weaker? Without waiting to make sure Ella knew what was coming, Ben sucked in a deep breath and readied his mind to push with a fervor even greater than the last time. And this time, he would target his missile into the mind of the alien. A surge of adrenaline

204

coursed through him as his mind began to open. But in the split second before he dropped the barrier in his mind and prepared to hurl the thought at the orbs, his eyes widened.

A bright blue light, more blindingly intense than anything Ben had ever witnessed, shot out and of all five of the orbs at once. The individual beams were no thicker than a pencil but they flashed together and converged at a point about two feet beyond the blue lined box. It didn't take more than a half-second for Ben to realize what was about to happen and he tried to scream but his throat locked with fear and anguish as he saw the combined beams reach their target.

Ella had been watching everything with wide eyes. She knew even before the beam hit her that it was intended for her but there was still no time for her to run or move or drop out of the way. The bright beam slammed into Ella's chest and brilliant stars of pain exploded through her.

THIRTY-FOUR

Ella's body rocketed backward from the force of the laser's impact. She would have crashed onto the hard concrete floor if she hadn't been flung into the Dan who was standing behind her. It was a miracle he didn't simply let her drop to the floor. He didn't owe her anything and his transformation had robbed him of what human compassion he had left. But in his surprise, he grabbed her as she sagged nearly to the ground.

Surrounded by the black pillars and the glowing orbs, Ben stared with fury as Ella's head lolled down onto her chest. He didn't see any blood, but he knew by the look of her that she was hurting. Knowing that it was his fault, his stupid delaying tactic, that caused them to attack her, nearly broke him.

In the instant Ben let down his guard, almost succumbing to his grief and guilt, the alien orbs took advantage of his weakness and renewed their assault on his battered brain.

"Tell us why you are Singular!"

Lifting his pounding head, Ben nearly blurted out the truth. He nearly told them everything. He almost told them that he had no idea what made him Singular. The hurt and the guilt added to his frustration of not knowing what was happening with Ethan and Amos. Why not tell them the truth and let them destroy him? It might be the only way to give Ethan a chance to save them where Ben had failed. It wasn't what he wanted and it wasn't the way he thought things were going to work out, but he couldn't let them hurt his family any longer.

He looked up sadly at Ella, his decision made. Ben smiled a defeated smile that didn't hold even a portion of the sorrow he felt deep in his soul. He had failed her. He had failed his family and he had failed the world.

Ben had never wanted to be the savior of anything. Yet the feeling of being special - unique in some way - had been a godsend for him. For a few short weeks he was more than just Ben Richardson. He had risen above being simply a warehouse worker who clawed against jamming a cigarette in his mouth every fifteen minutes. And the clarity of mind that came from continually focusing on what his next move would be had helped to ease his feelings of grief and sorrow and loss. His mom was long gone, but the loss of his dad was still fresh. But he had a new focus – a new goal. Keeping his new family safe had been his only goal. Giving up wasn't his way, but it seemed there was no other way left to him.

His mind began to slowly unblock the wall he had created to hide the pathetic truth. The truth that he might have been Singular, but he was also powerless and weak and he never had a chance to defeat them. Ben expected to see the hurt from his failure tattooed on her face. He held his breath and readied himself for it. But as she looked into his eyes, her pained expression softened and she thrust out her narrow chin and shook her head at him.

"Don't." She sent the thought to him like a piercing arrow.

Ben wanted to tell her no. He wanted to tell her that he loved her and Amos and Ethan and he was sorry for everything and he wanted to tell the aliens the truth and let it all be done. He wanted it to be over and he was afraid of what they were doing to his son. He was afraid he had made a huge mistake. But she kept shaking her head.

"Don't."

Ben clamped his jaw tight. The shake of her head told him his choices were no longer his own. From the moment that seemed so long ago yet was also like the blink of an eye to him, their lives and their future were intertwined. Every decision he made affected more than just himself and that responsibility weighted on his shoulders like a millstone. What Ben wanted to do was end it all. Actually, that wasn't a hundred percent true. What he really wanted was one last cigarette. The craving to feel the burn as the nicotine hit his tongue and taste the bitter smoke as it was pulled down into his lungs was stronger than it had ever been. Then after the cigarette? Then he would let them end it all. But Ella didn't want to give up. She wanted to fight and she wanted Ben to keep fighting.

Ben looked at his wife. Then from somewhere low in his gut, he dredged up enough strength to give her what she wanted. What she needed. He carefully began to rebuild the barriers in his mind and at the same time, began crafting a complex subterfuge of lies for the insistent aliens to feed on.

****

From his low vantage point on the opposite side of the hangar, Amos could barely see the box with the blue border and the five orbs inside. From that distance, Ben's face was a fuzzy mass that seemed to blur in and out of focus like an impressionistic painting. To his sorrow, Ella's face was clear. He could see she was being held roughly by the arms by an Other and the frown of anguish nearly broke Amos' heart. He knew she was in more pain than she was letting Ben see. She had always tried to be brave for him and for Ethan and it was clear she was trying to be brave for Ben.

Amos shook his head and almost ran toward Ella. In truth, he had never been brave or strong and his only reason for coming up with the plan was that he had been desperate to help Ethan. He couldn't let Ethan down. He had to get to his brother.

Crouching as low as he could, Amos jogged around the far side of the ship, his tennis shoes making a faint slapping sound on the concrete floor. Moving quickly around to the side where the long ramp protruded from the spaceship like some type of obscene alien tongue, Amos was once again struck by the size of the craft. His feet stumbled and the rubber soles of his shoes emitted a loud "squeak". He froze in place, his eyes wide and his fingers splayed out in front of him. His breathing sped up to the point he thought he might hyperventilate as he waited to be caught. After five long seconds when nothing at all happened and the Other never looked in his direction, Amos let out the breath he was holding. Jogging lightly on the balls of his feet, Amos ran quietly up the ramp and into the dark bowels of the spacecraft.

Amos was immediately drawn to the only door in an otherwise solid wall of silver. He didn't hesitate and rushed through the doorway into the room, pushing down the last of his fears. Ethan was there. He could smell him.

Without glancing around, Amos knew it was the big silver room just like in his dream. But there was one difference. In his dream, the room was empty. In reality, his brother Ethan was laying on his stomach on a piece of cloth. Amos recognized the cloth as Ella's shirt and his gut twisted once again at his decision to leave her in the hands of the Other. But just then, Ethan's tiny head bobbed up, unsteady on the still weak stalk of a neck. His eyes rounded when he saw Amos and the naked baby began wiggling with excitement and a soft chortling pushed through his lips.

"Shhhh. You have to be quiet." Amos chided and ran to pick up Ethan before he could make too much noise. Using both hands to lift him, Amos was surprised at the weight of him. He had never held Ethan by himself before, and for a little baby, he much heavier than he would have expected and very wiggly. Preoccupied with holding on to the unaccustomed weight in his arms, Amos didn't give any thought to the silver boxes mounted high up on the walls. Even if he had, he wouldn't have had any idea what the red dots in the center of each box might mean. That detail hadn't been in his dream.

Holding the baby tight to his chest, Amos started toward the exit. When the first laser struck him, high on his left shoulder, the pain was hot and bright and it stunned him completely. Ethan's fingers clutched at Amos and as the second laser sliced through the meat of his upper leg, Amos screamed out loud and slid to the floor. Realizing what was happening, Amos tried to push Ethan away from him but Ethan's tiny fists bunched tightly onto Amos' shirt and he wouldn't let go. Amos rolled his face away, turning onto his side, the pain shooting daggers of agony through his body and bringing hot tears to his eyes. Then, it was no quiet cooing or soft sobs that issued forth from Ethan. For the first time since being left with the aliens and being abandoned to the silver room, the baby drew long, deep breaths into his lungs and exhaled an ear splitting wail.

****

Ben had just finished creating what he hoped was the most convincing lie of his life when he heard the sound he had been dreading all day. The box had seemed to be soundproof but this was a sound Ben not only heard, but he felt all the way to the marrow of his bones. His newborn son wasn't just crying, he was screaming at the top of his lungs.

It had been a lifelong effort to keep his anger in check. It had been drummed into his young mind that his temper was dangerous and too many bad things could happen to him and to others if he didn't keep that part of him locked away. But Ben was an adult now. And he was angry and he no longer wanted to push it down. The rage built in him so quickly that blood red mist covered his vision in an instant. His brain exploded with imagery, replaying every wounding event, fueling the anger coursing through him. His mother's face leapt into view and he felt the hurt and injustice of her being taken so young and leaving him and his dad. His father's face swam past and then in a fast forward flash he saw Ella's husband lying broken and bleeding on the street. Once the face of Amos' transformed father jumped into his mind like a ghost in a b-rated horror movie, Ben's entire being blazed with a fury that consumed his thoughts and his emotions.

Heat shot through his body and he was sure if anyone had touched him in that moment, they would be burned to cinders and fall in a heap at his feet. The inferno inside him twisted and roiled like a caged tiger fighting to be unleashed. Ben tried to make eye contact with Ella to tell her to protect herself, to guard her mind but there wasn't any time. Over thirty-five years of pent-up wrath blasted through his frontal cortex and slammed into the glowing orbs with the force of a thousand suns.

Ben was beyond knowing or caring what would happen but when the red mist of fury cleared from his vision, he was struck mute at the effect of his massive burst of mental energy focused on the alien orbs. He let out a grunt of disappointment as the five orbs merely glowed more brightly for a half a second.

Was that it? Ben lifted his head to Ella and this time, he did see the disappointment in her eyes. It had all been so worthless. All for nothing.

But when Ella's eyes widened in fear, Ben didn't understand at first.

"Ben!" She whispered through a throat constricted tight with fear and pointed.

Ben followed her finger which was trained shakily at the orb directly behind him. He swung around but even as he swung, from the corner of his eye, he saw the glowing light of the orb begin to brighten with the suddenness of the flare of a match. As he stared, the entire hangar blossomed with light as one by one, the orbs began to shine until the light was blinding white and the heat that radiated from them made the skin of his face begin to blister and peel.

"*Get down!*" Ben hurled the thought to Ella and then dropped face-down on the cement floor as a whining hum swelled around him. The sound grew shriller by the second and in the instant that Ben clapped both hands over his ears, the five orbs exploded.

The explosion of the orbs slammed into Ben and just as he thought he might burst apart from the pressure, the direction of the force reversed. There was a huge, ear-splitting sound like a grinding jet engine and then Ben's arms were forced away from his head and away from his body as he was being sucked toward the five fragmenting orbs. The pain was excruciating. It felt as if everything in him was being pulled apart. Ben opened his mouth to scream as even his hair felt like it was being ripped from his scalp.

Then with a suddenness as if a light switch had been flipped off, everything stopped.

****

When the five orbs exploded, the shriek from Ella pierced Ben's brain like a lance. He was on his feet and running toward her without a single glance at the alien orbs or the blue barrier. It wouldn't have mattered anyway. More than having exploded outward, it seemed the orbs had imploded in on themselves. The concave tops of the black pillars were molten and mottled with flecks of black grains that continued to sink down into the pillar, becoming part of the pillar itself.

Ben raced to Ella, feeling like a man in a dream going in slow motion. He was aware of the Other lying flat on his back on the floor, its eyes wide open. Its head was oddly misshapen and dark red blood streamed from its ears as a testament to the violence the orbs' explosion had inflicted on it.

Ella lay on the floor, her eyes closed and one arm thrown back over her head as if she was reaching up to wave at him.

"Please don't die. Please." Ben begged and pushed the thought into her mind, trying to be gentle but he knew he was pushing hard. His head was spinning and he struggled to catch his breath. His last push at the aliens had taken nearly all his strength. *"Please don't die."* He pushed the thought at her again. She was his life. She couldn't be dead. Ben grasped her roughly and gave her shoulders a jarring shake.

"Stop it." Ella's eyes flew open and she grumbled out loud and shook her head, then shoved the thought back at him, laced with irritation. *"Stop it."*

Sobbing with relief, Ben clasped Ella to his chest. He didn't care that she saw his tears. In that second he didn't care about anything except holding her in his arms and never letting her go.

From the open door of the alien ship, Ethan screamed.

"Come on!" Ben yanked on Ella's arms and pulled her up from the floor.

Swaying a bit as she stood to her feet, Ben faced her and placed his hands on both sides of her face, forcing her eyes to his. There was no way to know what they would find in the hangar.

"I can go alone if you want to stay here." Ben's voice was urgent but soft.

"No." She shook her head. "They're my babies. I'm going."

They raced the length of the hangar toward the ramp, holding each other up as they went. Darting through the opening to the spacecraft, the layout was as they remembered it and they flew through the door together.

THIRTY-FIVE

A scream tore out of Ella's throat.

Amos lay on the hard silver floor, blood streaming from the many wounds the lasers had sliced deeply into his body. His small face was gray and ashen. Even before Ben reached down to touch him, they knew he was dead.

Ella couldn't move. She could barely breathe. Her body even refused to respond to her command to pick up her baby. Ethan lay tucked slightly under Amos' left arm, unhurt, his dark eyes round and wet as they blinked up at Ben.

Ben squatted down and gently touched a finger to Amos' throat, then his head dropped and his shoulders sagged. Ella was still locked in her position with both fists bunched over her mouth. How could Amos be dead? How could this have happened? That wasn't the way it was supposed to go. Ben was the Singular. He was supposed to destroy the aliens and everyone would be okay and they would live happily ever after as a family.

Ethan's tiny hands still clutched at Amos' bloody shirt and the baby stared up at Ben, his dark eyes masked with grief.

"Come on, kiddo. Come to me." Ben let one knee dip onto the floor as he held out his arms to lift Ethan up and away. Ethan's small head was resting on Amos' check and his fingers were balled tightly into fists that held firm to Amos' shirt. "We have to go, baby." Ben coaxed and tried to pry his fingers away.

As Ben's hand connected with Ethan's fingers, he noticed how warm the baby felt. It wouldn't have been surprising if he was sick. After laying naked and dirty in the cold, sterile room, it made sense Ethan might be sick and running a fever. But as his son continued to stare into his eyes, blinking back tears and yanking weakly on Amos' shirt, Ben finally understood.

Just then, Ella's paralysis broke and she stepped close and pushed roughly past Ben to pick up Ethan. She couldn't stay in that room any longer and she couldn't look at Amos' body any longer. She just couldn't.

"No. Wait." Ben stopped her with his tone.

Ella moaned softly and shook her head. "No." Her voice was barely a whisper. "Please. Let's just go."

Ben nodded his head at Ethan. "Just wait, El. Okay?" The baby reached out one pudgy arm and let himself be lifted onto Ben's lap. Ben then wrapped his other hand around Amos' blood covered neck. The sight of all the blood still pouring out of Amos' body almost made Ben physically sick, but he pushed down the bile and held his hand to the small, still body until he felt the warmth and tingling begin to radiate from Ethan, through him and into Amos' cooling body.

EPILOGUE

Ben stood with his hand on Amos' shoulder at the foot of the crumbling stairs. The house was dark and appeared deserted. But Ben knew it wasn't deserted. Coming back to look for his father hadn't been Amos' idea. It was something Ella had insisted on.

"If his father is still alive, now that everyone who had been transformed is free, we need to at least try and find him."

"But El? Amos knows his dad killed his mother. How can he go back and deal with that?" Ben had argued.

"We won't abandon him. We'll always be close by." Ella's hand had been so soft on his arm yet he felt the urgency in her voice. "We'll help him adjust if it's what he decides he wants to do. We have to give him a chance to try." She had left them no choice.

Amos' small frame trembled as they waited on the doorstep of the white house. The last time they had been there, Amos' father was covered in his mother's blood and the sidewalk was splattered with red.

There were no lights on inside, but a tightening in his gut made Ben lean his head slightly to peer into a narrow side window. He expected to see a view of the living room clouded by the grayish dirt on the window. But his view was blocked by the sight of a dark, haggard face that instantly jerked back from the pane. A dusty cloth curtain fell back into place and then all became still inside the house. Ben glanced over at Amos to see if he had been watching the side window. The young boy's eyes flicked quickly away from the window and Ben knew he had seen. Within a second, Amos' head was down and his attention seemed to be firmly held by the yellow laces woven through the eyelets of his new blue tennis shoes.

"I guess he's gone." Amos stared up at Ben and the hopeful look in his eyes nearly tore Ben apart.

"Yeah. I guess we should move on then." Ben said.

He could've said more. He could've tried to explain that sometimes grief wouldn't let you rest, and that seeing glimpses of his wife's countenance in Amos' face every day might be too much for his father to bear. He might have insisted that they knock on the door until his father either answered them or let his silence be their answer. But Ben didn't do any of those things. Some things were too far gone, too lost to ever recover from. He knew that, and it was clear Amos knew that too.

When the five alien orbs had imploded and crumbled into fine black grit, all the men who had been transformed into Others had awakened, stunned and grief-stricken over what had been done to them and what they had done. Some were too hurt to live with the guilt. Some retreated into dark places where their minds could lay numb and barren of any thoughts. And there were others who were determined to rebuild. Over the past few weeks, much had been restored although there remained so much more to do. Shattered infrastructures had to be recreated. Splintered governments were reestablished and basic water, food and electrical systems put back into working order. And all this was done with an urgency to get things going, to get things back to something that might hopefully resemble "normal."

There would be a new generation. The women who had survived the aftermath of the transformations were still coming out of hiding – wary and fearful – yet they came.

Ben thought briefly of Ella and Ethan, waiting for them a couple of blocks away at a newly stocked and newly opened grocery store. Somewhere in the future a confrontation likely waited for his son and Ben feared for Ethan, but he had made a decision. When Ethan was old enough, Ben would tell him all he knew about the time of fires in the sky and all he knew about being Singular. Ben hadn't been prepared at all. He didn't blame his mother; the cancer took her so fast, she had simply run out of time. But Ethan would be different. Ethan would be prepared.

A light smile touched his lips and his hand stroked down the back of Amos' head. The soft curls were fuller now and Ben would have to try and figure out how to give him a haircut.

"Let's get back to Ella and Ethan before they start to worry." Ben said.

"You know she's buying cheese, don't you?" Amos blurted as he spun on his heel and hopped down the cracked steps to the pavement.

"Yes. I'm sure she is." Ben smiled wider and reached down. Amos' fingers slipped easily into his hand.

"Take my hand, baby, Take my hand.
We can go on like this forever if you take my hand..."

www.ingramcontent.com/pod-product-compliance
Lightning Source LLC
Chambersburg PA
CBHW022058170626
46808CB00002B/491